WRATH OF ACQUISITION

CORE: BOOK FOUR

BY

MAQUEL A. JACOB

Published by
MAJart Works LLC
2001 NE Aloclek Dr Suite 211
Hillsboro, Oregon

www.majartworks.com

ISBN: 978-1-950438-17-4

Cover Art by Dar Albert
www.wickedsmartdesigns.com

ONE: A NEW REIGN

Lost Acquisition

Chardon stood amongst a field of tall yellow grass, the blades brushing against his knees as he watched the slow descent of an unknown ship in the horizon get closer. His long white robe under a brown sleeveless chamois fluttered in the soft breeze that intensified to a strong wind with the ship's approach. He breathed deep, taking in the grassy carried in the air, then exhaled slowly while narrowing his dark blue eyes.

Raising one hand to shield his face from the specks of dirt flying about did little good. A lot of it got caught in the strands of hair that swirled before his eyes.

For a moment, he became distracted, marveling at the deep, strawberry blond hair color, grown darker the last two decades. His vanity always kicked in at the most inopportune times.

The ship breached the horizon, blocking New Lassa's midday sun as it passed. An octagonal shape with soft edges, its dark grey underbelly accented the rest of the ship's lighter shade. The loud hum of its engines in hover mode reverberated in Chardon's head. The planet remained on high alert yet the faint sounds of everyday chores from the nearby village behind him filtered through underneath the distant whirring of the ship's thrusters shutting down. It took more than this to frighten Lassians.

"This is why you should have established a space hub with a scout tower," his mate, Halfar, standing beside him stated.

Though equal in height, he was in stark contrast to Chardon with bone straight, jet black hair and murky green eyes that made one think of forest mud.

Halfar gave Chardon's personal bodyguard, Modas, the leader of Lassa's Manbeast clan a dirty stare. At nearly seven feet tall, Modas was a formidable sight with short, black talons sharp like scalpels rested at his sides.

The massive mane of brown hair flowed down his back obscuring the blue robe with dark grey overlay.

Despite their mutual animosity, the two rivals were within a few feet of each other. Chardon found nothing comical about their little immature fights.

Chardon pursed his lips, dropping his hand from his face. "That's probably a good idea."

"I suggested it long ago. We could have been operational by now," New Lassa's chief scientist and spiritual guide, Ganna added.

He glanced behind him at her. That last part of Ganna's title was something to be scoffed at. Her eggshell shaded robes made her look the part along with the silver locks of hair jiggling in the wind. An amused expression graced her face, grey eyes wide in anticipation. It gave Chardon the chills.

"No one knows where our planet is except Azrom. I saw no reason to put security protocols like that in place." Chardon frowned. "And who doesn't use a gateway."

Modas' son Trinon remained silent next to him. Only a couple of inches shorter than his father, he was more deadly. A playful grin masking a readiness to kill spread across his face. Wearing all black, his childish demeanor belied the villainous look.

"Uhh, that would require them to have our coordinates," Trinon said, "and as you just pointed out..." He tilted his head towards Chardon, giving him a side stare.

"Well, it's too late now." Talas, the leader of the warrior clan, interrupted their silent tiff.

Chardon averted his eyes towards him.

Talas, All slender muscle on a barely six-foot frame, with fae-like features that completed his beauty. Blond, wavy hair fell past his waist nearly touching the top of his leather leggings. He tugged at the cuffs of his rust red leather jacket as he too stared up at the ship now extending its landing gear. A touch of envy grazed Chardon's mind before he dismissed the thought.

I'm more beautiful either way.

The gang's all here, he thought in the Earth term. Except for his cousin, Jaron who immediately went to assemble the council when the transport gate sent an alert. Whoever or whatever stepped off the alien ship would not be getting off alive if they came to fight.

Chardon glanced back at the gate operator's hands running across the console hitting icons and buttons, never looking up.

"Update?"

"Scan complete," he answered.

"Weapons?"

"On board but no signature. They are powered down."

"Let's hope they come in peace and that ramp doesn't open up with a barrage of firepower." Halfar flexed his hands to loosen up the tension.

"If you feel incapable of handling a fight, get behind me and stand back out of the way so I can move freely." Modas delivered deadpan.

Trinon winced. Chardon turned towards the two and saw Halfar's face contort in anger. Modas, as usual, was a blank canvas.

"Stop it." Chardon's eyes narrowed. "This isn't the time."

The loud hum of the ship brought their attention back to it. Up close, he could see the odd shape of the dome, like the shell of a tortoise. Three fat prongs were extended from the underbelly and pierced New Lassa's soil causing a vibration under their feet.

"Well, let's see who has come to visit us." Talas smirked.

The ship completely shut down, a rectangular outline for the opening appeared. It grew wider as it formed into a ramp that lowered onto the ground. Chardon took another deep breath.

Three figures stood at the top. Each one a different race. They walked down the ramp almost tentative. The one in the center raised his hands, palms already up before him in surrender. His skin was a reddish tint with some hints of green. His eyes were brown yet glowed somehow. He wore a long white robe beneath an emerald colored one.

"Please, we mean no harm." The being said as the three stopped at the foot of the ramp. "We wish to speak freely with you." Seeing Chardon's group not move, they continued towards them.

The alien on the right caught Chardon's eye. He felt Modas bristle. In a knee length loin cloth open at the sides and a thick leather breast plate, the alien was easily six feet five with a thick mane. Green eyes like jewels expressed a warning.

Behind him, a long reptilian tail swished back and forth, moving the dirt around.

"Razznian?" Halfar asked unsure under his breath.

The alien heard him.

"No. We are originally from there. We evolved, differently, and had to leave."

Chardon noticed the difference. More bipedal human than reptile, the skin was smoother with more aesthetically pleasing facial features. His manly demeanor gave Modas a run for his money.

The alien on the left came across as timid, not making eye contact. A short blade lay in holsters on each side of his hips. The blond tendrils instead of hair cascaded around their shoulders. He appeared to be wearing a uniform. A dark red kefta with gold overlay designs, black knee-high boots and gloves.

"Interesting," Talas mused.

They halted a few meters from Chardon's group.

"What brings you here to New Lassa?" Chardon asked.

The middle alien stepped forward. "Our solar system, Tolitha, has been attacked and ravaged the past two decades by a race we have no knowledge of. Their targeting seems to be random."

"Like they are testing each planet's might," the reptilian alien added.

"We waited a few years before making our arrangements to come here. So far they have not attacked since then but…" The alien on the left hung his head further as he stopped talking.

The reptile took up the story. "We spotted a fleet of their ships on the outskirts. They will probably hit us again soon."

"And this involves New Lassa how?" Chardon asked.

"We have come to plead for aid against a new threat," the middle alien replied matter of fact.

Talas' eyes went wide. Halfar stared at them incredulous.

"You want us to assist in your battle against this race of scavengers? Again, why?" Chardon squinted in confusion.

The three looked at each other then back to Chardon. The middle raised his arms to his side.

"You are our Regent. Who else would we ask?"

Chardon reared his head back as if slapped.

"What do you mean?"

"Our system was brought under the rule of New Lassa through a deal with the Dreridians and the female called Sestis."

"Is she not present for a reason?" The timid alien looked over them, certain none of them were her.

"She's dead," Chardon snapped fiercer than he'd liked.

"Oh." The timid one's head went back down.

"It looks like Sestis' deeds bloomed to fruition after all," Ganna said.

A darkness fell on Chardon's face. He clenched his fists. "And how did you find us?"

"We contacted the Dreridians, and they gave us these gate coordinates. They said any political or military inquiries must go through our assigned Regent." The middle one lowered his arms.

Halfar placed a hand in the small of Chardon's back. He leaned over and whispered in his ear. "Calm yourself."

"I would like to know about this enemy." Talas pivoted sideways and nodded towards the village. "Shall we?"

His anger momentarily deflated; Chardon regained his stance of authority. He pointed at the ship. "First, let's deal with that."

"You wish to move our ship?" The middle alien seemed perplexed.

Chardon turned to Ganna.

"Find a place for it away from the population."

"Absolutely."

Ganna walked past the three and headed up the ramp.

"Was this not the landing area?" The middle one pointed to the gate console. "I assumed it would be because of that."

"We don't have a spaceport," Modas replied.

"Yet." Halfar stared Chardon down.

"Oh, it's definitely in the works now," Trinon laughed.

"Please, follow me." Chardon led the way with Talas and Halfar while Trinon and Modas took up the rear. "I'm sure you would like to relax first. Have a drink."

"That's a given." Halfar scratched his right temple. "We all need one."

They walked in silence the rest of the way. The closer they got to the village, the more scrutiny they received from the people. Chores had slowed to a crawl the moment the ship appeared in the sky. There would be so many questions.

Behind them, the ship's engines engaged. The thrusters fired, scorching more of the terrain. Chardon tried not to react. They took so much pride in getting the soil back in good health from the last attack on New Lassa. Seeing the burnt grass hurt his heart.

The ship rose and turned towards the mountains where, on the other side lay a shipyard with their own vessels docked there. Chardon saw the three aliens glanced around, not being too conspicuous as they took in the environment.

"It seems so peaceful here," the middle alien said. "I feel no strife."

"We try to keep that down to zero." Talas turned his head to address them. "We're not really a fighting race." He nodded to Halfar. "That's more his territory. Right, former Supreme Ruler?"

Halfar gave him a dirty look.

"Supreme Ruler?" The reptilian alien's gaze fell on Halfar.

"That's right, we haven't introduced ourselves." Trinon clasped his hands behind his head. "The dark haired moody one before you is Halfar of Azrom." They all stopped, with horrified expressions. Chardon and his entourage stopped. "Oh, and by the way, we are allies with the Razznians."

"I...we...had no idea." The middle alien looked from Chardon to Halfar.

"Then you have more might than you claim," the reptile alien said to Talas.

"Hmm. Perhaps."

Talas resumed walking and the rest followed. He was mindful of the small field creatures scurrying about, forcing their guests to do the same.

The stares eventually ceased and daily tasks continued. Some of the children remained curious, fascinated by the reptilian's tail in constant movement. Many had to step out of the way to avoid getting whacked.

To kill time until Ganna returned, Chardon showed the aliens around the main village. The only place they didn't go was the core garden. He did not trust the aliens' motives yet. For all he knew they could be a Trojan Horse. Halfar gave him a knowing glance. He was just as paranoid.

Jaron, Chardon's cousin, and strategist met them at the entrance of the compound where the council rooms were.

Her face showed distaste at the group. She locked eyes with Chardon as he came within a few feet of her.

"What's the matter with you?" She seethed. "We have no idea who these creatures are, and you give them a tour of the land like they're special."

"Calm down," Talas raised a hand to stop her. "Nothing was going to happen." He tilted his head back slightly at her mate, Modas and son Trinon. "Give them some credit."

"I am sorry this has caused such chaos." The middle alien bowed his head then raised it. "We only did what was required."

"Required?" Jaron frowned.

"If you would be so kind as to lead us into a council room, I will explain, cousin." Chardon gave her a forced smile.

Jaron turned to the dimly lit corridor and walked down. The group followed her to one of the bigger rooms. Inside was a large rectangle table set low to the floor with cushions surrounding it. They all settled onto them while Trinon and Modas stood guard in separate corners. Servants came in with carafes of drink, glass tumblers, and small platters of food. Their guests were impressed.

Ganna arrived with three other council members. The heads of Engineering, Politics, and the Military sat at the table with similar looks of disappointment on their faces. That riled Chardon, knowing that is how they felt about him in the not-so-distant past.

"Is that really necessary?" Ganna asked the reptilian. "Is it a nervous tick or can you not control your tail?" She sat across from him.

"I do not get nervous." The reptilian's reply was soaked in ire. His tail went limp, curving around his right thigh.

A tumbler was placed before each individual and filled with the pale orange drink from the carafes. The middle alien picked up his glass and scrutinized it.

"What is this made of?"

"Don't worry," Ganna said. "After visits to many worlds, we found this concoction is pleasant to every species. A blend of nutrients, fruits and water." She raised her glass. "To new relations."

Everyone raised their glasses high in the air.

"To new relations!" They all took a sip.

"Mmm." The middle alien smacked his lips. "This is quite tasty."

The timid one took a bigger swig. "It's refreshing."

"Or we've been poisoned and don't know it yet," the reptilian added.

The room went quiet. Jaron leaned over the edge of the table, her hips lifting off the cushion.

"We don't need to poison you. If we wanted to dispose of you, we would have done it in haste." Her eyes glowed with blue electricity. Strands of bright red that streaked through her dark hair fell forward.

The reptilian lowered his glass close to the table. "My apologies. I am on edge. Where you do not trust us, we cannot put our faith in you as well."

Jaron sat back on her cushion. Her expression softened.

"As it should be." She turned to Chardon sitting at the far end of table. "So explain."

Talas cleared his throat to get everyone's attention.

"It seems that Sestis received a prize during her negotiations tour." The head council members scoffed in disgust. "New Lassa has been bequeathed with an entire solar system. Possibly a handful of planets as well." That caused a few gasps. Jaron was visibly upset. "An enemy has appeared threatening said system." Talas extended a hand gesturing towards their guest. "Hence why these representatives have come to request aid from their Regent." He moved his hand to Chardon.

"Such madness!" The head of engineering shook her head in disbelief.

"We do not have a true military force." The head of militia looked over at the guests. "What are you expecting in terms of support?"

The middle alien set down his glass. "A scouting party to assess the situation for starters. If the situation can be remedied without a fight, that would be ideal."

"From the little you told us, I find that wishful thinking indeed," Chardon said. "This enemy sounds like the type who attacks first and retreats if the work gets too difficult."

"Galactic bullies." Ganna met the reptilian's gaze. "I'm surprised your race hasn't pushed back."

"We tried. These beings are monsters. They had just as many casualties but their numbers against us was ten to one."

"It was like a sea of destruction coming at every planet." The timid one gripped his glass hard, causing vein lines to surface.

Halfar was intrigued. Of the three in the alliance, Azrom had power in numbers and artillery. The Razznians came in second, their ships forming a swarm that struck fear in the galaxy. To hear of an unknown rival raising havoc made his blood heat up with excitement. A need to conquer stirred in him. Raising his headfound himself staring in Talas' eyes.

He understood.

"That can be arranged." Chardon glanced over at Trinon. "You don't mind having a look see. Maybe get your talons wet if necessary."

"Not at all." Trinon grinned. "How many should I take with me?"

"That's for your mother and Talas to decide."

Jaron's lips went thin.

"We'll discuss it later." She addressed the middle alien. "Which planet is the next target?"

"That would be Andal. It is the largest in size and population. They did not send a representative due to needing everyone ready for battle when the enemy arrives."

"So, they have hit the smaller ones and realized they need to cripple the bigger obstacle in order to intimidate the others." The head of Science nodded while he contemplated. "They are smart. Relentless too."

"You may need to ask Romnus for a loan on an armada ship," Halfar said. "At least show a symbol of might."

Talas rolled his eyes. From Chardon's face, he saw the leader was on board with the suggestion. "Now." He clapped his hands loudly. "How about we do introductions before we get too far in the weeds on this?"

He hadn't pushed the subject since no one seemed to care. With a plan forming, it was necessary to have names to go with it all. Jaron sputtered at the realization. Their guests appeared shameful. The middle and timid one rather. The reptilian couldn't have cared less.

"Our apologies." The middle alien bowed his head. "We should have done that in the beginning. I am Ambassador Lombis of Suma Andal."

The timid one raised his head again.

"I am General T'Halgar of Andal IV. My position is third in our army. The enemy is going after our ruling planet where our King resides."

Silence fell and everyone turned to the reptilian. He caught their gaze as he took a sip of his drink. Lowering it, he grasped it with both hands.

"I am Emperor Xanic of Nasfir Second in Command. I opted to come myself to make sure our people's voice is heard. Our planet lies on the outskirts of the Tolitha system."

"With that out of the way." Ganna reached for a chunk of bread on the small plate in the center before her. "We should take some time to strategize and let them rest. The guards can lead them back to their ship."

"Or," Chardon retorted. "They can stay in the village. We have plenty of room."

"We couldn't possibly impose," Ambassador Lombis started to protest. Chardon raised a hand to cut him off. "If you insist."

"Good." Chardon pointed to the servant who remained by the door. "Bring something stronger to drink." The servant left in a hurry.

"Libations? So early in the day?" The head engineer sat straighter, her head tilted back in surprise.

"Absolutely."

The servant returned with two more carrying large green bottles bulbous at the bottom with long narrow necks. They went around filling empty glasses, waiting for the individual to finish the previous drink before doing so. When everyone had a more potent serving, Chardon raised his glass.

"To a new venture and a swift resolution."

They all toasted in the air then drank. It was going to be a long day. They may as well enjoy it. Chardon had a knot in his stomach.

A Sense of Dread

New Lassa's night air had chilled by the time the moon shined its eerie glow on the surface. Off in the distance, the dark outline of the mountains were visible against a burnt orange and navy-blue sky. Small creatures scuttled under the brush making hushed rustling sounds. The village was quiet. Everyone should have been asleep in anticipation of the work ahead.

Chardon was not. He crept out of bed, careful not to wake Halfar, and ventured out in only an outer robe. The cool breeze penetrated it, nipping at his skin. He walked aimlessly as he thought about the implications of what Sestis had done.

I barely rule this planet.

It certainly crossed a few of his council members' minds. Strands of his hair whipped around into his mouth causing him to look up while pulling the chunk back behind his ears.

Ganna's lab was a few yards away. The outer lights were on. A motion lens swiveled towards him and he saw the eye zoom. Of course, this is where I end up. He decided not to dodge the inevitable and walked up to the doors that opened for him.

The pristine lab with all white counters and equipment felt cold. The healing pods were empty and had been for months. A good sign. Ganna sat at her workstation staring at a holographic DNA chain that slowly spun around giving her a four-dimensional view.

"Do I want to ask how you got that?" Chardon pulled a rolling chair from another station and sat not far behind her.

"Why are you surprised?" She didn't turn around. "They are a new race we have not encountered. All information is necessary."

"And this is?" Chardon half pointed to the hologram.

Ganna's face lit up with joy.

"This is the reptilian creature's strain. He's not wrong about his species being similar to Razznians. But they are on a completely different level."

Now Chardon was intrigued. "How so?"

"They are indeed more human than reptile. It makes me wonder how that happened."

This time she did turn to him. Chardon was horrified and his expression must have conveyed it. She smirked and looked at the hologram again.

"Please don't elaborate."

"Such delicate sensibilities." She let out a laugh. "And they seem to have only two or three traits in contrast to Razznians who run the gambit of reptile variety."

"And now we are responsible for their planet and countless others." Chardon leaned back.

"Oh? Are we addressing the elephant in the room as Earth people say?"

"You're not surprised. All the schemes Sestis took part in you benefitted from."

Ganna spun around in the chair and locked her glowing silver eyes with his. Chardon flinched at the rage in them.

"I have said this before but maybe I need to explain." Her tone was venomous. "Everything I do is for the sake of Lassa. Sestis and I did not share the same goals. Did a few align with mine? Of course. But she was greedy, messy," her face scrunched, "and did not love Lassa!"

Her face softened, not by much, and she crossed her arms. Chardon sat back straight in his chair. The two always fought over his deceased mate's actions. Even in death, there were repercussions to her antics.

"Why didn't you stop her?" Chardon tilted his head.

"Why didn't you?" Ganna scoffed. "Instead of drowning in lust with Halfar, you could have cut her off at the knees."

Chardon's skin grew hot. He leaned forward. "That was uncalled for."

"I know what I said," Ganna snapped. "Tell me I'm wrong!"

She wasn't. Chardon had no comeback. He had turned a blind eye to Sestis because he had no love for her. From the beginning, she made her ambitions known. It was why they were mated by his parents' decree.

"I wish…" Chardon started.

"It's too late for that!" Ganna cut him off. "What we need now," she stopped. "You know what needs to be done."

"As do you. I authorize whatever it is."

Ganna's eyes went wide. "Are you certain that's wise? I will do what I deem necessary."

"As much as I despise a space port ruining the aesthetics of our planet, I guess it must be done."

"It doesn't have to be subpar in taste. We can use the gate as a prescreening."

Chardon met her gaze. "I hadn't thought of that."

"Yes, well, that's a given. I'm smarter than you for a reason."

"Ganna." Chardon took a deep breath to calm himself.

"And an actual military force. I suggest we utilize the alliance for that."

"Makes sense."

Movement at the door startled them. The two turned their attention to the sound and saw Trinon leaning against the frame. The door slid closed behind him.

"I will never get used to such stealth." Ganna had a hand on her chest. She had stopped breathing for a split second out of fright. "I guess he can't sleep either." She relaxed, letting her hand drop in her lap.

"The problem is we are not some great army like Azrom or Razzna." Trinon stepped further into the lab. "We are a group of warrior clans. Despite our numbers, which are vast, we are but a third the size of a regular fighting group."

"Because we are still recuperating from your lover's near massacre of our race," Ganna said to Chardon.

It was still a sore subject. Halfar regretted sending the planet bomb to their original home world, killing everything, scorching the surface black. Ganna and her servants were able to save half the population's cores. To this day, some of the people scorn him when he walks past.

"First, we need to establish how many planets are under our Regency."

"Right. Before we go checking out enemy lines." Trinon crossed his arms and tapped the bottom of his lip with a finger. "If they are indeed going across the galaxy looking for a worthy fight, we will encounter them elsewhere."

"Lassa will find them foolish if they challenge Azrom." Ganna smiled.

She wanted to see such a battle. Chardon and Trinon could feel her desire.

****

The morning brought a flurry of activity. Their guests were up and about congregating with the council at breakfast in the dayroom. Servants flowed through filling drinks and replacing empty platters. Chardon and Halfar arrived late due to Halfar's incessant need for morning mating. That was Chardon's reason for being in female form. She sat at the end of the table, Halfar next to her and waited for a servant to come.

"This is unexpected." Ambassador Lombis looked over Chardon's appearance. "I was unaware you were a shifter species."

"When you said you were mated to Halfar, it didn't register. Now I see," Emperor Xanic added.

"We have a lot to discuss. That is not one of them." Halfar leaned away as a servant filled his glass then Chardon's with a dark red brew. "Our mating is advantageous for you."

Trinon came into the room with his father. Modas and Halfar gave each other a terse nod. They had decided long ago to accept the fact that they would never be friends. Trinon glanced sideways in the air. The two took a corner each in the back of the room, grabbing the larger cushions to sit on.

"Not to kill the mood," Trinon said. "But I have a bad feeling about this."

"And you voice this now after agreeing to be a scout?" Jaron asked angrily.

"I had time to think about." Trinon shrugged. "We have no data on this enemy. And even if we did, clashing with them in real time is a whole different story."

"I agree." Halfar stabbed a piece of sliced meat from a nearby platter and plopped it on the small plate set before him. "You can know all the stats of the enemy, but it all means nothing until you come face to face."

General T'Halgar perked up. "Yes, but still. I do have data collected from the last battle. Who will receive it?"

"That would be Jaron and I," Talas replied from his seat at the middle of the table. "No need to go in completely blind."

"New weapons can be manufactured in a short time if needed." The Science council woman took a sip of her drink. Her gaze was fixed on the table. "I would want assurance that we can get in and out with minimal injuries. No casualties." She looked up with a determined expression.

"No casualties," Talas repeated. "I will guarantee it."

"That's not feasible." Emperor Xanic retorted. "No battle…"

"When our strategist says no casualties, he stands by his word," Chardon interrupted. "We have fought many battles and so far we have been," he paused. "Somewhat victorious."

Halfar and Jaron stared at her for a moment, testing to see if she was serious. Chardon bristled.

"Dear leader," Jaron said. "Let's not exaggerate. I concur that when Talas declares no death, he delivers. But this is a new wrinkle, and we cannot be so optimistic."

Trinon took the plate of food and glass of brew from the servant. Guarantee or not, he still had no faith in his scouting mission going off without a hitch. His father glanced over at him. There was no fear for his son. Instead, it was a look that said, 'get it done'.

****•****

The village to the East was Manbeast territory although other clans resided there due to mating. Trinon strolled down the main road until he came to the youngling playpen where little manbeasts in various stages of growth occupied the bins. The newest ones were a cluster of round puffs resembling hedgehogs. They sniffed each other with tiny black snouts wet with snot.

He remembered when his litter was tiny. His brother Und had sniffed him and backed away as if he was rotten. Their sister, Una, never came near him. Thinking back on it made him sad. He loved his siblings. Why didn't they love me in return? Or am I overthinking it?

There were five in his litter. Two energy users and the others manbeasts. The energy users rarely came around to check on their other siblings. Same for the second litter their parents had. A loving family dynamic was a pipe dream. Trinon understood he was different. He felt it in his very core. And it stemmed from his mother. He didn't know how.

His brother, Und, was talking to one of their energy user sisters. They both glanced over at him approaching. To Trinon's surprise, she merely nodded towards him and left. Und's face went blank. Trinon stopped walking. He stood in the middle of the road struck with hurt though he refused to show it.

Mustering all his mental strength, he cracked a smile.

"Found you!" He chimed.

Und let out a deep sigh and turned to face him. His droopy lids added to the look of annoyance. The long sleeveless robe covered a full body battle suit.

"What brings you here, Trinon?"

"I can't come say hi to my own family?" Trinon asked playfully.

Und frowned in disgust. "That's not what I meant, and you know it!"

Trinon raised his hands before him in a defensive stance.

"No need to get angry."

"What do you want, Trinon?"

Arms dropped to his sided, Trinon moved closer.

"There's going to be a scouting party for our guests' home worlds. We want to show a little intimidation and force to scare off an enemy."

"There have been rumors spreading. Something about New Lassa being Regent to other planets." Und's expression went dark. "Another drop in the bucket from Sestis."

"Yep." Trinon crossed his arms. "Talas and mother are drawing up a plan. Halfar will ask Azrom for an armada ship with plenty of weapons."

"They want a battalion of manbeasts."

"And I figured you would want to be in on the fun."

"How many?" Und crossed his arms as well.

"I say about fifty. We would split the lead. Same amount of energy users will be under Mom's second in command."

"That's a lot of muscle for a scouting party."

"Oh, well, the enemy seems to be quite relentless. They don't like being told no."

"Hmm?" Und almost looked interested. "Fine. Just don't get in my way and try to dictate how I run my men."

"Wouldn't think of it."

Und uncrossed his arms and walked off without another word, leaving Trinon alone on the road.

Barbon, his father's right hand, came and patted him on the back.

"You all need to figure this out. It hurts all of us to see your family in such a state. As our leader's horde, you all need to set better examples."

"I'm trying." Trinon dropped his arms. "They won't meet me halfway."

"Keep trying. Don't back down yet. And your father needs to step in at some point."

Barbon slid his hand from Trinon's back and headed to the main hall. Trinon averted his gaze to the playpen.

Since I'm here.

He went towards the tiny things mewing, helpless to fight back against the terror he was about to inflict on them for sport.

It was a rite of passage.

✶✷✶

Modas watched the footage of the battle General T'Halgar had brought along with Jaron, Talas, Chardon and Halfar. A tiny chip sat on the 300mm data retrieving platform in the center of the table. A holographic feed was displayed in midair. The resolution was a bit grainy and flickered from time to time. It was a miracle the footage had been captured at all given the chaos of the battlefield.

From what he could tell, there wasn't much to go on. Most of the images were blurred, the colors blending into a smear of grey. Some of the footage hinted at the enemy's fire power while the rest gave more detail on their appearance.

Ugly.

That is what came to mind the more he scrutinized them. The Dreridians, with their craggy skin, had more appeal. And the enemy were huge. Taller than his own nearly seven-foot frame. And bulky. Bulging muscles layered atop each other covered their bodies. Thick feet swathed in nanoskin, short, discolored talons, and squatted faces with sharp rows of teeth. Those faces contorted in fury as they bashed in the skulls of their prey made it much worse.

The footage ended and they all sat in silence for what seemed like minutes. Talas finally spoke.

"Nasty."

Jaron sputtered out a laugh. "Indeed."

"Not a laughing matter, unfortunately," Halfar said. "Close contact is not an option."

"What?" Chardon squinted at him. "You've defeated far worse than this."

"Which is why I know hand to hand combat is certain death with these creatures."

"They are quite formidable," General T'Halgar said. "We were only able to drive them back because they seemed bored after attacking for hours straight."

"So, they like toying with their targets." Talas seemed not happy about that.

"And we don't know what other weapons they may have in their arsenal." Jaron leaned over the feed controls and reversed the footage until it showed one of the enemy ships. She froze it there and zoomed in. "What are those for?" She pointed to a mechanism mounted on the front.

"No idea." T'Halgar hung his head. "As I said, they didn't really engage us full on."

"It was a test." Halfar and Talas replied in unison.

"Every attack was a test." Talas leaned back using his arms to hold him up. "They probably feel your system is ripe for the taking."

"All they have to do is take down the larger planet as stated." Halfar tapped the edge of the table. "They have no idea you are under a Regency."

"And didn't bother to find out either," Jaron added.

"What now?"

T'Halgar looked around the room at everyone.

"We proceed as planned." Chardon rubbed the side of her head, messing up her hair.

"With more ships." Halfar addressed Talas.

"What?" Chardon asked, stunned.

"You are not sending a scouting party. It will be a full unit with three armada ships."

"Fully loaded, huh?" Talas said. "That sounds about right."

"Showing that kind of force would send a different message," Jaron protested.

"Exactly." Halfar lowered his head and brought his eyes up in disdain. "Don't touch what doesn't belong to you."

Chardon slumped her shoulders in defeat. She wasn't about to argue. Modas was glad. For once, he agreed with the former ruler. No reason to go in halfcocked hoping for a peaceful resolution. He could tell the enemy was not one to listen.

"First things first," Chardon finally said after regaining her composure. "We need to have a talk with the Dreridians about our Regency."

"Yes, like how many do we have." Jaron shut down the feed and removed the tiny chip from the data platform. "For all we know, Sestis could have acquired a hundred planets."

Chardon went visibly pale. Modas hid his own sick feeling that crept up.

Sestis.

He never liked that female. Nor she him. That was the only good thing about Halfar destroying their home world; it took her with it.

"I will arrange transport with Ganna. Would you prefer a small entourage?" Modas turned to Chardon and waited for her reply.

"That would be best. I don't think we'll end up in a fight with Dreridians."

"Don't be so sure," Talas said.

Chardon gave him a dirty stare. Modas met Halfar's. Just in case.

A Ruler's Responsibility

The entourage formed two rows in front of the gate for transport. Chardon in male form, stood next to Halfar and behind them were Ganna, Modas, Talas, Trinon, his sister Mara, and Chafar, Chardon and Halfar's son; a Lassian warrior in training. Modas had personally chosen each person to accompany Chardon.

The Lassian ship appeared over the mountains and made its descent towards them. Sleek in design with muted colors of tans and greens, it nearly blended into the forest ahead. Ganna beamed at it proudly. She was the head of development for the project when it was being built. It never ceased to amaze Modas how talented yet mind boggling corrupt that woman was.

As the ship hovered, it created a strong wind that blew their hair and robes straight back. They shielded their eyes from flying dirt and grass until the ship was on the ground and the wind died. The ramp extended and they boarded in two single file rows.

Instead of heading to the personal chambers, they all took seats in the main cabin located in the same corridor as the bridge. Strapping into their seats, there was tension in the air. Modas knew why. Dreridians were schemers with too much power. They controlled the galactic trade, making them the first and last authority on regulations.

From the nearest porthole, Modas could see the gate operator hitting the coordinates. The ship lifted off and eased towards the swirling black void that would send them to the outer boundary of the Dreridian system. What would take weeks was now cut into hours. Modas took a seat near the door and connected the restraints. He glanced over at Chardon already looking anxious. Space travel was not his friend.

*****

The ship shot out of the vortex into Dreridian space and slowed to a crawl. Security ports were scattered around the entire perimeter of the main planet with space hubs closer in. Cargo ships cruised past them and docked for inspection before being allowed on the surface. A security drone came alongside the Lassian ship and did an initial scan. The tiny beams of light ran over the ship like a strobe. When it was done, the lights blinked out and the drone sped off to the nearest hub.

A row of lights creating a runway appeared in front of the ship. It traveled down following them all the way to the planet surface onto a true ramp. The ship was guided to a docking station at the palace.

Chardon and his entourage exited the ship amid workers rushing about securing the clamps that locked it in place. At the bottom of the ramp was Lord Greggor to greet them.

A stout creature, he was an anomaly among his race. The average Dreridian was tall, slender, and elegant despite their appearance. His stature was rumored to be caused by his diet of exotic food fair. Which was also rumored to be other species.

"Lord Chardon!" Lord Greggor raised his meaty arms in the air jubilantly. "How good of you to visit on such short notice." His eyes twinkled with mirth under the craggy skin.

"I didn't have much choice after you sent those representatives from the Tolitha system."

"Ahhh, well." Lord Greggor lowered his arms and shrugged. "It is protocol after all." He clapped his hands together. "Come. Lord Pondur awaits. We have a nice feast set up for you."

"Oh," Ganna smirked. "I bet you do."

"Such distrust," Lord Greggor replied slyly.

They followed him to the personal lift that would take them up to the main floor of the palace. It was a tight fit with Lord Greggor's four guards and Chardon's people totally twelve. The silence felt awkward yet no one dared to break it. There would be enough conversation to go around when they got to their destination.

The doors opened to the main corridor bustling with servants carrying various plates of food to a room down the hall. Chardon remembered it being the conference room where they had a huge misunderstanding years ago.

Right as they entered, the servants had finished setting the room and hurried out. At the end of the table, front and center, Lord Pondur sat sipping from a delicate bejeweled chalice. He wore an impeccable suit tailored to his slender frame. The craggy skin looked freshly cleaned. He halted mid sip and glanced over at his guest. Lowering his chalice, he gave a warm smile.

"Ahh, the Lassians. And Halfar," he said with pity.

Chardon stiffened, not looking Halfar's way. He didn't have to. He could feel the malice coming off the former ruler.

"Lord Pondur." Chardon gave him a respectful head bow.

"Please, sit. Relaxed. We have much to discuss."

The spread of food and drinks on the table resembled a mini banquet. Chardon knew instantly it was to appease them for the lies to come. Modas stood in the corner while Trinon sat at the very end of the table to keep a full view of the room.

"What seems to be the problem?" Lord Pondur crossed his hands over his lap.

Chardon glared at him. "Besides being surprised by a group of off worlders calling me their Regent?"

"You sound put off by it. What issue besides the random attacks makes you upset?"

"How many?" Chardon slammed a fist on the table. Lord Greggor's craggy brow raised. "Tell me what you gave her." Anger filled his tone.

Lord Pondur met his eyes with equal hostility. Talas drummed his fingers on the hilt of his dagger secured at the hip. He had relinquished his sword at the door.

"Lady Sestis negotiated for real estate on many occasions. Of course, she didn't always get what she desired." Lord Greggor grunted in amusement. "In the end, she was granted Regency over three planets previously held by the Razznians, own bwing Nasfir, the Tolitha system, and four scattered around the Rendal system."

The silence spoke volumes. Ganna stopped eating mid bite. Chafar kept his head down but a frown formed. Mara sat with her mouth gaped open. Chardon's expression went from fury to defeat. His fist slid off the table as he sat straight in his chair.

For a long time, he stared at nothing, contemplating what to say next. He finally looked around the room and got back on track.

"First," he leaned forward, "those planets under Razzna will go back to them."

"That is not how…"

"You will reverse that decision."

"How about you ask the Razznians if they still want those said planets?"

Chardon balked at him. "Why wouldn't they?"

Lord Pondur shrugged, raising his hands at his side.

Flustered, Chardon nonetheless continued.

"Fine. I will ask Lord Kraznan. As for the others. Why did you not help them? That enemy horde could easily come for yours."

"They would be daft to do so. And I could not give aid without their Regent's permission."

"Gah!" Ganna dropped her half-eaten cake on her plate. "That's a lie, and you know it."

"Careful," Lord Pondur wagged his finger.

"They are moving laterally." Halfar said. "It's only a matter of time before they arrive in your system."

"Oh, but they would have to pass Azrom. I'm sure that armada would nip those miscreants in the bud." Lord Pondur smiled, retrieving his chalice.

Halfar's eyes went wide. He sat back.

"You expect Azrom to do the dirty work."

"That's a crude way of putting it," Lord Greggor retorted.

"But he's not wrong." Ganna glared at the portly creature.

"Why do we have to venture so far out of our system to fight an unknown enemy when the mighty Azrom can wipe them out before then." Lord Pondur took a sip of his drink. "Saving the galactic trade."

They all stared at him, marveling at his audacity. The conversation would go downhill from there. Chardon seethed inside.

****

The Lassian entourage exited the lift and onto the dock platform with a haste that bordered on running. I have to leave. Now. Chardon barely contained his rage. Their ship was ready, the ramp already extended down. No one acknowledged them as they marched up.

Inside the main cabin, he plopped into his seat and strapped in. Talas stood over him.

"What? If you have a complaint about how I handled that, say it," Chardon spat.

"Not at all." Talas moved to sit three seats down from him. "I only wanted to say calm yourself. We can find a way to remedy the situation."

"That pompous ass knew exactly what he was doing." Ganna settled into her seat, already in the restraints. "He better hope Azrom is victorious. That's the only way the Dreridians avoid a fight."

With everyone ready for travel, the ship lifted off and headed back to the void of space. Once it passed the checkpoint, a vortex opened back to New Lassa.

****

Waiting in the council room when they arrived were the three aliens along with Jaron. Drinks had already been poured and set on the table before each cushion seat. Chardon sat cross legged on the cushion at the end and took a sip. He coughed, not expecting the harsh liquor.

"I figured you all would need something stronger after a meeting with that self-centered aristocrat." Jaron snorted at the look on Chardon's face turning bright pink.

"And you were right." Talas took a swig and exhaled. "It was quite a show."

"I wanted to rip the crags off his skin!" Halfar tossed back a good amount. He immediately caught his breath, tilting his head side to side.

"What was the outcome, if I may ask?" Ambassador Lombis leaned forward as he addressed Chardon.

"We're going to have a look at our new enemy," Ganna replied.

"And hope it doesn't come to war," Halfar finished. "Now it's my turn."

****

Night had fallen which suited Halfar fine. He didn't need a long send off. The gate guardian was at the console setting the coordinates for Azrom. The vortex appeared ahead and he began his walk into the void. As usual, he would arrive on the roof of the main palace. Stepping out on the other side, he was greeted by General Kur.

The seven-foot-tall warrior stood with arms crossed. His forest green hair flowing down to his waist. The full body battle suit hugged his slender muscular frame. His signature longsword, in an ornate sheath was attached to the sash at his waist.

"Halfar. This is unexpected." Kur stepped forward, meeting him halfway. "What brings you here unannounced?"

"A strange, yet dire, predicament."

"Oh? Does it involve carnage?"

"Possibly."

"Sounds interesting." Kur tilted his head and gave him a slight smile. "Come. We are in the emperor's lounge."

They fell in step with each other and walked down the stone staircase to the next level.

"No fires to put out today?" Halfar squinted at the sunlight bearing down on him. It was midday on Azrom. "Is my cousin slacking off?"

"He couldn't even if he wanted to. Your child is pregnant with twins. He is running on fumes trying to multitask."

"Twins?" Halfar stopped walking. "Is she alright?"

"Is that a real questions?"

Halfar grinned. His daughter Farin was never not moving. Always in flux and a deadly fighter. He should have known better than to ask.

"I warned Romnus."

Kur snorted. "We all did."

They rounded the side of the building and entered the doorway leading into the main sector of the palace. Soldiers marched down the corridors in full armor. Servants moved out of their way, careful not to drop their wares. At the end of the long hallway, the two turned off into a dimly lit corridor. Towards the middle, light shined out from an open door.

Halfar's cousin, Romnus, the current Supreme Ruler of Azrom sat on a section of the plush seating surrounding a small round table inside the lounge.

Next to him was General Rass, Kur's mate. Halfar sat across from his cousin and Kur took the seat by Rass.

"Really, cousin?" Romnus leaned back in his chair. His massive body filled every inch of it. "No warning?"

A devilishly handsome being with dark curls that brushed the top of his shoulders and full lips, he was nearly twice Halfar's size in muscle mass. He wore his usual black cloak with thick, black fur lining the collar. Underneath he wore an all black bodysuit. His boots had a lackluster shine, dirt caked at the tops. He's been in the fields again.

"It's a dire matter that may involve carnage," Kur offered.

"That's my expertise," Rass said.

"Which is why I have come to ask a favor." Halfar settled into his chair.

"That does not bode well." Kur's eyes narrowed.

"Do you remember the deeds of Sestis?"

The others stiffened at the mention of that woman. Kur's lips curled in disgust. Romnus simply nodded in slow movements. Those jeweled eyes burned with fury. Rass rolled his eyes, not wanting to think about her.

"Now what?" Kur asked. "It never gets any better, does it?"

Halfar took a deep breath and exhaled.

"During her times gallivanting around the galaxy, she managed to negotiate Regency of an entire solar system and a slew of other planets."

Romnus' eyes almost bulged from their sockets.

Rass actually sat straight. "You're joking."

"With her death, the Regency falls on Chardon." Halfar continued without replying. "New Lassa is now the proud rulers."

"For the love of…" Kur began.

"What's the favor?" Romnus cut in.

"You see, there is a new enemy raising havoc on the five systems. The one we hold Regency over, the Tolitha system, came for help by suggestion from the Dreridians."

"Uh huh. I don't like that part either," Kur said.

"When asked why they did not assist," Halfar paused for effect. "Lord Pondur eluded that when the enemy moves this way they would have to pass Azrom and you would obviously wipe them out for the sake of galactic trade."

"Is that so?" Romnus was not amused.

Azrom's dealings with the Dreridians was nothing short of a lesson in thievery. They had demanded an exorbitant amount of product to cover lost revenue and still ended up penalizing Azrom. There was no love for the trade tyrants.

Halfar pulled a chip from the small insert of his jacket and placed it on the data platform embedded in the table. The battle feed from before played. Rass leaned forward, getting a closer look. Kur crossed his arms. Halfar could see his fingers digging into his forearms. When the feed neared its end, Halfar paused it.

Romnus reached into his cloak and pulled out a small orange fruit. He rolled it in his hand for a while before taking a bite. Its juice wet his lips and he licked it off slowly. The fruit was mildly poisonous, like a neurotoxin, causing paralysis in most. It only calmed Romnus slightly, acting as a sedative if he took too much.

"I am requesting three armada ships for the scouting party to show a force of might." Halfar waited for an answer. Romnus appeared to ignore him. "Cousin." He said sternly.

Romnus glanced over at him, still chewing the rest of the fruit he shoved in his mouth.

"That would only add fuel to the fire." Romnus used a finger to remove any excess juice from his lips. "What good is a scouting mission if the goal is a fight? Cousin."

Halfar looked at the shadow lurking in the dark corner.

"How long are you going to keep quiet? I'm sure you have an opinion."

The figure moved into the light. Farin, his daughter, now Queen of Azrom, was beautiful as ever. A prominent belly protruded beneath the dark robes. Eyes like her father amid her mother's features gleamed.

"How did you know I was here?" She seems perplexed.

Romnus laughed. "You're not as stealthy as you think."

"I knew the moment you entered." Halfar smiled. "It's good to see you, my child."

Farin blushed. She walked over to the table maneuvering past Kur and hugged Halfar,

"It's good to see you too, father." She stayed standing. "As for my opinion. I think a small battalion is ideal. The goal is not to pick a fight but avoid one."

"If they listen," Rass said.

"And they don't look like they would," Kur added.

"If it all goes south, we go back in with true Azrom power." Farin rubbed her belly. "As an alliance, we can't have New Lassa seen as weak."

"I understand that," Romnus replied, heatedly. "This seems like the wrong tactic."

"Hit hard or not at all." Kur said.

Rass sat back. "But there lies the dilemma. We have no idea what reinforcements they have."

They remained silent not looking at each other. Halfar finally spoke.

"So what is your answer?"

Romnus stared at him with disinterest. He could sense Farin tense up behind her father.

"I'll have to think about this. The last thing Azrom needs is another war."

"Yet, it will come to you whether you want it or not." Halfar stood. "I can find a guard to escort me back to the gate."

Farin grabbed his arm, stopping him from moving. "You're not leaving!" Halfar turned to her. "You haven't visited my son or the rest of my people."

"If the Supreme Ruler agrees, I would love to stay and visit for a day or two."

Romnus glared at him. "Tread carefully, cousin." Farin slowly turned her gaze on him. "It's not even a question. Of course you can stay. What are you implying?"

"Nothing at all. Cousin."

"Really?" Kur said exasperated. "This game the two of you play is getting stale."

"Has," Rass retorted.

Halfar took his daughter's hand in his. "Lead the way."

As the two left the room, Halfar peeked behind him at the feed frozen in midair. Rass reached over and hit the replay.

Good. See what I see.

******

A transmission came through the gate console and the operator skimmed the contents. It was a message Halfar had been waiting for. He copied the feed on to one of the tiny recording chips before paging another guardian to come retrieve it. The handoff complete, he resumed his tasks. He had some anxiety about the upcoming mission.

While he calculated how to maneuver the vortices, he wondered if Halfar still had the same burning desire for carnage as he did when he was supreme ruler of Azrom. As much as the operator despised him, he understood Halfar's needed expertise.

"Don't let anyone stop you," he called out to the other guardian already yards away. "That message is important."

The guardian waved a hand in the air as acknowledgement. He made his way to the commons where Chardon and Halfar resided in their personal chamber. Using his knuckles, he tapped on their door. Halfar flung the door open, startling the guardian.

"What brings you here so early in the day?" Halfar did not look pleased.

Wearing only a pair of leggings, his hair in disarray, he appeared to have just rolled out of bed. His murky green eyes bore into the guardian.

"I am to deliver this urgent message from Azrom." The guardian held out the chip.

"Oh." Halfar's demeanor changed. He smoothed his hair back with both hands. "Give me a moment.

He shut the door. The guardian heard muffled voices and people moving around. He waited patiently in the hall. When the door finally opened, Halfar was dressed with Chardon walking up behind him.

"Give it me." Halfar held out a hand. The guardian placed it in his palm. "Thank you. I am grateful. Please wake the rest of the council and have them meet us in the war room."

The guardian bowed and left the commons. He too didn't like the idea of their leader sending a scout party to hostile territory. *Haven't we suffered enough?* Back outside, he looked up at the yellowing sky signaling daybreak. *This was not Lassa.* He sighed and continued walking. *No need to dwell on the obvious any longer.*

By sunrise, everyone involved with the mission were gathered in one room. Halfar had already read the message. He sat next to Chardon at the center of the table. Jaron came in rubbing her eyes. She sat across from Talas who had already downed one glass of his breakfast drink.

"What is so dire that we had to crawl out of bed at the crack of dawn?" She stretched while yawning.

"My request for three Azrom ships has been approved."

"Then the planned mission is a go," Talas exclaimed in delight. He clapped his hands together and eyed Jaron on the other side. "Are you ready?"

Ambassador Lombis clasped his hands together on the table. "I have sent a secured message to the ruling planet in our system. They await your arrival."

"Our political councilman and I will be on the first ship to negotiate along with energy users. Trinon and Und will be the leads on the second ship in case a fight does break out. The third ship will have most of the weapons to lay cover fire if it gets nasty."

"Huh." The head of science's mouth downturned. "A three tier mission. I like that. Would you mind letting me ride along? I want to get more data on their tech."

Ganna immediately protested. "If that's the case, I should be going as well!"

"Absolutely not." Chardon didn't yell, his harsh tone effective. "We need you here to coordinate any emergency actions."

She almost pouted. Talas fought back his anger. He never liked her either. Could never trust her. Every time something sinister happened on Lassa, it always led back to Ganna. He looked away from her and met Jaron's gaze. She had the same look on her face. They both fell in a silent disdain.

"I want detailed reports." Chardon leaned against the table. "The more information we get, the better. If possible, get a hostage."

General T'Halgar's head snapped up in horror. "You can't be serious!"

"They would probably die first than be taken by their enemy." Emperor Xanic said.

Halfar's eyes narrowed. He felt the bloodlust fill his veins.

"All the more reason to capture one."

The three aliens flinched at the expression on his face. Talas tilted his head to one side as he took at the former ruler's demeanor. Oh, yes. He was coming on the mission.

No doubt.

Bad Blood

Three Azrom armada ships waited on the outskirts of New Lassa's stratosphere for their crew to be beamed up. Each one spanned close to three hundred meters in length and fifty meters wide. Their dark metallic gray hulls were accented with maroon markings beneath the Azrom symbol. Purple lights ran down their length on both sides.

On New Lassa's surface, four blocks of fighters and representatives stood in formation. The two on the end were split at the center with Trinon commanding one group and Und the other. Talas, Chardon and Halfar led the center block and the third were a group of energy users led by Jaron's second in command along with the head of science. Behind him were General T'Halgar and Ambassador Lombis.

Halfar tapped his wristband and it blinked blue.

"Ready for transport." He waited for a response.

"Commencing retrieval. Stand by for allocation of the first ship."He turned to Talas and nodded.

Behind them, the political advisor fidgeted with his robes.

"Nervous?" Talas smiled at him.

"What?" The advisor smirked. "Pfft! Not at all. I was just thinking maybe I should have worn my short sleeved robe in case I had to fight after all."

"It's too late now," Halfar said.

A wide beam of light shot from above and engulfed Talas' group. Each person disappeared as it narrowed into a thin line. When the blinding light died, they found themselves in the main docking area of an Azrom ship.

"Let's get ready for departure." Talas led his group down the corridor towards the bridge.

He could see the other groups get beamed up to their designated ships as well.

*****

Jaron and Ganna watched from the lookout on the hillside. Both had grim expressions on their faces. A sick feeling came over Jaron and she mentally pushed it away.

I have to think positive!

"This is going to end badly." Ganna's outburst somehow echoed in the wind.

"How about not sending bad omens to our people as they go into unknown territory."

Ganna rolled her eyes. "No need to get testy. I was merely stating the obvious."

"That's part of your problem," Jaron seethed. "Not everyone wants to hear that."

Ganna turned from the ledge and made her way down the narrow walkway.

"I'm going to prep for incoming wounded. No need to fumble that protocol."

Jaron spun around and was blocked by Modas. She hadn't heard the manbeast approach. She never did. Modas towered over her.

"Don't. It's not worth it." Hands clenched, Jaron nodded. She knew better than to let that woman get to her. "Everyone will come back alive."

"But not unharmed."

"No."

****

Trinon did a walkthrough of the ship to get familiar with its features. Und had reluctantly followed, seeing the benefit. He was miffed that Trinon was the one to suggest it first. Did it really matter? The manbeasts and fighters in their charge steered clear of their verbal attacks on each other. Trinon ducked around the arch of a high beam and continued down the corridor towards the weapons room.

"So, great superstar of manbeasts, are you about satisfied with your inspection?" Und's voice was filled with venom.

"What does that mean?" Trinon glanced behind him at Und. "And it's not MY inspection. If things get bad, we need to know where everything is."

"Of course. You are always so observant."

The condescending tone was not lost on Trinon.

He let out a loud sigh.

"I am not going to fight with you, Und."

"Good. Then don't assume you know everything and dictate what my unit needs to do."

"I never…" Trinon was not allowed to finish.

He saw Und turn around and went back towards the main cabin. At the cross section he veered off course for the weapons bay. The amount of weapons could determine if they got out alive.

Brute Force

Small projectiles fired from an angle outside the vortex rim rained down on the left bow of the armada ships as they eased out into the system's main planet space. Red and gold lights criss crossed between the enemy ships holding position in an arc around the planet and the military forces defending it. Land to space weapons fired at will knocking a few of the enemy ships out of orbit.

It wasn't enough.

There were at least fifty enemy ships bombarding the surface. Talas was certain there were ground troops causing destruction. The armada ships had the advantage due to their unexpected arrival and size. The puny rounds merely left scorch marks on the hull where they hit. The ships cruised forward to find a landing on the surface. Halfway there, he decided on a different strategy.

"One of these ships needs to stay in orbit," he addressed the head of science.

"We would be sitting wide open!" The man balked.

"True, but this ship has more fire power than the enemy. They are not going to stop fighting just so we can plead with them to do so."

"The whole reason for the mission…"

Talas held up a hand to stop him. "Our forces will transport down. You will get to see the planet up close and personal."

"And you?"

"As much as I want to get my hands wet, I will stay here."

"Fine." The science leader turned from him and headed to the transport bay. "I wish you luck."

Talas' lips went thin. He stared at the massive amount of firepower pummeling the planet. It was nonstop; relentless. The other two ships sped passed a group of enemy ships and punched through the atmosphere in fiery glory. To his dismay a handful of enemy ships followed, training their weapons on the ships.

The bridge rocked, tilting hard to the right. Alarms went off and the overheads flickered. He managed to keep his balance. The main screen changed to show a group of ten enemy ships had turned so their weapons were dead locked on the armada ship. Talas glared at the screen.

"Damage report?" He called out to the technician.

The tech turned his head so fast, Talas almost thought it would keep going one hundred and eighty degrees. A look of terror covered his face.

"There's a breach in the hull!" He pointed to a group of smaller enemy ships clamping on. "They're attempting to board!"

"Have the science leader and all the energy users been transported?"

"Yes."

A sinister smile spread on Talas' face. "Good. Lock down the bridge. Send the order for our soldiers to assemble near the breach."

"Of course." The tech went back to focusing on his station.

Talas motioned to the five soldiers standing near the doors. They nodded and went out before him as the doors slid open. Guess I'm going to get to play after all.

****

The first armada ship managed to land at the capital where the majority of the attack was occurring. It seemed the enemy was dead set on wiping it out first. The main building was already in ruins from multiple rounds over the past year. Royal guards were barely keeping the enemy at bay. Chardon and Halfar met the representatives racing out of the ship and took cover near a group of fighters positioned by a stone staircase that led up to the top of the building.

General T'Halgar pointed to a man perched near the top, laying rounds of laser fire onto the enemy below.

"That is His Majesty Cogar Wenthril!" He called out. "I have never seen him outside the palace in a battle."

Hearing his name and title called in the hot wind, the ruler of the planet glanced down at them, his hand never leaving the giant gun's trigger. Chardon stared at him in awe.

The man was indeed majestic in every way. Even with his royal garb dirty, torn, and bloody, he stood with authority, a bicep exposed through a large tear showing off muscles. Half of his dark blonde tendrils had come out of its ponytail and waved in the air as if reaching forward. Grey eyes squinted in rage.

"We have to get to him!" General T'Halgar yelled.

The ruler made a tsk sound. He was out of rounds. Climbing down, he landed close to Chardon at the middle of the staircase.

"This is what you deem reinforcements? Forgive me for sounding ungrateful but…" he swept an arm across the landscape. "They won't stop."

Halfar stepped forward and met his gaze. "These are Azrom ships. They can handle this much."

"So you say." Cogar was not impressed.

The Lassian political leader held up the translator.

"Have you been able to decipher their language?"

"They didn't give us a chance to."

"We started sending a cease message to allow negotiations. To let them know this planet is under New Lassa Regency."

"And?" A royal soldier handed Cogar a new cartridge. He ejected the used one and slapped the other in.

"Something is odd." The political leader watched the translator go through its database and flicker blue multiple times. "It's like it found it but didn't."

The translator went solid blue. Enemy rounds seemed to lessen as if in slow motion. They looked up at the sky, witnessing a backdraft of smoky air. There was an eerie silence blanketing the planet. The translator clicked. The blue light turned red, losing its signal.

And the enemy unleashed a round of hell. Like a meteor shower, the ships in orbit resumed firing onto the surface with increased intensity.

****

The leader of the energy users immediately called out formation. They all scattered to encircle the palace and the royal soldiers within the perimeter. Hands raised, glowing with blue pulse energy, they collectively blocked the onslaught. The strain was harsh.

She felt her arms start to burn and pain shot through them like they were about to break into pieces. She held on for as long as she could until her bones snapped, howling in pain as the enemy blast receded from being repelled.

Chardon rushed to her side and dragged her out of the formation. Both her hands were broken along with all her fingers. The tips of her forearm bone stuck out from the skin. Chardon looked around and found a few more energy users with the same injuries.

A loud ping made Chardon look over his shoulder. Halfar had one arm morphed into a claw in the air. Tiny black dots smoldered on its shell.

"Get down!" The moment he said it, a barrage of laser fire came at them.

Chardon watched in horror as a few hit Halfar. Seconds later, he felt a few of them penetrate his body as well. Two hit the already down energy user. Not deterred by the onslaught, Halfar located the enemy soldiers firing on them from below and jumped into the fray. Chardon dragged the leader the rest of the way to a collapsed stone corridor. It would act as a shield for now.

Angry, Chardon stood and stared at the sky. Another round was coming at them. Wide, bright orange and capable of wiping out the capital, it sailed forward like a phoenix of death. *Not while I stand!* Chardon conjured up a ball of energy that expanded to nearly the same size as the blast. He would stop it at all costs.

****✳****

Trinon got his troops off the ship and made his way to the center of the field covered in debris. Up ahead, the enemy was still firing on the planet soldiers. Und was leading his unit the opposite way towards the right behind Trinon.

"Where are you going?" Trinon shouted over the sounds of destruction. "We need to lay an offense."

Und stopped and turned to him.

"You don't dictate strategy for me."

"This is not…" Trinon gave him a dire look. "Your unit needs to go around," he pointed to the area behind the enemy further out on the left, "and take out the enemy from that side while I…"

"I will command my men as I see fit. I don't tell you how to lead!"

"Und!" Trinon was getting impatient.

The whole argument saddened him.

"You want to go play hero, I won't stop you."

Und walked away.

Trinon turned to his own unit of manbeasts. They all seemed embarrassed for him. And ashamed of the dysfunctional display.

"Let's go. This planet needs our help."

As they moved towards the area, a group of enemy fighters spotted them. Here goes nothing. Trinon extended his claws. He hit the first one that came at him and his talons scraped off the hard hide. Like armor, the enemy skin was close to impenetrable.

Trinon realized he had to hit a lot harder. He dodged the crude, short blade, bending almost ninety degrees backwards. Still low, he swiveled to the side and brought his talons up into the enemy's abdomen where the exposed skin was not as tough.

The enemy let out a horrid shriek, making Trinon wince, as it continued to try and strike him down. Trinon pushed deeper even as he felt the short blade slice into his back behind the shoulder. Finally, the enemy slumped. He pushed them off, letting the innards spill out. The enemy's grip on the blade went slack and Trinon pulled it out, tossing it away.

A slew of them came for him and he fought them off, clearing a path for his manbeasts towards the struggling planet fighters. That foreboding didn't subside. He managed a reprieve and stood in an empty space looking up while his men fought around him.

He saw the enemy fire streak across the sky towards the surface. Madness. Then everything seemed to stop. The hairs on his body rose. The streaks dissipated and a split second later, he saw the heavy stream shoot down. Some of his manbeasts were hit including the enemy's own fighters. They were all defenseless in the open fields.

He glanced over at where Und had gone to gain position. There was no way his unit would get out of it unscathed. As he had envisioned, the enemy moved swiftly towards Und's troops. Trinon already had an advantage on his end.

He motioned for his second in command. The manbeast dispatched an enemy and turned to him.

"Continue to the designated point. I am going to try and divert the attack on the other side." The manbeast gave him a sorrowful stare. "I know. Despite how much of an ass my brother is, I can't leave him to die."

"Understood." The manbeast whistled to two others. "Take them with you."

Trinon half smiled. He nodded and the three of them headed for Und. As they got close, Trinon noticed one group of enemy fighters switch out their weapons. Instead of the medium sized guns and short blades, they heaved a larger weapon with a wide barrel out of their battle cruisers. Ugly metal with what appeared to be tentacles wrapped around its body.

Planet fighters had formed a defense line ahead and the enemy aimed right for them. Trinon had no way of stopping it. He had no choice but to watch the red tendrils fired from the new weapon hit them head on. The tendrils lassoed around their bodies and started to burn into their uniform down to the flesh. Smoldering skin resulted from their insides being cooked.

The tendrils invaded their bodies like tree roots, destroying tissue as it went. The fighters barely had time to scream, and it was cut short as they fell to the ground.

Trinon squeezed his eyes shut as he continued to flash step towards Und's location. He could hear more of the new enemy weapons firing. Above, he saw the wide beam of light spread over the capital. This mission was a bad idea.

An enemy grabbed Und from behind and he stabbed his talons into their head. There were already three of his manbeasts down. Protecting them was priority. When the fight shifted after the weird silence, he knew he had made a mistake. He would never tell Trinon that. The new onslaught had him barely holding his own. I will not die here!

Out of the corner of his eye, he saw a planet fighter hit with a glob of red veinlike things. The horrified scream cut off as the red tendrils moved into their body made Und stop dead in his tracks. His eyes went wide in disbelief; and fear.

What is that?

He was about to move to take down the enemy that shot the stuff when he saw Trinon and two other manbeasts coming towards him. They halted a few feet from him.

"What are you doing?" Und spun on him.

"We came to assist."

"I have this under control!" Und snapped. "Take care of your own people!"

"This is not the time for this," Trinon replied calmly. "They have a new weapon."

"Yeah, I saw it. I'm about to take that thing out."

"It's more than that one, Und."

"Then you go get the rest yourself!"

"Und, you need to listen to reason."

"Get out of my way, Trinon."

Und stepped past him, heading for the enemy, and found himself shoved back, sailing in the air. As he passed Trinon, he saw the red tendrils open like a web towards Trinon. Right as he landed on the burnt surface, the tendrils wrapped around his brother and began embedding themselves. Trinon did not scream, his face almost blank, as he stood with his arm still out from pushing Und away.

The smell of burnt cooking flesh filled Und's nostrils. Trinon fell to the ground, his body seizing violently. Bloody foam oozed from his mouth. The tendrils snaked through every crevice inside, eating away at it.

Und's vision blurred into a red haze. A fury rose in him more vile than anything he had ever felt. He heard his own animal growl fill the air as he launched blindly into the direction of the enemy that took down Trinon. Despair and pain lay beneath all that rage. He had gotten his brother killed. If it meant his life in return, so be it.

He would have his vengeance.

****✳****

Chardon steadied himself on the top of the palace and held the energy bubble in place. When the blast was close enough, he reshaped it into a shield spanning nearly half a mile. It was taking a lot out of him but he refused to lessen its strength. The blast hit and Chardon felt the weight of it in his whole being.

A battle of power commenced.

His feet were pushed back a few inches but he kept the pressure on. When it felt like a stalemate, he used everything he had to push the blast back on the path it came from. Multi colored speckles shimmered from his body. No. Not that! He fought to contain his power while getting more leverage.

Down below, he found Halfar in the throes of battle. He turned to Chardon, a look of fear on his face as he knew what would happen if he unleashed any more energy. A blade went through Halfar's shoulder, forcing him to arch back in surprise.

They locked eyes. Chardon had enough. This ends now. He pushed more and the blast bounced back into space.

Drained, Chardon fell to the ground. He had no strength left to save Halfar or any of the energy users still fighting. Shit! His eyes fluttered closed.

****

Talas took a deep breath as he braced for another round of enemy forces trying to make their way further into the ship. He was already wounded worse than he thought and had no time to triage himself. The enemy was true to the data. Relentless, yet they were starting to wane.

From the viewport near the breached hull, he could see out into space. It lit up in a ball of orange. Talas stared out in awe. He traced its trajectory and watched the wide beam of light hit the front line of enemy ships in one large arc. The ships were knocked back, the bridges caved in.

All attacks abruptly stopped.

A vortex opened and from the planet came a slew of cruisers and battle ships. The entire enemy fleet literally backed out of the solar system without a declaration or cover fire. Talas let out a raspy, chuckle, coughing up blood as he sat slumped against the bulkhead. The enemy ship stuck to the armada ship ripped itself off leaving a gaping hole. The ship's repair system initiated a thin membrane to seal it temporarily.

It's over. Talas fell unconscious. He let the glorious darkness wrap around him.

"…get up!…leave now!"

Talas startled awake. The science leader stood over him yelling in desperation. A medic was tying a bandage under Talas' arm and around the shoulder. He winced in pain and tried to sit up.

"What are you saying?" Talas tasted blood in his mouth. He spit some of it out.

"We need to get the wounded to New Lassa now!"

"Huh?" Talas felt out of it.

"They'll all die!"

Talas shot up abruptly. The pain screamed at him. He gritted his teeth.

"How many?"

"Doesn't matter. The enemy had a weapon we didn't know about. It's not pretty." The science leader took a sharp intake of air. "A lot of the manbeasts are down."

"What does Trinon say?" The science leader went silent. Fear gripped Talas as his chest tightened. "Where is Trinon?" He grabbed the science leader by the front of his robes.

"Trinon is one of them as is Und."

Talas fell back against the wall. Stunned, he found he couldn't catch his breath. His eyes stung painfully. This is not happening. Why is this happening?

"Come." The science leader and the medic helped him to his feet. "We have to get you strapped in for the jump."

"Jump?" Talas frowned. The science leader nodded to the breach. "Oh."

They made their way to the main cabin. As he was set in the reclining seat, the medic injected healing gel into his wound. Looking out the viewport he saw the other armada ships awaiting jump sequences as well due to the massive damage they sustained.

I didn't keep my promise.

****

Four attendants struggled to hold Und in place on the bed platform inside the medical bay. His lips were drawn back exposing gritted teeth that did nothing to stop the loud growl emitting through them. Tears streamed down his face, his hooded eyes barely slits. Blood seeped through the white gown at the shoulder, midriff, and upper left leg. His wounds had reopened from suddenly awakening in a panic.

Ganna came rushing in with an injection gun. She found an opening among the multitude of arms and shot Und in the side. He seized for a moment then went limp.

"You need to remain still!" She chastised him. He wailed, the crying almost unbearable to hear. "I haven't sealed your wounds yet. Just did a bit of triage until I could come back to you."

"Tri....non," Und managed to get out before falling into a deep sleep.

Ganna pursed her lips. It was too late for that. She understood his guilt and had no pity for him. Serves you right. She nodded to the attendants. Two of them left while the other two stayed to assist her in cleaning him up to seal his wounds. The moment the armada ships arrived and beamed down the wounded, she knew it was worse than she could imagine. Every medical bay on New Lassa was filling up.

Jaron burst into the medical wing like a wild animal. Her hair was in disarray and her eyes bulged. She was manic. Ganna tilted her head sideways towards her.

"Not now, Jaron. I need to finish this and he will rest for the next few days."

That stopped Jaron midway to the bed.

She looked confused at what to do next. Her hands shook. The tears were endless. With Und's wounds sealed, Ganna dismissed the attendants and turned to see Jaron had not moved.

"All you can do is wait. Your children are stronger than you realize." Ganna saw the pain and terror, no, felt it permeating the room. It poured out of Jaron's whole being. To her own surprise, Ganna wrapped her arms around Jaron. The woman sagged against her. "And you need to be just as strong."

Jaron begin to slide down, losing consciousness. Ganna tried to hold her up then she went light as a feather. Behind

Jaron stood Modas. He lifted her effortlessly into his arms, alleviating Ganna's plight. She could see weariness on his face.

"I will take her home." Modas turned away. "Take care of my sons."

"Of course." Ganna watched him leave then went to help the rest of the wounded being brought in. "This was a bad idea," she whispered to herself.

****✳****

Chardon was livid at himself for miscalculating the risk which Talas shared the blame. They were both angry at the enemy. To have such a horrific bioweapon that invaded then destroyed living organisms was beyond the pale. Even Halfar wasn't prepared for something he saw as monstrous. A planet bomb seemed civilized in comparison.

They sat in silence in the war room with Barbon, Chafar, and the Science head. The servants had brought two carafes of strong liquor and one was already empty. Chardon took what remained in his glass like a shot, wincing at the burn.

"I'm sorry," Talas whispered. He tinkered with his glass half full.

"For what?" Chardon snapped. "You kept your promise."

"And that was a miracle in itself," Halfar said.

Talas found no solace in their praise. He maneuvered his body at an angle to rest his wounded arm on the table, wincing at the pain. It had been grazed by the red tendrils.

The only reason he still had it was due to the thick leather forearm bands he always wore. One of the energy users still on board had ripped them off right as they struck. That no one else was hit by it was due to Talas hitting the button to barricade the corridor behind him where other fighters had retreated.

"You have to get that treated properly," Barbon said

"I will." He glanced at the amateur bandaging wound over the length of his forearm. "It doesn't hurt as bad as it looks."

"I know we determined the enemy was relentless" the Science head began, "but this was on a different level. Bordering on insanity."

"They just kept coming." Chafar stared at the wall in a trance. A patch on the right side of his forehead staunched the blood from a deep cut. "They wouldn't stop coming."

His hands shook.

Halfar's face contorted in rage. To see his own son shell shocked from a battle was too much to take. Then he thought of Jaron and Modas. The room went silent. He realized the others felt the same. Chardon got up from his cushion and went to Chafar, embracing him.

"At least we were able to push them back to the outskirts of the system." The Science head took a sip of his drink. "It was clear they weren't prepared for such an intense fight."

"And we only had three armada ships," Halfar responded proudly.

"We still have no idea the size of their forces." Talas said. "For all we know, this could have been the equivalent of ours with thousands more in the wings."

"Let's not think about that right now." Barbon stood, his massive frame blocking the hover light behind him. "We must focus on healing and assess the damage later."

"I'm going to stay here and finish this carafe of liquor," Talas said.

"Might as well," The Science head added.

He dragged the carafe closer to the end of table where they all had congregated. Barbon hesitated for a split second then sat back down.

****

Modas' horde crammed into the family commons hut where the infant playpen sat in the far corner. All his younger children were present and looking miserable. A blanket of sadness, remorse, and shame filled the room. Not one of them spoke.

Mara, Mota, and Jakar entered the gloom and they frowned in disgust. Mara snorted. Now they feel something for Trinon? She glanced over at Una huddled against the wall with red, puffy eyes. How dare you. Mota placed a hand on her shoulder. When she turned to him their eyes met. She could tell he was thinking the same. Jakar's face was blank as usual, yet she felt his anger.

"What's this?" She yelled. "Not rejoicing that your sibling fell in battle?" Some of them stared at her in horror. "You call him profane things, belittle him," she paused. "Disrespect him! And now you sit here shedding false tears."

Una extended her talon and blue light spurted from the energy user girl's hands. Mota raised a hand while he blocked them from Mara.

"Tap down." His said sternly. "Have you lost your minds?"

"Is she wrong?" Jakar asked nonchalant.

All ten of them hung their heads.

Una retracted her talons. The energy user sister powered down. There was nothing they could say. Mara didn't want to stay a moment longer. She left the hut and headed back to her own chamber quarters. She needed to hug her children.

"Trinon is different," their energy user sister finally spoke up. "We just don't understand him."

"And you never bothered to try either," Mota retorted.

"He knows that." Jakar crossed his arms. "It's why he doesn't press any of you to engage him on a personal level."

"We never…" Una started.

"Wished him harm?" Mota stepped closer, fists clenched. "You're a liar. We hear it from your mouths almost daily."

This time Jakar had to calm Mota by grabbing his shoulder. Mota wrenched away from him then also left.

He was fed up.

"You all should know how this looks to the other clans. The leader's horde not close knit like theirs. Distrust and in fighting." Jakar's eyes narrowed. "Figure it out."

He left his younger siblings to contemplate their past actions. His demeanor may not have shown it, but his blood boiled with fury. This is not how his family should be.

****⁎****

Und winced in pain from trying to turn on his side in the medical bed. His head was swimming and he felt nauseous. I have to go! The attendants had stopped treating him days ago. It was up to him if he could manage getting around on his own. His sealed wounds still hurt. Sitting up sent a pain in his chest so he opted for rolling on his side.

Like static electricity, the pain shot through his body. He caught his breath, counting in his head until it subsided.

Move! Slamming his fist on the edge of the raised platform, he pushed his hips closer to the ledge so he could swing his legs over.

Okay.

He exhaled hard then came upright. The room went off kilter and he braced himself with his hands gripping the bed, arms straight.

He fought back tears. So weak. He had never felt that before. Every battle he had been in saw him victorious even when injured. But not like this. These wounds were life threatening. I almost died. Enough of that. There was only one thing on his mind that needed to be done.

Sliding off, his feet hit the floor. The coolness steadied him. Now stand. That was not so easy. The moment he put his full weight on his legs, they buckled. He was able to catch himself a split second before hitting the floor. He turned to grip the edge of the bed and held on.

"For the love of Lassa!" He yelled in frustration.

Calmer now, he forced himself to stand. The white robe was dingy yet still white. He didn't care how he looked. With painstaking steps, he made his way to the critical ward where the more severe cases were kept in cryochambers.

The wing was dimly lit by a few hover lamps in the ceiling corners. It didn't take long to find the right one. Slumped in a chair next to the one near the back was his mother in a sour sleep. Her face was scrunched up and her fingers twitched. He reached over and moved a lock of hair from her forehead. She didn't wake up.

Thank Lassa!

Und got closer to the cryochamber and looked inside. There lay Trinon, his body a mess. The red tendrils had eaten through down to the bone. Nanobots ran all along the deep crevices repairing the damage. Bile rose in his throat. He slapped a hand over his mouth. Tears came.

I don't want this!

His body faltered and the vomit spewed forth. He retched loudly. A hand touched his back. He looked up from the mess he was making and saw Jakar standing over him. No longer able to control himself, he cried harder, causing the vomit to worsen. His older brother stayed by his side, rubbing his back.

Their mother woke up startled.

She checked her surrounding then saw Und. Without a word, she went to the storage cabinet for the suction tool to clean up the mess.

She grabbed a few wet wipes and bent down near him, wiping his face like he was a baby beast. Jakar took the suction tool from her and handled the vomit.

"I'm sorry," Und cried.

"Shh." His mother held him close to her bosom. "I know."

TWO: THREATS

Far from Normal

News of the failed Lassian mission was contained within the first royal house. Romnus didn't want rumors to flow outside the palace for good reason. The three ships had arrived covered in scorch marks, one having sustained damaged to its hull on the left side. The signs of a fierce battle. The dock crew worked through four day cycles repairing them.

Kur came into the throne room wearing his full royal military uniform. The black and red clashed with his hair. Gold fasteners kept his cloak attached at the shoulders. The longsword at his hip swayed with each step he took. At the base of the throne, he bent to one knee and bowed his head.

"Lord Romnus." He then stood and met his gaze.

"General Kur." Romnus glanced over at the royal council waiting in the wings by the side entrance. "We have much to discuss."

They always remained business like in the council's presence. After the last two rounds of betrayal, trust was not given freely. More footsteps echoed in the throne room. Rass came to Kur's side followed by Batis who went to his left. The two knelt and bowed. Getting back up, they eyed the council as well.

Romnus gestured to the royal advisors. They went towards the throne stopping a few yards from Kur's group. The first to speak stood on the end at his right.

"My lord. It has been confirmed that the enemy encountered by the Lassians is indeed moving towards Azrom. We seem to have piqued their interest."

"They were coming this way regardless," the next in line said. "If we were going to stop their advance, we should have sent a full fleet."

"There is new footage of the enemy weapons." The third one held out a viewing bubble and let it float above his hands. It grew larger for everyone to see. "Quite nasty, if I may."

The red tendrils shot forth tangling themselves around a fighter from the planet. They watched how it ravaged the body before the fighter fell to the ground half dead. Rass covered his mouth with his forearm. Batis turned away in disgust.

"Have we established a means to counter it?" Romnus found his hands gripping the sides of the throne makign his knuckles go pale. He took a deep breath and relaxed, letting his hands lay on his thighs. "I want a full analysis."

"Yeah," Batis looked over at the bubble. "I want none of that business."

Kur stood rooted, struggling to find some sense of calm and failed. What he ended up with was a horror-stricken face. His lips were slightly parted as if he wanted to yell while his eyes, though narrow, conveyed his feelings.

"Were there any casualties?" Kur finally said, regaining his composure.

"The strategist, Talas made good on his guarantee," the fourth councilman replied.

"Which might as well be moot considering the level of wounded." The fifth advisor moved closer. "I do believe we may be able to use the alliance better going forward. Razzna would also be on their route following us."

"They would never get to Razzna!" The second advisor bellowed. "We are not letting them do as they please. We are Azrom!"

Batis looked up at the ceiling in embarrassment. That part was one of Azrom's problems. The elite thinking in the old ways. That Azrom was indestructible. Unbeatable. Romnus concurred. He had been trying over the past few years to correct that sentiment.

"While we may feel this to be true, it still bears we have weaknesses like any other race." Kur rested a hand on the hilt of his sword. "Lassians have never been a race of warriors. They had to become one to defend their home world."

"Until we blasted it into the void," Rass added.

The silence was heavy. No one needed to be reminded of Halfar's selfish deed. The first advisor cleared his throat, breaking the mood.

"Yes. They have no battle ships nor a sizable army." He clasped his hands before him. "Do we really want them to develop such things?"

Romnus thought about New Lassa. A peaceful population with no real strife. Only delivering might when provoked. No. He didn't want to see the Lassians become a hardened race. It would break Farin's heart.

"To avoid such a fate, we need to be their army," the third advisor suggested. "A new plan set in place." The viewing bubble lowered into his hand and winked out of existence.

"Generals?" Romnus addressed Kur and Rass. Then he turned to Batis. "Commander Batis?"

"I say we wait." Batis crossed his arms, standing akimbo.

"Are you daft?" Kur looked over at him. "We don't want them coming here."

"I think he means to wait and see if they veer off course," Rass said.

Batis nodded. "Their interest may be piqued, but my guess is they want their next fight to be less grueling. Whet the appetite."

"That sounds equally as bad." The second advisor frowned. "Raising havoc between there and Azrom would throw off trade."

"Good!" Romnus exclaimed, startling everyone. "Then the Dreridians can see the consequences of not acting in the first place."

"Oh, come now!" The fourth advisor scoffed. "They would never lift a finger to do dirty work unless it was on their turf."

"I need one of you to visit New Lassa and get more details." Romnus leaned back on the throne, resting his head on the top ledge. "And make sure my cousin is alright."

"Really?" Kur raised his brow. "You think Halfar would allow himself to be injured in a battle? Do you know him? Have you met?"

Romnus glared down at him. Kur's playful expression lingered as the corners of his mouth twitched upwards in an attempt to smile.

"He's not invincible."

Kur cocked his head to one side. "No. But he is stubborn and doesn't like to lose."

"Are you volunteering?" Romnus snapped.

"I'll go. Can I include our Science Officer?"

"That is a given." Romnus raised his head. "Is that acceptable, council?"

The five bowed their heads in acknowledgement. They turned and left the throne room through the side door.

The moment the door shut, Romnus stepped off the throne. He got within a few feet of Kur.

"I don't have to tell you how bad this looks."

"No. We've conquered worlds before with only three ships. This is unprecedented." Kur dropped his head down. His eyes shifted. "Where did these things come from?"

"Exactly." Romnus turned to Batis. "I want full tracers. I'm sure New Lassa is doing the same. If we can combine our findings, we'll get an accurate location."

"On it." Batis pivoted towards the main entrance and marched out.

"I'm starving." Romnus followed Batis out.

Kur and Rass stayed for a moment. Both contemplated what all the current incidents meant. A new enemy from some other part of the galaxy? Why now? They turned around and went to catch up with Romnus.

"He's supposed to wait for us to escort him."

Rass chastised him silently.

"Do you really think we are protecting that behemoth?"

"He's not that big," Rass tsked, waving the thought away.

"Not like your father, no." Kur smirked. "Now that is a monster."

Rass gave him a shocked face, dropped jaw included. Kur tilted his head away from him.

"I'm not wrong."

He got a wild idea in his head. Maybe he could take his father-in-law to New Lassa. It would scare the hell out of the manbeasts who hadn't witnessed such a species. He grinned mischievously.

****

The gate guardian frowned at the console activating on its own. From the incoming signature, he knew it came from Azrom. Most likely General Kur. When the portal opened to let a small entourage walk through, his guess was immediately confirmed. There was no mistaking the seven-foot-tall monster. Behind him was an even bigger monstrosity. The guardian gaped at what he felt could only be a beast.

The group arrived at the platform centered in front of the gate as it powered down. The guardian made eye contact with General Kur.

"If you had sent a communication ahead of time, I would have gladly opened the gate for you." The guardian's eyes narrowed.

"Where's the fun in that?" General Kur gave him a lopsided grin. "Where is Halfar?"

The guardian placed his hands flat on the console. "Resting like the others." He was certain General Kur knew about the failed mission.

"Is he injured?" General Kur asked, surprised.

"Nothing serious. He's more angry than hurt as I see it."

"Hmm. That makes sense."

"What," the guardian cleared his throat, feeling nervous, "is…I mean…who is that behind you?" He tried not to stare too intensely.

"That!" Mota called out as he approached from the fields, "is Rass's father, Commander Abras."

The guardian stood straight, shocked at the revelation. There was no way. He looked up past General Kur to the massive Azrom soldier and saw the resemblance.

"How?" He breathed. Startled that he said it out loud, he stepped back, embarrassed.

"Mota," General Kur addressed the manbeast. "I would have expected Trinon to greet us."

"That's not possible." Mota's expression went dark. He turned to the guardian. "Please continue to keep watch. We may have more visitors over the next few moon cycles."

"Of course." He watched General Kur's entourage follow Mota to the main compound. Commander Abras walked past him and blocked all light. Such power. The guardian stared at the bulging muscles until the group disappeared over the hillside.

Kur waited for Mota to explain about Trinon and none was forthcoming. As they reached the edge of the village, he broached the subject.

"What stops your brother from greeting us, Mota?"

The manbeast stopped, not looking back to face him.

"My brother was one of the critically wounded."

Kur halted in shock. He saw Mota's hands ball into fists.

"How bad?" Kur wanted to think it was not as dire as it seemed, yet he braced for the worst.

"Bad." Mota relaxed his hands. "The enemy's weapon were these red tendrils. They wrapped around his whole body."

Kur went pale. The battle footage had seared in his mind. Seeing what those red tendrils did to that one fighter, he couldn't fathom Trinon being caught in something like that.

"Your family." Kur dropped his head.

"Is a wreck, actually." This time Mota did turn his head and smile; the sadness clear.

They resumed their walk and arrived at the main compound. A manbeast family strolling along the road slowed their pace as they caught sight of Rass's father. The same happened with others who came across the entourage. It didn't faze the soldier in the least.

At the far corner of the building, the group turned onto a stone path that led to the common area and private chambers. Mota halted at the door inside the main corridor. He tapped the side of the frame.

"Halfar. You have visitors." Mota looked over at Rass's father. Would he even fit in the door? He tapped again, harder. "Halfar."

The door swung open. Chardon in female form stood wearing a plain manilla colored lounge robe. Her eyes were puffy and slightly pink. She had clearly been crying. Her gaze landed on the group behind Mota.

"This is," she sighed heavily. "Not unexpected." She moved out of the way and gestured for them to enter. She saw Rass's father. "You may want to lower your head first."

Halfar lay sleeping on the bed with beads of sweat covering his forehead. Bandages, with dark splotches, were wrapped across his bare chest. His breathing sounded labored.

"We're waiting for a medic to come." Chardon sat next to Halfar on the bed. She reached into a basin full of water on the nearby side table and wrung out a rag. "We let the worst injured get treated first. I didn't know how bad his were. He never said anything." She wiped his brow.

Kur became angry. Not only about the enemy. It was Halfar's stubborn nature.

"Of course not!" Kur spat. "He has too much pride."

"I will go check on when the medic will get here." Mota did a half bow and left the room.

Kur grabbed one of the straight-back chairs gathered in the corner and pulled it closer to Chardon. He sat down and leaned into it.

"It was more brutal than reported then."

"I wish I could take it all back. Start over with a better plan." Chardon's hand fell onto her lap. "I have failed my people once again."

"No!" Kur's outburst made Chardon flinch. "You will not blame yourself for this."

"I was naïve. I thought even if we couldn't bring them to listen to reason, with three armada ships, the balance of might would tip in our favor."

"And on any other occasion, that would be true." Kur let one of his arms hang to the side of the chair. "This enemy is more formidable than we anticipated."

Halfar opened his eyes and glanced over at Kur. He tried to sit up. Chardon and Kur instinctively pushed him back down.

"You stay," Kur ordered. Halfar bared his teeth. "Still got enough in you to fight?" Halfar's eyes glazed over. In seconds, he was back asleep. "I thought not."

A medic waited to be acknowledged at the open door. Chardon waved them in.

"Please." Chardon moved off the bed. "Take care of him."

"Of course, leader."

Kur rose from his seat. "Good. We need to talk. Now."

Chardon nodded, taking one more look at Halfar while the medic used a portable scanner to check his vitals.

"Let's go. I will send for the others." Chardon led them out of the room.

Rass's father once again squeezed through the door frame, hunched down at an almost ninety-degree angle. Chardon glanced back at him in pity. Along the way to the conference room, she stopped a servant and told them to gather the council.

Azrom's science officer, Lt. Treshur, looked around the room, taking in its simplicity. Kur understood his fascination. He too marveled at the minimalism of the Lassians. Though he had heard about Chardon's parents being quite flamboyant, Sestis following suit.

Kur sat dead center on the left side of the large oval table. Rass's father took to the cushions in the far corner reserved for the manbeasts. He fit snug on top of them. Chardon sat across from Kur while the science officer sat next to Kur. Within minutes, the council arrived followed by servants bringing drink carafes and small plates of food.

Not long after, Talas came in.

The warrior's hollow appearance struck Kur. His face was gaunt, and his arm was bare in a sling, though no wounds were present. Talas noticed him looking and managed a tight smile.

"It's healed, but it still hurts like it's not."

He sat next to Chardon.

The council members spread out around the rest of the table. Everyone waited until they all had their glasses filled before taking a drink. The servants left the room.

"Let's start from the beginning, hmm." Kur said, setting his glass down.

"The only ones in this room who were there are Talas, Chardon, and I," the head of science replied. "There is no other way to explain it except to say the brutality was unmeasured. They had no regard for even their own fallen."

"Savages," Talas blurted as he took a sip of the warm liquor. His demeanor softened as it coursed through him. "I've seen wild animals more civilized than them."

"We were able to obtain footage from the battle." Kur lowered his eyes. "It was horrific." He raised his head. "I heard Trinon was badly wounded."

"That is an understatement." The science councilman snapped. "He protected Und which didn't do much good. Und lost his bearings and ended up injured nearly as bad."

Kur placed a hand on his chest. He had not been prepared to hear that.

"I was not aware." He stared at Chardon slumped miserably against the table, holding her drink as if already drunk. "My regards to Jaron and Modas."

"What will Azrom do?" The head of politics asked.

Lt. Treshur leaned forward. "I would like to first get my hands on one of those weapons."

"That's obvious!" Ganna rushed into the room, causing a small breeze. She was out of breath as she dropped onto a cushion near Lt. Treshur. "I tried to convince that one," she pointed to the Lassian science councilman, "to grab anything considered a weapon so we could reverse engineer it. He said that wasn't part of the mission."

"We barely got out with our cores!" The science council man roared.

"Yet," Lt. Treshur raised a finger. "She was not wrong. Don't you agree?"

The room went silent. The Science councilman, flushed with anger, tapped his fists on the table.

"In hindsight, yes."

"The enemy is on the move." Kur crossed his arms. "If they breach our system, we go on the defense. Where three ships failed, an entire fleet will be victorious."

"I always admire your race's modesty," Ganna said sarcastically.

"When has it not been true?" Lt. Treshur glared at her.

"You've only been lucky so far. Every empire gets to meet its match. Your comeuppance has arrived."

"How do you figure?" He snorted in defiance.

"General Kur said it himself. Azrom has conquered entire worlds with less. But this time, you couldn't defeat a small horde."

It was a slap in Azrom's face. Kur felt the sting. She seemed to relish in it, knowing how her words hit. Chardon's head snapped to attention. Her face contorted into something ugly as she looked over at Ganna.

"You will not disrespect Azrom in my presence." Ganna stopped drinking and eyed her over the rim. "I will only tolerate your ill tongue for so long before I remedy it." Chardon's stare didn't waver, and neither did Ganna's.

Kur waited for the two to finish their tiff. He couldn't care less what came out of Ganna's mouth. He established his dislike for her long ago. They broke eye contact at the same time and resumed drinking. Liquor may have been a bad idea. Talas gave him a knowing look.

Indeed.

Lieutenant Treshur shook his head. Strife had landed on New Lassa and he didn't like what he saw. Abras sat observing as well. Kur felt at a loss.

Making a Home

New ships and weapons were on the agenda before Kur and his entourage were escorted to a separate building for housing visitors. With Ganna in the lead, the science council man, and Lt. Treshur left the conference room, headed to her lab to brainstorm ideas. Chardon was visibly drunk as was Talas though he seemed able to handle himself better.

Kur settled into his designated chamber and watched the two stumble across the fields to the main commons. What a mess. He turned away from the window and plopped onto the bed. His body sank down. He could never get used to such fluffiness. A bed should be firm.

Light tapping on the door made him look up. Who could that be? Kur sat upright and swung one leg over the edge of the bed.

"Enter."

The door eased open until he could see who stood on the other side. Halfar, dressed in a loose tunic, black leggings, and short boots walked in, pushing the door shut. There was malice in his eyes and his haphazard hair did him no favors. He moved stiffly as if trying not to hurt himself.

"You should not be moving around, I'm sure. Did Chardon not make it back to your chamber? She would be livid if you weren't there."

Halfar wasn't paying attention. He sat slowly on the chair next to the bed, wincing as he settled down.

"You will not tell Romnus of my condition." His tone was even, calm, full of fury.

"Is that it?" Kur swung his other leg off and sat on the edge of the bed. "I don't know what you think Romnus feels about you. I can you tell it's wrong. I will not hide it from him. He specifically told me to check on you."

Halfar turned his head away, still angry.

"That's just part of his duty."

"Stop." Kur gripped the mattress. Halfar looked back and saw his reaction. "The same blood runs through you as his."

"I do not show weakness!"

"Yet you have. And there is no shame in that. It all depends on when and why."

"That race. Those weapons." Halfar whispered, hanging his head.

"They haunt you." Kur nodded. "I know. They do the same for me." He leaned back, placing his hands flat behind him. "I despise Ganna. What she said is probably correct."

"And what did that pariah say?" Halfar's brow furrowed.

"That we've met our match. Azrom will no longer be invincible."

Halfar tried to get comfortable in the chair. "Will Azrom come to New Lassa's aid?"

"I wouldn't be here if the answer was no. Razzna is also part of our alliance. Have you forgotten?"

"This won't be easy."

"No. But first." Kur grinned. "We have a request from all the lead scientists."

"I fear to ask."

"Get one of those weapons red tendril weapons."

Halfar's eyes widened in awe. "That is…"

"Audacious." Kur smiled wide.

"Outrageous!"

"Same thing." Kur sat back up, waving a hand at Halfar's outburst. "I brought Commander Abras for a reason."

"You mean besides showing him off to the manbeasts?"

"It was that obvious?" Kur saw the look of exasperation from Halfar. "We are going on a short combat mission." He slid off the bed and stood towering over Halfar. "While the enemy is still fleeing in disarray."

"That's madness." Halfar stared up at him. "Rass would desecrate your corpse for leaving him and your children."

"Talas is not the only one who can guarantee no deaths."

Without warning, Kur lifted Halfar off the chair and slung him over one shoulder. Halfar hissed in pain.

"What are you doing? Release me!"

Kur opened the door, walked down the narrow hallway, and headed out towards the fields. He kept a firm grip on Halfar the whole way to his and Chardon's chamber.

Once inside, Kur found Chardon half off the bed, arm and leg dangling, sleeping sloppily.

He bent over and let Halfar roll off his shoulder onto the bed. Chardon didn't move.

Halfar struggled onto his side and took hold of Chardon's arm. He pulled her to him until she was back on the bed next to him.

"I won't be able to accompany you on the mission."

"Exactly." Kur turned away. "Your place is here on New Lassa now. Let Romnus take care of Azrom."

He left the two of them to rest. By the time he got to the door and glanced back, they were in a deep sleep.

****•****

One Azrom armada ship sat hidden behind the third moon of the fifth system inside Dreridian trade space. This one differed from the main ships. Its shell was a darker gun metal, close to black, that cloaked its appearance amid the void. All the running lights were off, making it a shadowy blob next to the moon's brightness.

Moving through the center of the system in a seemingly sloppy diamond formation were the ten enemy ships. They were in no hurry, cruising past each planet without deploying an assault.

Curious. Kur watched the procession from the bridge of his ship. In full battle armor, he contemplated the reason. The enemy had no qualms about attacking any planet. The representatives' system happened to be along the way from a previous scourge they initiated. But now. Not so much as a recon ship to scout the potential.

Commander Abras stood a few feet away, his gaze glued to the enemy ships. From what little information Azrom and New Lassa had obtained, if they attacked one of their ships, the rest would certainly not assist. Kur glanced back over his shoulder at his father-in-law. That blank look that somehow simultaneously conveyed malice made him shudder.

Their mission was beyond dangerous. He folded his arms and raised one hand to his chin. If the situation went south, there would be at minimum a handful of deaths. He wanted none. Visions of Halfar and Talas nearly broken from their fight angered him.

"Let's wait a day to see what we have," he suggested to Commander Abras.

"We attack the ship on the tail end." Abras looked toward the end of the diamond. "They would have the weapons on hand as rear guards."

His deep, booming voice that vibrated in the air always amazed Kur. Rass's was deep and raspy. Nowhere near the same level of intensity.

"It has to be quick and dirty." Kur tapped his chin. "We find the first of those things, wrench it out of their hands if necessary and retreat."

"By the time we jump, they will know are objective."

"I don't think they care." Then Kur stopped.

In the previous battle, he found it strange that none of the fallen enemy who possessed those weapons no longer had them when the main fleet fled.

"Or maybe they do. Limited supply or secret technology? That is the only explanation." He continued.

"Both," Abras boomed.

The two left the bridge to the crew and headed to the docking bay. They would continue to view the enemy from there and launch a fight cruiser when the time was right.

Kur sat in the back of the fighter strapped in along with twenty Azrom soldiers. Abras was a pillar of calm across from him. The enemy ships had passed the moon hours ago at a steady clip. It would take no time for the fight cruiser to catch up. The pilot tapped icons on the virtual console displayed before him while the navigator did the same next to him.

"Initiating launch. ETA one hour."

Kur looked around at every soldier, their faces obscured by the helmets' face shields. "The moment that ramp opens, we will be in enemy territory. No one dies." He took a deep breath. "Victory!"

"Until Death!" They shouted.

He grimaced at the automatic reply.

The cruiser shot out of the port like a bullet, heading straight for the enemy ship that lagged the rest of the fleet. An equally ugly ship that suited the race. Bulky, spiky hull with mottled colors. Lights all over it in an almost random arrangement.

"Do a short jump," Kur commanded. "I don't want to give them any time to prepare."

"As you command." The pilot nodded to the navigator. "Jump sequence ready. How close do you want us?"

"Right up their ass," Kur replied with the Earth term.

The fight cruiser shimmied, becoming a multicolored blur, then winked out of sight. When it reappeared, they were indeed directly behind the ship. Klaxons sounded.

"Proximity alert." The AI announced.

Lights sprung on along the rear of the enemy ship.

"Head for that section. They see us coming." Kur braced against the bulkhead.

"Grappling hooks functional." Long tethers extended from the cruiser and rammed into the hull, piercing deep. "Docking sequence engaged."

The main cannon fired, creating a bigger hole in the enemy port already opening as the cruiser's ramp opened to let them out. Kur saw a group of enemy fighters get blown back.

"Advance team, take your positions!"

Ten of the soldiers barged through the center, then split to cover both sides of the doors leading into the ship's corridor. A group of enemy fighters got through as the team shot down more coming from behind before jamming the door.

"Barricade secure!" The team leader reported through his suit's commlink.

The other ten surrounded the enemy. It looked like an advantage. Kur immediately realized it wasn't as the enemy spread apart like rodents and attacked with sheer abandon. Azrom fighters were ruthless. This was much worse. Within seconds, four of his soldiers were badly wounded. The enemy was hell bent on making their deaths as cruel as possible.

No! Kur entered the fray.

He sliced through the first enemy who had a downed soldier's arms clasped together at the wrist, prepared to sever them. The Azrom soldier went limp. Grabbing him by the ankle, Kur dragged him back and flung him next to the cruiser. He went for the other three enemy fighters on the verge of similar fates.

In desperation, Kur managed a flash step to the last one before it was too late. The enemy had removed the soldier's helmet and dug its claws into the side of the soldier's face. It was peeling it away at the muscle, exposing tendons. The scream almost made Kur falter.

Azrom warriors don't cry out in battle.

Kur positioned his blade at an angle as he came close and cut the enemy's arm off at the elbow. The severed limp went flying into the air. Not deterred, the enemy pulled out a long dagger and impaled the soldier to the floor. Kur felt his body heat rise with rage. With one swing, he cut the enemy vertically. There was no blood splatter as both halves fell in opposite directions.

He glanced around and saw his men getting slaughtered. Abras used a regular sized sword which looked like a dagger in his hands to take down a group of enemy fighters in one swipe. His blade sliced them in half at the waist. The advance team was trying to retreat. Some remained pinned down at the jammed door.

This is not good. Kur got to them, somehow managing to make a path. He had not counted how many of the enemy had gotten through the door. His unit was outnumbered two to one. Shit!

"Get out of here!" He yelled into his commlink. "This is not a victorious day."

The soldiers inside the cruiser, who only sustained minor injuries, laid cover fire as Kur and Abras made sure the rest of his men were at least on the cruiser's ramp. The jammed door burst apart. Two enemy fighters stood, each holding red tendril weapons at the opening. They fired.

Kur saw the thin lines of shimmering red shoot towards them. There was nowhere to dodge it. The tendrils spread across his vision like a spiderweb. Then there was darkness.

Abras stepped in front of the ramp with his own long sword in hand. Its reach was nearly the same size as the ramp, the width ten inches. He turned his blade flat before him and swung. The tendrils struck, blocked for a split second, then Abras volleyed it back to the enemy.

Kur saw their surprised, putrid faces as the tendrils wrapped around them. Right as they fell, Abras took out a grappling gun. To Kur's amazement, he shot it towards one of the weapons. It took hold, and he reeled it onto the ramp.

"Mission accomplished." Abras turned, stepping onto the ramp, and hitting the seal icon.

The ramp closed, engulfing them in black.

"Grappling hooks released." The pilot said. "Initiating reverse sequence. Prepare to jump."

The fight cruiser jerked hard, removing itself from the hole it made. Small ships came flooding out from the bow of the enemy ship. Too late. The fighter cruiser cleared the rear of the ship and jumped back to the moon.

The moment the cruiser arrived near the armada ship, a tractor beam guided it in for speed up delivery. Docking clamps met it on approach and locked it down.

"Ship secure." The AI said. "Prepare for jump."

Kur breathed a sigh of relief, then pain seized him as he coughed up blood. What? A deeper dark engulfed him. His body fell sideways on the ramp. The armada ship shot forth through a vortex, missing the enemy ships that were in pursuit but still too far away to make any difference.

****

"General Rass will not be pleased."

The medical officer stared down at Kur's body on the floating stretcher. He had given the General a powerful sedative to keep him from waking up. The pain would be excruciating. Multiple wounds covered the length of his frame.

"I would brace for an outburst," he added.

"It won't just be General Rass." The medic on the other side of the stretcher nodded up ahead to the entourage coming at them down the main corridor.

Lord Romnus and a very pregnant Queen Farin walked briskly to the medical bay with stern expressions. Behind them were Batis, Biandra, and Lord Aloni.

They all stopped in their tracks as another stretcher came past the two medics carrying the soldier with half his face torn off. A blob of healing gel covered the wound, pulling the flesh back in place.

Queen Farin covered her mouth with one hand, bending forward as if about to retch. The first medic grimaced at the sight. Yeah. It was bad. The stretcher continued into the bay. Lord Romnus appeared stunned. He didn't move except to grab hold of Queen Farin's arm to stop her from falling.

From the other side of the corridor, General Rass came in a rush, pushing soldiers out of the way. He got within a few feet of Kur and his father blocked him. Commander Abras was like a stone wall. Rass became confused, stepping back from him.

"Calm yourself." Commander Abras' voice carried.

General Rass struggled to keep his composure. He slid to the floor in a daze, then looked up at the medics. "How serious is it?"

The medics looked at each other. The first took the lead.

"From the way the wounds seem to have been inflicted, he probably had no idea he was hurt. There are puncture marks, broken bones, deep lacerations, and bruises. Combined," he paused. "General Kur is in a dire state."

The second medic nodded. "We will keep him in stasis until at least eighty percent of them are healed." He gestured to the medical bay. "May we take him?"

"Please." General Rass went to stand and faltered.

Not wanting to witness what would already be deemed weakness, the medics guided the floating stretcher into the bay with the rest of the wounded. They had not seen such devastation in centuries. And it was only a small battalion.

Romnus walked over to Rass and placed a hand on his shoulder. He turned to Abras.

"Was it as brutal as expected?"

Abras looked down at him. "Worse."

Romnus gritted his teeth. "So the mission was a failure."

"No."

That made Romnus cock his head in surprise. "You were able to retrieve one of the weapons?"

"Yes."

"But, was it worth it?" Farin went past Romnus and helped Rass up. "Why is this happening?"

Rass came back to his senses and stood on his own.

"We are getting back what we have subjected our enemies to tenfold."

"No matter how bloody a fight, this is beyond reason," Farin exclaimed.

Rass met Batis' stare and the two silently agreed. Batis had been on many campaigns as well and knew the despair and carnage Azrom dealt in battle.

"This day was bound to come," Batis said.

Romnus turned away from them. "I didn't think to see it in my lifespan." He made his way to the war room. "Let me hear the whole account. Where is the weapon?"

"In a vault case being transported to the science wing," one of the injured soldiers replied. He stood behind Abras, his right arm in a sling and a gel patch on his eye. "You had to see it to believe it. Commander Abras was glorious."

Rass, Abras, and the soldier joined Romnus' entourage. Biandra handed him one of the small orange fruits. He took it and shoved the whole thing in his mouth. More would be needed before the day was done. The neurotoxin coursed through him, calming his nerves.

Easy Target

Not many things made Ganna happy. She reserved her joy to advancement in the sciences. It was easier that way. So, when she received the communication from Lt. Treshur that one of the enemy weapons was in their possession, she jumped out of her seat and yelled out, startling the other lab technicians. She heard a clank and turned to see one of them had dropped their utensils while staring horrified at her.

Ganna smiled, slowly sitting back down at her station. She finished reading the rest of the message. There would be a summit meeting with the alliance leaders and scientists to discuss the next steps. The details were to be kept from the Dreridians. Good! She got up and addressed her assistants.

"I will be at an emergency meeting with the council until around sunset. Keep me posted on any dire developments."

She sent a message to everyone necessary before shutting down her terminal and headed out.

The fresh afternoon air hit her at the lab entrance. She breathed in deep, exhaling slowly. It was going to be a wonderful day. Off in the distance, she could see the other council members making their way to the commons. Chardon was still looking haggard, continuing to walk around in female form. That was nothing compared to Jaron's appearance.

The strategist was almost rail thin, her robes not fitting properly. They dragged on the ground; the hem getting dirty. She didn't care to take notice. Talas walked beside her, no worse for wear. Ganna felt a pang of sympathy, causing her to clutch the front of her robe.

However much she longed for New Lassa to be a super power that could defend itself, she didn't want war. Turning Lassians into military might was not the goal. Sestis had been misguided, corrupted by the lure of power presented to her by greedy rulers.

****

Ganna's exuberance met a slow death as she sat at the conference table with the rest of the council. For the first few minutes, while everyone accepted the usual service, she remained silent.

What am I doing?

She balked at her own thinking to let them steal her joy. Mustering her voice, she tapped her hand flat on the table, getting their attention.

"You must not fret, my dears," she said in a loud, cheerful tone. Frowns fell upon her. "I have brought some uplifting news."

"The enemy has fled our galactic corridor and found new prey?" The political councilman snorted. "Other than that, we are still in danger."

"Pfft!" Ganna waved her hand. "Not if we can drive them out ourselves. It would be more satisfying."

"Spit it out, Ganna." Jaron had little patience. She took a drink, her eyes barely open in slits.

"Azrom has confiscated one of the enemy weapons!" Ganna cried out.

Her outburst startled a few council members. Talas sputtered, spraying his drink on the table. Chardon and the head of science almost dropped theirs.

"What? How?" Chardon asked, wiping drops of liquid that jumped out of her cup from the front of her robes. She turned to Halfar. He looked concerned. "What is it?"

"Please, explain." Halfar set his drink down.

"Apparently, they went on a mission. Small unit, I believe. Only twenty or so. They ambushed one of the enemy ships."

Halfar's face scrunched, his expression darkening. Ganna realized her mistake. The rest of the message was not what she wanted to bring up. As if tapping into her mind, Halfar locked eyes with her.

"There were no casualties?"

Ganna forced a grin. "Not a one."

"No wounded?" Not just Halfar gave her a stern look. His gaze didn't waver.

Ganna hesitated. That alone gave them a clue to what she was hiding. She sighed heavily and lowered her head.

"There were many wounded. I would say not one escaped unscathed."

Questions erupted, jumbling together to the point where she couldn't discern what any of them were. She slammed her hands on the table, stopping the verbal flow.

"That is not the issue! We now have an advantage. Do you wish to throw away all their efforts? Dishonor the fight they went through to get it for all our sakes?"

Silence. Halfar clenched his fists.

"That being so," he said. "How bad?"

Ganna pursed her lips, exhaling through her nose. "General Kur was near death when they arrived back on Azrom." Gasps rang out. "The only one with hardly a scratch was Commander Abras."

From the back of the room, Modas let out a gruff snort. Talas managed a grin.

"Yes, well," Talas laughed. "It would take a whole lot to bring that monster down."

The mood lifted, becoming lighter. Ganna felt relief. Now they could focus on the task at hand. She seized the opportunity.

"Lt. Treshur has arranged a meeting place for the alliance scientists to disassemble the weapon and review the findings. This is to be kept from the Dreridians, of course."

The head of engineering frowned.

"For all we know, they have yet again given some race forbidden technology. I never trust those things."

"Nor should we ever," Chardon added. "How long do you think it will take to find a counter for its effects?"

"Or eliminate its threat completely," their science council man said.

"This is a complicated piece of weaponry." Ganna stared up at the ceiling, contemplating the answer. "I'd say about two years, give or take."

"That's quite fast. Are you certain it can be done?" The head of engineering asked.

"With three of us and our technicians, I don't see why not," Ganna replied.

"Then safe journey." Chardon raised her cup. "I look forward to seeing what we can accomplish to rid ourselves of this scourge."

The others raised their cups as well, Jaron being the last. She still had a hard time praising Ganna for, well, anything.

Just you wait! Ganna raised her own cup. *To my success.*

Separatists

Wrapped in billowing waterproof parkas, the patrolling soldiers' grim faces were accented by the less than sanitary area sprawled wide around them. The dark grey sky dumped dirty rain that stained the streets and buildings. An arctic wind forced the soldiers to bend forward, heads down, so they wouldn't get a face full of the nasty water. The pelting rain made it almost impossible to see through their goggles. They were essentially walking blind.

This is what planet Barrima looked like three quarters of its yearly cycle. The small regions where it wasn't raining dealt with extreme cold or heat. Barriers to combat the planet's insane environment had long fallen apart. Makeshift shelters had been built over the last two centuries.

The soldier in the lead gripped the front of his parka with gloved fingers. A promise broken. The Dreridians had come announcing they were no longer responsible for the planet. Another race would take Regency. To flood resources into the economy to cover the repairs. Their planet would thrive once more.

Lies!

All the former leaders had died from disease or fallen from the harsh weather. He was the only one left with some authority. The people looked to him to fix it. The new Regent had visited once. He remembered the diabolical demeanor that erased her beauty. Statuesque, and powerful.

Sestis.

Her smiles were disingenuous, her words like poison; she promised a new era. And then she left, never seen or heard from again. The planet Barrima languished. They struggled to make the minimum loads of goods for trade. The Dreridians would not hear a word to the effect of not being able to meet their demands.

Galactic trade must move.

The charcoal-colored stone building acting as a central hub for the planet loomed ahead. His men trudged forward, determined to make it before the storm picked up. There were times when the wind could lift one of them despite being tethered together beneath their parkas, and snap the tie, sending the poor soul into the sky.

At the doors, the leader punched a code into the keypad embedded on the side. The doors rumbled open, shaking the ground.

"Hurry!" He called out. His voice only went so far, dying in the wind. It didn't matter. His men knew the drill. "Keep hold of the tether!"

His men crawled up the broken steps to the entrance, encumbered by the parkas and tether. A stray creature clawed its way through the rocky hillside near the building. The wind picked up, peeling the creature from the rocks, and snatched it up. Desperate to hold on, its limbs ripped apart, leaving the clawed paws. He watched it disappear into the sky, no telling where it would eventually land, and hoped it would be dead before that.

He hit the panel on the inside of the door to seal it shut and silence engulfed them. The cavernous corridor was pitch black and still. They waited, huddled together while untying the tether and removing their goggles. The leader pushed his hood off his head and wiped his face with one hand.

Overhead, hover lights flickered to life, illuminating the area with a soft, pale glow. He breathed a sigh of relief. Safe. More than a few men had lost to the storms. The worse happened in the hot regions. Cold, you could layer and stave off. Extreme heat, one could do nothing about.

"Let's get to the hall. I'm starving." He led the way down the corridor.

"Think the communications crew got a hit while we were out?" His second in command trailing behind him asked.

"Hope so." He scratched the side of his head, messing up already tangled brown hair that reached below his ears. "We need some kind of news to get us out of this rut."

They all stepped into a tiny alcove where they shed their parkas, over boots, and gloves. Underneath all the gear, they wore plain fabric jumpsuits. The greyish brown color was a light shade that made them look a tad dirty.

Many of the soldiers rubbed their hair to fluff it, using their fingers to comb it back.

From there, the group proceeding towards a light at the end of the corridor. Past the threshold lay a sprawling cafeteria. Although dimly lit, it was still brighter than the other rooms.

Half the tables were empty. His group had returned later than the others. The cook looked up from his station and nodded to the leader. It was the last batch of the breakfast run. Enough for about twenty more people.

Single file, the leader and his group lined up at the counter, grabbing a tray as the cook pushed them out onto the rail. The steaming meat smelled amazing. The one thing his people would not give up was decent food. They didn't get it all the time, but it was consistent.

The last bell rang, signaling the end of breakfast. No one else was out patrolling. The cook gathered his crew. They all took a serving and came from behind the stations to sit at the tables, along with the others. Not wanting to taint their meal with doom and gloom conversation, everyone ate in silence.

The last bite consumed, utensils down, the cook spoke.

"Hate to say it, Master Aden, but we're going to be short on meat next cycle. Going to have to start rationing again."

Aden nodded. No reason to cite his disappointment. It happened at least five times a year. Each season, they had to reevaluate their supplies.

"A diet every once in a while never hurts."

A few of the men snorted. There wasn't an overweight person on the entire planet. They ranged from fairly healthy to emaciated.

"I'm gonna' go clean up." The cook stood. "Do you want a lunch service today?"

Aden shook his head.

"Let's just do a late dinner. Light on the fare."

"Good choice." The cook went back to the kitchen area, his crew following.

Aden also stood, picking up his tray. "Time for us to get moving as well. Check communications."

They deposited their trays in the washing bin, each in a slot that kept them upright. The machine slammed shut and the loud wishing sound of it cleaning filled the room. Aden and his group walked back to the corridor and hung a left towards another spot of light.

As they got closer, the communication room loomed ahead. Of the twenty or so stations inside, only six of them were being used. A full functioning one took too much power from their energy grid. This skeleton crew kept it at a small footprint.

The head of communications was a young male of one hundred and forty named Emar. He hadn't been born, let alone thought of during the wars. That's what made him ideal for the task. He had no preconceived notions, though the plight of the planet angered him too. In his research, he had grown to despise the Dreridians. Not necessarily Sestis. She was merely a greedy tyrant.

He heard the footsteps of the group enter and glanced behind him over one shoulder. They looked exhausted. As always. He sighed, returning his gaze to his screens.

"Happy Daybreak," he greeted them. It was silly since the sun had not come out in days. "I have some interesting finds for us."

"Is that so?" Aden took a seat close to him while the others scattered around to sit at the empty stations. "Tell us."

"There seems to have been a big fight over in the next quadrant."

"Really?" Master Aden perked up.

"It seems that rogue empire attacked another planet under Sestis' Regency." He frowned. "Apparently, they sent representatives to ask for help."

"And none came?"

"Not sure. But probably not." Emar swiveled in his seat to face the leader. "Here's the interesting part. A caravan of ships is moving towards our sector. Looks like their rear ship was damaged in a fight."

"I don't understand."

"The ship that attacked was an Azrom fight cruiser. The victims were the ones who attacked the planet under Sestis."

He could see Master Aden trying to piece it together.

Azrom was so far from their sector that they had no reason to monitor them. Known as a mighty war race, they had nothing to do with them. Nor the other planets in the other quadrants. All due to their economic decline. They were on no one's radar.

"Hmm. Explain."

Master Aden seemed to have given up.

"From what I could gather, it seems Sestis and her mate have a child. That child is currently the Queen of Azrom."

Master Aden's eyes went wide.

"They gave their child to that monster who rules Azrom?" He cried out.

"It appears so. With the attack on a planet under her Regency, it would be fair to say Azrom would retaliate in Lassa's steed. I found the Lassian race does not have a military. Just a couple of warrior clans."

"So Azrom is their army."

"To be clear, much of my findings are at best speculation and possibly outdated."

"But closer to the truth than not."

"Correct."

Master Aden leaned back in his chair, clasping his hands behind his head as he let the information sink in. Emar was sure he would suggest what he too had been thinking. He looked at him.

"Where is the caravan of the enemy ships?"

I knew it! "Still moving. The rear ship is lagging due to damage."

"Maybe we should give them a hand."

"They don't seem to be the kind to negotiate."

"Oh, I think they are smarter than we think." Master Aden removed his hands and slapped them on his thighs. "Send a translation message in a loop and see which one they respond to."

"All of them?" Emar asked. "Even the unknown ones?"

"Especially the unknown ones."

"Will start the sequence today."

"Good. Let me know when you get a hit."

Master Aden stood, motioning his group to get up. They left the communications room. Emar went back to his duties. He tapped the far-left screen, and it came to life, displaying a code relay in progress. I've already started.

*****

Two weeks after starting the sequence, Emar finally got a hit. The caravan was almost near the edge of leaving their space when it came. He contained his excitement as he examined the translator's data. It was one of the unknown languages from far outside the five quadrants. Maybe even a different galaxy.

He had sent a message to Master Aden. Not surprisingly the man came running into the communications room, three of his men in tow.

"What do they say? Are they hostile? Do they accept our assistance?"

Emar tilted his head and gave him a wary stare. Master Aden stopped at his station, instantly aware of how he sounded.

"My apologies." He exhaled. "What have we got?"

"An unknown language captured centuries ago. They are not from our five systems at all."

"Sounds right."

"They do indeed want to know what our assistance entails. They will annihilate us if they so choose."

Master Aden went pale. "That's not an option."

"They are scanning our planet as we speak."

One of the leader's men scoffed.

"Then they will know we are not a threat. Attacking us will give them no satisfaction."

The sad truth of that stung. Emar looked at his middle screen. It filled with gibberish in long strings of code. When it stopped, he turned to the leader.

"They are sending a convoy and the damaged ship. I have alerted the maintenance crew at Sea Dock of incoming."

"Good. They will see our expertise," Master Aden said proudly.

Barrima didn't just make parts for ships, they were also one of the best repair planets in the Dreridian Trade system. That was part of the problem. They were so good at it they didn't get many customers. Sometimes it would be decades before another order came through.

"What do you think?" Master Aden turned to his second in command, Ryben, who stood behind him.

"Bring up our main cannons as a precaution. Have a troop ready near the docks and outside our base perimeter."

Master Aden nodded in agreement. Their race was down and out, but not defenseless.

A small chime rang out from under the left screen. Emar reached over and picked up four tiny discs barely half an inch in diameter.

"Translator devices. Can't have any misunderstandings."

"You're good. Yes, that's right," Master Aden smirked, taking the discs. "What's their ETA?"

"Eighteen hours."

"Plenty of time to prepare." He smiled.

A sinister expression spread.

****

The enemy convoy hovered over the Sea Dock not leaving until the damaged ship was clamped down. Maintenance workers scrambled towards the ship, eager to assess the problem and get their eyes on a new alien vessel. The convoy turned and headed towards the main base. It landed at the designated area a half mile from it.

Too close. That is what Commander Ryben thought. He understood Master Aden wanted to show trust and a lack of fear. He was scared. Emar was able to get some images of the fight. Even the leader reared back in terror. And now those things were on their planet.

The massive aliens came thumping down the open ramp of their ship. Their armor blended into their flesh, the two in the rear carrying large barrel guns. One of Ryben's men took a step back, then another. More did the same.

"Stand still!" He hissed angrily. Master Aden glanced back and frowned. Commander Ryben grabbed the first soldier. "You will not show fear in this moment!" He said in a low voice.

The alien leading the others stopped a few feet from Master Aden, scanning the entire group.

"We welcome you to our home," Master Aden spoke. The translator spewed out an electronic sounding noise.

The alien leader seemed confused for a moment, then spoke back. It was harsh, difficult to hear without cringing. Commander Ryben fought to not cover his ears.

"What is your agenda?" The translator filtered to their language. "Why have you invited us here?"

"Well, it's not wrong," Commander Ryben said.

"We are a repair planet. We also make parts. It would be against our beliefs to let a crippled ship pass us and not assist." Master Aden replied with a straight face.

Ryben and his men were impressed. He was certain the communications kid was nodding in approval in the room.

"Then what is the price for repair?" The guns held by the two in the rear lit up with tiny red lights around the six inch wide barrels. "Or are you stealing technology?"

Master Aden stood shocked. These creatures were not stupid. Commander Ryben grimaced. Are we that obvious?

Regaining his confidence, Master Aden raised a hand in protest. "Not at all. How about we talk inside?" He gestured towards the base entrance.

The guns powered down, and the aliens followed him to the base. Ryben fell in step next to Master Aden while the rest of his men took up the rear behind the last two aliens.

"We need to tread carefully. They sniffed us out good."

"I know!" Master Aden whispered, leaning closer. "We just have to play dumb for now."

The group walked through the great corridors and entered a large war room, unused for decades. It last acted as a conference room for seasonal updates. Hastily cleaned to the best of its condition, yet still dingy, it served its purpose.

"Please, sit." Master Aden waved a hand to the long rectangle table in the center.

With everyone seated, the alien leader's beady eyes… narrowed. Aden wasn't sure about its expression.

"Your planet is shit." The translator interpreted.

"That's a harsh thing to say to a race who is accommodating you." Master Aden's tone filled with fury despite him saying it half-jokingly.

"You have nothing we want."

"That may be true," Master Aden grinned. "But I think maybe not."

Emar came in holding a tablet. He sat down across from the lead alien, no fear in his demeanor. He tapped the tablet to turn it on.

"You were attacked by a race known as Azrom. One of the deadliest armies in the five quadrants." The alien leader seemed intrigued. "There is an explanation as to why."

"The deadliest? No. We have fought better."

That made them all sit at attention.

"The planet you attacked was under the Regent Sestis. We, too, are part of her possessions."

"They tried to stop us. To talk. We were not interested." The alien stared at the kid. "Why did they cowardly ambush our ship?"

"Well, you see." Emar gave the biggest smile. "The Queen of Azrom is in fact the child of our Regent. So, your payment," he paused. "Is more of a gift. Vengeance against Azrom. And we know how to get it for you."

The alien's eyes narrowed further. Even with all the folded skin and armor, it was obvious. He didn't trust them, but the thought of destroying Azrom sounded sweet.

Aden watched the aliens leave the room to be escorted back to their ship. He waited until their figures were mere shapes in the distance before letting out the breath he was holding. His commander did the same, slumping back in his seat and sliding down a bit.

"That was not for the lesser of will." Ryben sat straighter. "Those creatures are terrifying."

"And those weapons are not to be toyed with." Aden leaned over the table and drummed his fingers. "We need to be capable of striking at both ends." He squinted as he thought. "One to take down Azrom by way of that Queen."

"And the other for our Regent's home world."

"First, we have to find it."

"Not a problem," Emar piped up. "The Dreridians are obligated to give us that information since they do not handle conflicts outside of their purview."

"Ah, that's right!" Ryben bent forward. "We can lead the enemy straight to them."

"I like it." Aden smiled. "I would love to see the look on that female demon's face when she realizes her mistake in abandoning us."

The group grabbed their glasses and raised them.

"To the return of glory for our people!" Aden raised his glass higher.

They all took a celebratory drink.

THREE: REUNION and BONDS

Secret Vows

Deep within the core garden past the edge of the field lay buried hidden ones. Ganna made her way towards them in the dead of night. She had hiked up her robes and tied them between her legs to avoid brushing against the foliage, which would cause sound. Behind her was a floating stretcher. Its near inaudible whir made her wince.

Everyone should be asleep, though she was certain a manbeast lurked somewhere. They always roamed the planet, sneaking about like insects.

Her foot landed on a branch protruding from the soil snapping it in half. The sound echoed in the air. In a panic, she stopped, her eyes widening for a second. She breathed slowly. Looking around and seeing no one, she proceeded past the field and onto a patch of earth that was less moist, almost hardened.

Removing a portable hoe from the carrier bag slung across her back, Ganna walked further in. She fully extended its handle and started digging in a spot she had marked decades ago with a diamond shape. There were others scattered about.

I only need this one for now.

She toiled for nearly an hour until the tool pressed into something soft. There you are. She got most of the dirt from around the edges. Grabbing hold from underneath, she pulled. It was stubborn at first then gave way. The body slid out of the ground, and she hefted it onto the stretcher.

What a mess.

It was close to destroyed. Parts of the limbs were missing and the ones intact, broken. Half the face was gone. The flesh itself had patches where no damage was visible. The rest was charred black in contrast.

At the bottom of the gaping hole sat a separate mound. She reached down and brushed dirt from the top. The round, glowing bud came into view. Using both hands, she dug it out the rest of the way.

She set down a piece of cloth from her sack and set it on the ground. Careful not to jostle the core too much, Ganna placed it on the cloth and wrapped it up tight. She wiped her brow with the back of her forearm then clapped her hands together to get rid of any excess dirt. Satisfied, she walked back to her lab with her prize.

Now for the rest.

Inside her lab, Ganna went to the back wall and touched its edge. A secret panel opened to her personal lab that only she had access to. She didn't turn on the main lights, instead using the glow from the stretcher as a guiding light.

An empty cryochamber sat in the gloom. She tapped the icon to open it and the floating stretcher eased vertically into it until reaching the end. Then it backed out, letting the corpse slide off onto the flat surface. Ganna set the bundle inside and unwrapped the core. She picked it up for a moment, admiring its soft orange glow.

Smiling, she placed it back inside the cryochamber and sealed it. On the side console, she entered the adjustments and configurations needed to complete the cycle. It would take months to complete the sequence. That gave her plenty of time to set the other plans in motion.

All for the sake of Lassa.

She went over to her desk and powered up her system. For the first time in centuries, she remembered her father. A revered scientist and fiercely loyal to Lassa. He was the one who figured out how to defend their home world. And brought the manbeast project to fruition. Not your greatest achievement, father.

It wasn't the idea that was flawed. She had concluded over the years it was the DNA strands used to create them that were the problem. Making sentient warriors out of a small creature hell bent on survival by any means and capable of extraordinary feats sounded good, but in theory, no.

Ganna frowned, hating herself for getting off track with nostalgia. She had no time for that. Maybe one day, she could finally be able to settle down. Find a mate of equal mind and skill. She even had someone on her radar.

The system finished booting up. Linking it to the cryochamber, she dove into repairing the long dead specimen. It needed to fuse with the core to start regeneration.

You're going to be so angry when you wake, she chuckled to herself.

****

The young manbeast wasn't looking where he was going. Jaron watched him walk briskly towards the commons to catch up with the other children. He was a little shorter than her, his brown skin like a creamy mocha. She could drink him up. It almost made her want another litter just to see if they would turn out like him.

As expected, he glanced back behind him and ended up slamming right into her. His eyes went big as saucers as he looked up. She smiled, holding his arms at the biceps. Then his expression turned to fear and shame. That angered her. He had no reason to feel such things.

"I am so sorry, Elder Jaron." His voice quivered a bit.

"You never have to apologize to me. Just be aware of your surroundings or your father will scold you."

He simply nodded. Before she let go of his arms, she gave him a big hug. He didn't resist, forgetting for a moment that he was treating her differently. Then he snapped out of it and pulled away from her.

"I'm going to be late for my lesson."

"Then go."

His mother, Salara, came rushing up as he ran off. Tall, with a darker complexion, she was striking. Her dark hair was a deep brown, thick and wavy that she kept wound up in a bun set back atop her head. The light-colored chimere made of canvas cloth complimented her skin. Her striking green eyes were full of sadness.

"I am so sorry. I don't know why my son gets so distracted." She bowed her head. "Please forgive him."

"Stop that." Jaron's tone was harsher than she wanted. The mother raised her head, startled. "There is nothing to forgive."

The tall female manbeast hung her head in shame. Jaron inhaled hard, letting her chest expand, then exhaled to calm herself. This had been going on for years. She was about done with the whole charade.

"I know. You always say that. Thank you."

Salara turned away and headed back to the housing sector. Others in the field stared at her shameless attire. Jaron understood the reason. Many times, she herself had run out in only her top robe to chase after one of her children.

Jaron balled her hands into fists. She wanted to bring her back and hug her as well. Once again, she chickened out and ended up standing alone in the fields. *Why do I always do this?* She looked to her right and saw Modas give her a knowing stare.

****

High-pitched wails followed by rough coughing filled the small chamber. They had been going on for days with no relief in sight. Four infant manbeasts lay cuddled together, shivering, their pelts damp with sweat. The cries were painful to their parent's ears. The two had moved into their tiny room to keep watch.

None of the remedies worked to cure whatever was ailing the little ones. Salara felt defeated, at a loss. She had stopped crying so hard before daybreak, now sniffling softly; letting the tears fall freely. Her hands shook as she caressed them in the large, cushioned wicker basin.

A boy from their first litter, the one who always wandered aimlessly about, came into the room and didn't get close. He was clearly distraught, wanting to help with no idea how.

Jakar sat on the edge of the small bed, head in his hands. He looked up at his son.

"Go get my mother." The boy stood stunned. Salara turned to him in surprise. "I should have done that in the beginning." Jakar hung his head. "I was wrong to keep this from her." When his son didn't move, he glared. "Go!"

The boy turned and fled the room. He got to the edge of the field and halted, scanning the area. Finding his target, he went straight for them.

Jaron heard the rushing sound of tall grass being forced together. She rose from picking flowers and saw the boy who always bumped into her come running towards her. His grief-stricken face made her chest tighten. He stopped a few feet away.

"I'm sorry," he said, out of breath. "My father needs you."

"Calm down." Jaron cupped his face in her hands. "What's wrong?"

"My baby siblings, they're sick. Our mother tried everything she could think of."

His tears set Jaron in motion. She released him.

"Don't ever apologize! I am your elder mother. I will always come when my family needs me. Come. Let's hurry."

He led her to Jakar's home. A place he never let her visit since he found his mate. She could hear the wailing the moment they reached the outside of the building. Inside the room, Jaron caught her breath. Jakar looked exhausted. Salara appeared spent as she held one of the infants in her hands.

"I know you're angry." Jakar said. "When they didn't get better, I remembered you were the only one able to fix it when us other children were sick. I'm sorry."

Wheezing. Jaron heard the little one trying to breathe. Salara looked up at her in terror.

"I can't get her to...please...help me." The pain in her voice, Jaron knew well.

"Give her to me." Jaron held out her hands.

Using the tips of her fingers, Jaron pushed down into the infant's abdomen and made circular motions until they let out a labored, raspy cough. The little one shuddered and began wailing.

"Good girl." Jaron rubbed the little beast's head. She placed her in the basket with the other siblings and hefted the whole thing up. She turned an accusatory stare at Jakar. "You should have told me from the start." She glanced at Salara. The tall beauty sat slumped on the floor. "Get some rest. I have this handled."

Carrying the basket in front of her, she headed to the sandbox near the family commons. If Jakar had not been so secretive, he would have been living with the rest of them. That way, she could get to the children easily the moment they got sick.

The sandbox had another litter of manbeasts inside one of the square bins near the entrance. They perked up as she entered. Jaron sighed. She looked around and found one in the back far enough away so others wouldn't catch whatever the infants had if contagious. From what she could tell, it was not a virus.

She set the basket next to the square and lifted the infants out one at a time into the section covered in mounds of soft grass atop sand with tiny cushions. The basket cushion was soaked through. It would get cleaned and sanitized later. Right now, her focus was on getting them comfortable before going to mix up a remedy.

Modas stepped inside and came up behind her. She could feel the apprehension coming from him as he towered above. He bent to her level and stared at the little ones. Their wails subsided a bit from weariness. They would cry themselves to sleep for probably the umpteenth time.

"Their strong." Modas reached over and caressed one of them. He turned to Jaron. "How is Jakar?"

"Devastated. Not as much as his mate. She's too far gone."

Modas nodded. He rose, running his fingers through her hair. "I know you'll heal them."

"As I always do." Jaron stood. "I have some herbs to pick."

Jaron went around him and headed to the fields again. She had left her basket of flowers. Now she had more important things to add.

While she went around selecting herbs, she felt the pull of the frown that etched on her face. No chance of alleviating it until she was certain those infants were recovering. Others in the field steered clear of her. She imagined she looked fiercer than normal.

"You're scaring people again." Mara's voice was close.

When did she sneak up on me? Jaron looked behind her, then up. She rolled onto her knees and stood, brushing off the bottom of her robes.

"I don't care."

"Oh, I know." Mara laughed. She glanced at the basket of medicinal herbs. "Uh oh. Who's got a sick litter?"

"Jakar."

Mara's brow furrowed.

"So now he wants to acknowledge his family? Because we can help his children?"

"Stop it," Jaron chastised.

"No!" Mara replied, indignant. "He basically shut us out and now his litter is sick, and we jump to his aid?"

"Yes!" Jaron snapped. "Because we are his family. And so are they."

Mara looked crestfallen with shame, lowering her gaze. "You're right. I'm sorry."

"I wish everyone would stop saying that."

"Yeah, well. We don't know what else to say." Mara glanced at the herbs. "I'll go get the rest. The sandbox?"

"Yes. I'll meet you there then."

Jaron lifted her basket and headed back. In the back corner, she found her mortar and pestle set with a carafe of water. The wicker bed was gone, along with Modas. As she predicted, the little ones were asleep from exhaustion. She could still hear their labored breathing. She started on the first remedy batch, carefully mixing them into a paste. The concoction was for their bellies to calm their insides and cool them down.

Mara came in and set the rest of the herbs next to the others. The second group of herbs was for an elixir. Jaron nodded and Mara was off again. One of the sweet fruits would make it bearable for them to consume. Jaron had yet to make a remedy that tasted any good. She heard footsteps coming. Who is it now? She looked over her shoulder and found Jakar's eldest son standing far from her.

"I may look angry, but I'm safe. You can get closer."

He did as she suggested, and she grabbed him into a hug. Stunned, he didn't have time to react. Then his body sagged. She felt the wetness of tears soak through her robe.

"Shh. It's alright. See." She eased up enough so he could turn his head. "They're asleep. I'll have them better in no time." He nodded, burying his face back in her bosom.

Mara stopped in her tracks at the entrance, a berry bunch in her hand. Her mouth opened and her eyes widened.

"I thought so!" she exclaimed. "He looks like Jakar."

The boy raised his head in surprise. Jaron snorted.

"You really think we couldn't tell who your parents were?" She caressed his head, flattening his mane, then released him.

He wiped his face inside his elbow, smearing snot on his robe. Jaron frowned at that. This was partly Jakar's doing. She had little doubt the two of them frustrated his mother.

"That's disgusting. Don't do that." Jaron pulled him over to the washbasin on the other side of the sandbox. "Wash that off."

Mortified into compliance, he removed his robe, isolating the area where he wiped and began using the cleaning agent atop the basin to scrub it. Mara had a closed mouth grin on her face. Jaron turned around and whacked her on the arm.

"Ow!" Mara covered where she had been hit.

"Whatever you were thinking, the answer is no."

"You're no fun."

"Have you forgotten?" Jaron stared her down. "We have a more important task to do."

Mara straightened; her expression turned serious.

"Right. Let's get down to business, then."

Mara went past her to the infants. Jaron shook her head. As she walked back, she caught sight of the other little ones in the front section, leaning with intrigue over the edge of the wooden square.

"Stay put and go back to playing or whatever it was you were doing."

One of them simply stared at her while chewing on a piece of grass, not giving any indication they were listening. Its sibling next to him sort of lowered himself down until his nose touched the ledge. The third looked over at the first with curiosity. The last one had a sheepish grin. Jaron gave them a sinister look. Not one of them budged.

Whose little ones were these?

Jaron was miffed that her scare tactics, which worked on everyone, including adults, appeared to not work on them. Little demons!

She sat down next to Mara. They continued to mix the medicines. The first one done, Jaron scooped up a good-sized wad onto her fingers and began to swath her charges bellies. She applied more on the one who had trouble breathing earlier, including the forehead and behind the legs. She was still too warm for Jaron's liking.

"They're really sick, mother." Mara picked the berries off their stems. "What is it?"

Jaron didn't want to say it out loud in front of the older sibling still at the basin. The one thing she knew that needed to be done was for their mother to be admitted to the medical bay.

****

The medical technician held a tablet in one hand while they stuck a sampling needle in Salara's arm. A thin line of blood appeared in the tiny chamber. The tablet beeped. Its screen changed to show an analysis chart. Each line graph rose at various levels. A few of them turned yellow, showing something being wrong.

They extracted the needle and disposed of it by detaching it from the sampling end. Salara sat slumped on the examination table, her hair a mess. Big puffs were under her eyes and stress lines covered her brow.

"You seemed to have come in contact with one of the poisonous plants in the forest. It won't kill you, but it has nasty side effects. It being in your system, it went through your feeding ducts. With your litter being so small still, that amount could indeed kill them."

Her face crumbled; a surprised expression full of pain.

"I didn't know." She sobbed, gripping the table's edge.

"It's not anyone's fault." The technician caressed her shoulder. "As I said, it didn't harm you at all. Be glad we were able to detect it before any more damage was done."

She nodded.

"What now? What should I do with my litter?"

"It seems Elder Jaron has already given them the proper remedy. This is not that uncommon on this planet. We still have a lot to research." He picked up an injection gun and placed the muzzle on her upper arm. The tiny needle pierced the skin, administering an antibody. "This should get it out of your system."

The technician motioned her towards the door leading out of the medical bay. She slid off the table, towering over them, and trudged out into the early evening.

Sunlight had already waned, changing the colors of the sky. She looked up and inhaled shakily, letting it out as steady as she could. Somewhat calmer than before, she headed to the sandbox at the family commons.

After a heated yet loving argument, Jakar had vacated the tiny two-room quarters hut along with their belongings and into the main family building.

Children ran around the side, getting their last round of frolicking done before evening meal. The older manbeasts and energy users from teen years to elder roamed the property, waiting for the dining hall to open.

She could smell the aromas of food mingling in the air. Despite her thoughts of not eating, her senses said otherwise. Her mouth watered, her stomach agreeing.

She turned the corner and entered the sandbox. In the nearest stall, four little ones were climbing unescorted out of the sandbox. The first one stopped, one leg over the ledge and stared up at her. She tilted her head in amusement. Were they really going to escape into the fields on their own? The other three halted as well, waiting for what she expected was the older of them to decide.

The look of indifference combined with total disregard for rules made Salara snort. There was no way she was letting any of them get out of the sandbox. The first moved closer over the edge, tempting fate. His other leg was bent, ready to swing over.

A gust of wind passed through the entrance, causing Salara to cover her head, stopping it from undoing the messy hair. She didn't want to deal with trying to rewind it back into a stable bun. A quick glance behind her found the manbeast who had flash stepped inside.

Barbon went around her and stared down at the sandbox. He and the first child made eye contact. Slowly, defiantly, the boy slid back and brought his leg into the stall. The others essentially hid behind the stall's wall.

So he had another litter.

She tried to remain calm in the presence of her estranged father. When she and Jakar became mated, it was to be kept a secret since Modas had made it known that as much as he respected Barbon, the feeling was not mutual; having soured on her father's end.

There wasn't a hint of awkwardness between them.

"I wouldn't have let them pass me," she said.

Barbon turned his head to look at her and frowned, scanning her up and down.

"In your state? I doubt it." He did a head tilt towards the stall. "This one is sneaky. Always calculating some kind of coup."

She attempted to keep her hair atop her head. Do I really look that bad? Although she felt a little better, there was no mistaking her pain.

"Well, at least you know he may be a brilliant strategist someday?"

Barbon huffed. "Or a menace." He leaned over the stall. "You will stay here until your mother comes with your meal. Understood?" His tone cut deep. The little ones cowered down onto the grassy bedding. "Good."

"You came running for that?" She asked, stunned.

"I had a feeling." Barbon walked out of the sandbox.

When he was gone, she eyed his litter. They all looked guilty. And plotting another deed. She stepped away, glancing back a few times, and making eye contact with their leader. He was patient, she'll give him that. The stall in the back had a small hover lamp in the corner set on dim.

All four of her litter was asleep, curled up against each other. Their little bodies rose and fell in slow rhythm, making their fur spikey, then flat. She knelt beside the stall and used a finger to caress them, smiling as they moved as one towards her touch.

"I'm so sorry, little ones," she whispered.

"Enough of that," Jaron spat. "I won't tell you again."

"I…" She pursed her lips. "Please. Don't yell at me."

Jaron placed a hand on her head. "I know. But it's not your fault. They'll be fine." She moved her hand and held it out. "Evening meal is ready. Let's get you something to eat."

She nodded, taking Jaron's hand, and stood. Jaron led her out to the dining commons. On the way out, she saw Jaron eye Barbon's litter. They were getting a reputation.

******

Jakar stood in the packed dining common and motioned Salara to him. Jaron released her hand. She maneuvered around the giant table and went to sit by his side. Seeing the family all together in one place made her realize the size of

Modas' horde. And that she had struggled alone needlessly. A spark of anger rose in her.

As if sensing her feelings, Jakar placed an arm around her. He leaned over and gently kissed her temple. He understood the blame as lying solely on him. That wasn't true. She, too, could have defied his wishes and announced their union.

The other siblings made quick glances at her, knowing who she was. The rumors that were spread suggested she had not found a mate since none was present, instead having random manbeasts' litters.

Vicious words accosted her and sometimes her children. Yet Jakar would not budge. The hushed conversation around the table conveyed suspicion.

Modas slammed a fist onto the table, rocking the platters. The drinks swished, spitting droplets over the carafes' rims.

"You will not bring that disgusting nonsense into this room. She is of our horde, mated to Jakar. You will treat her as your sister. Is that clear?"

Mara was silent for a long while, bringing attention to herself. Modas looked over at her. She met Jakar's stare.

"Why would you allow this?" Her tone was cruel. "To have the village and your own family disrespect your mate and children? I expected better from you as our eldest sibling."

All around the room felt her cruelty. Mota reached over and poured himself a drink. He took a sip and set it down.

"She's not wrong. I feel the same. What was your end game in all of this?"

Jakar's stonelike expression wavered. His eyes narrowed as if in pain. It frightened her. He covered his face with one hand and kept it there longer than she could bear. Placing her hand over his, she yanked it away.

"I am also to blame." She addressed the family. "We thought this was the best way to avoid conflict with my father. We were wrong. We see that now." She raised her tear-stained face to them. "Will you continue to condemn us for it?" She turned to Mara. "Did you help our litter out of some family obligation because your mother demanded it?" Gasps erupted. "Or do you truly think of them as loved ones?"

Mara stared at her in awed resentment. She nearly rose from her seat. Her mother grabbed hold of her wrist and stopped her. Und exhaled loudly. He glared at them both.

"That was uncalled for. Mara would never think that. None of us would. As far as blame, yes. You are both in the wrong. The rift between Barbon and our father should never have been a factor. I am also disappointed in you, brother."

Mara's eldest child looked around the room, then at her father, Dellus.

"Does this mean we can't eat yet?" She had her fork poised ready to stab the sliced meat on a platter closest to her.

Everyone paused, reminding themselves of where they were and why. Jakar looked shamed. Mara eased back down, looking the same. Jaron smirked.

"Are we done slinging insults at each other?" Heads hung in defeat. "Good. Children first. We who are old enough to know better can wait our turn."

****

The hillside was quiet in the dead of night. Only a few critters chirped in the distance. Behind it, the mountains were giant black shapes against an equally dark sky. Four manbeast stood atop the hill watching over the village. Two had spread out on each side. The other two were a few feet apart, silently brooding.

Modas crossed his arms, standing akimbo next to Barbon. He sniffed the air and went to turn towards the other. Barbon raised a hand to stop him.

"The topic is silly at best," Barbon said before Modas could speak.

"I don't find it a silly matter."

"Modas, you broke a trust with our clan. Your horde is in disarray. As our leader, it looks bad. Sloppy. Incompetent." Each insult made Modas squirm. "That said, it has nothing to do with my daughter mating with your son."

"They seem, no, are, conflicted about your feelings. To go to such an extreme means we both gave them the impression we would not recognize their union."

Barbon nodded in agreement. He frowned. "She looks spent. She's not well."

"No. Jaron is caring for the youngest litter."

Barbon turned to him with concern.

"What has happened? Is their condition worse?"

"No," Modas waved one hand before tucking it back in. "They are getting better. Slowly."

"What is it?" Barbon crossed his arms.

"Poisonous root from that forest." Modas nodded towards the dense trees below. "We need to find the roots. They appear to be scattered throughout the region; not growing in one section."

Barbon's lips thinned as he exhaled through his nose. "Has Jakar and Salara settled in the commons?"

"Yes."

"Then I shall visit soon. Then Jakar must come to introduce himself and feast with my horde to welcome him."

"Of course." Modas paused for a moment, hesitant to speak. "I will show you my resolve to lead better. My horde needs healing. I will make it right."

"That is all I can ask of you." Barbon held out a hand. "We are bonded as one family."

Modas clasped his hand tight with his own.

"To raising a mighty horde."

They released each other's hands and continued to stare out into the night. Out in the distance, near the medical compound, they saw Ganna's lab lights on.

What is she up to now? They both thought.

Facing Truths

Visitors in the royal nursery admired the small bundles in the clear rolling boxes set on the other side of the viewing glass. In the first container were the Queen's twin boys and the other held General Rass' small boy. It was an auspicious day on Azrom with the children born two days apart.

Royal guards stood at each end of the viewing portal with two more positioned inside in the event an attempt on the newborns' lives came about.

Kur walked down the hall towards the group ogling his own and Farin's children. He never liked the whole spectacle of showing off the royal bloodline. It lacked taste.

The group caught sight of him coming and bowed while stepping away from the glass.

"Congratulations, Lord Kur!" they said in unison.

Kur grimaced, fighting back an insult. He smiled curtly.

"My heart feels with gratitude. Thank you."

The two guards ushered the visitors out of the hall. Viewing was over. Relieved, Kur turned into the door of the nursery opened by the guards inside. He leaned over his son and visually checked him for any signs of illness. Seeing none, he picked him up and held him close to his chest. The little one yawned, not opening his eyes. Instead of tiny hands were pincers wrapped in thick gauze to prevent him from hurting himself and others.

Tufts of forest green hair stuck out of the blanket. Kur grinned despite his hard demeanor. His older son resembled Rass. This one's mine. He poked his son's cheek with a finger.

"There is a sight not seen by many." Batis came up behind him. "If the masses saw such a face, they would drop dead from shock."

Kur frowned as he turned to him. The motion was stiff, making him wince. His genuine affection for his child being noticed was nothing compared to what they already said about his appearance.

He was not easy on the eyes at the moment. The visitors tried to hide their surprise and failed. They were in awe and frightened.

His recovery had been slow, spanning months, and he didn't get to be at the birthing that happened weeks ago. Even after waking from cryosleep, he was a mess. Rass was furious. Angrier than he had ever seen his mate. The chastising went on for hours until he finally burst into tears, startling Kur, and the medical attendants. I don't ever want to see that again. Kur gently rocked his son up and down.

"Why are you in here?" Kur leered at Batis.

"It's my chance to get a gauge of those two infants' health. I don't trust the findings of the royal doctors these days."

Kur's lips went thin. He was there for the same reason. There had been some discrepancies of late in diagnosing infants. Something on Azrom made newborns sick via the mother's system. They had no symptoms yet transmitted it to their unborn. He remembered something similar happened on New Lassa.

"How is the mother?" Batis asked as he caressed the twins' heads.

"Rass has slept for two days. She is exhausted from meetings with our military leaders. I will take her place later today."

"Like that?" Batis looked up at him in shock.

Kur frowned. "There have been worse after a battle."

"But not you." Batis stood. "The first time, no one really saw your defeat at the hands of Modas courtesy of Rass. This time is different. The people fear the fall of Azrom."

"Azrom will not fall!" Kur yelled.

His chest tightened, causing him to bend over coughing blood. It flecked onto the blanket and the front of his tunic. He kept a firm hold on his son even as his hands felt weak. His body felt drained, like he was about to pass out. Batis caught him, nodding to an attendant to get the newborn from him.

With his son back in the clear basinet, Kur took hold of Batis' arm and tried to rise.

"Not yet." Batis glanced over at the viewing port. They were far enough down that anyone passing would not notice them. "Got some pariahs approaching." Three members of the fourth royal house strolled by, taking a quick look at the infants, their faces scrunched in disdain, then moved on. He helped Kur to his feet. "Let's get you back to your chamber."

The two left the nursery and made their way slowly down the hall. At the end leading to the outside, Kur's entourage stood waiting. They fell into a flanking formation that protected them on all sides.

Kur and Rass' dark chamber h suited him fine. He wasn't fond of sunlight today. Batis helped him onto the bed, and he lay still fully clothed, not wanting to move. Batis went over to the small basin on the other side of the room and wet a cloth. He came back and wiped the blood from Kur's face.

That added insult to injury. Kur felt helpless; weak. Tears threatened to fall. I will not! His body felt heavy, like a boulder. He couldn't keep his eyes open. Darkness closed around him.

Rass witnessed Batis taking care of Kur as she came into the chamber. She stared in amusement until she saw the watered-down green blood on the cloth he held. Angry and scared, she went to his side.

"What has happened?" She demanded.

"Stay calm." Batis folded the cloth over to a clean side and wiped off the tears making their way down the side of Kur's face. "He pushed himself too much. I found him in the nursery being all smiling and affectionate."

"He's not a monster. Of course, he feels that way towards our child." Rass snapped.

"And who has seen that side of him besides you or I?"

Rass scratched the side of her head with two fingers, mulling over the question. It was true neither of them showed much emotion besides fury and blood lust. She knew what the people were thinking and saying. Efforts to prevent leaks of information regarding the mission had failed.

"No matter. What's done is done." She pulled off Kur's boots. "I will take over from here." Batis set the cloth on the edge of the bed. "My thanks to you."

Batis shrugged. "We can't have our pillar of strength down any longer." He turned his head at the entrance. "By the way, he was going to take your place at the war meeting."

"He's not going anywhere," Rass huffed. She started on stripping Kur naked.

"That's what I figured. See you there."

Batis waved goodbye as he rounded the corner onto the promenade.

Rass got Kur's clothes off and tossed them on the floor. She would take care of them later. Grabbing him by the legs, she swung him around and tucked him under the sheets. He didn't stir. His breathing was still labored. Stubborn. He had insisted on being released from the medical bay against the doctors' recommendation.

She straddled him and caressed his face before kissing him softly. "Sleep, my beloved. There's no rush."

Rass climbed off and left the chamber.

****

Batis wandered off into the fields near the first royal house and found Biandra picking more of the tiny orange fruits that kept Romnus from being murderous. He watched her carefully examine each one before placing it delicately in the basket hooked over her forearm. She appeared oblivious to his presence, but he knew better.

"Are you going to stare at me indefinitely yet again?" She didn't look his way.

"Well, you are pleasing to the eyes." Batis leaned against a wooden stake that marked the start of the poisonous plant's area. "You keep dodging me."

"You're not known for you courtship skills."

"Oh, so you've noticed?" Batis perked up with intrigue. "Then you'll take me seriously?"

This time, she did turn to him. "Not in the least."

He grinned. She was challenging him. There were many he could take for pleasure, or even as a mate. None compared to Biandra. A former warrior wounded in battle and taken out of commission to live the rest of her days as a servant. He frowned at the thought. That particular rule had never bothered him until recently. It had been long abandoned, no longer feasible.

Biandra was inches from his face. He blinked, startled that he had not seen her move, and stumbled back, catching himself.

"What are you thinking about that's upsetting you like that?' Her tone was calm.

Batis regained his posture, adopting a playful expression.

"Nothing for you to worry about." He pointed to the basket. "You better hurry and get those in the bowl by night fall. Our Supreme Ruler should keep a calm head."

She didn't budge, staring deep into his eyes. Liar. It screamed at him from her being. He lowered his eyes, severing the connection. He had come to toy with her, flirt a bit. Damn.

"I will see you later, after the meeting." Batis backed away until he was far enough so she couldn't see his face. "Don't keep me waiting," he called out.

He could feel her stare burrowing into his back. She was not going to let it go. I messed up again. Batis was by any stretch a considerate lover. Romance was not his forte. For Biandra, he would try.

In his own chamber, he took off his gloves and threw them angrily on the bed. He placed his hands on his hips and stood silent, not thinking for a bit.

"That bad?" Farin stood in the entryway with a look of pure enjoyment.

"Are you laughing at my pain?" Batis replied, heated. "Making light of my failure?"

Farin blanched at his verbal assault. "Not at all. Why would you say that to me?"

Batis turned to her and flinched at the hurt expression.

"I'm sorry."

"You have to be more patient." Farin stepped further into the room. "Your reputation precedes you." Her closed lips rose on one side, her eyes squinting.

"I know that!" Batis sat on the edge of the bed; one leg bent next to him. "She's toying with me. It's like she can see right through me."

"Then change." Farin stood before him. She flicked his forehead like a child.

"Stop that." He gently slapped her hand away.

"She deserves better."

"I know that too." Batis fell back, staring at the vaulted ceiling. "She's worth the wait."

*****

The late-night meeting was held in the war room deep within the main palace. A group of soldiers escorted Romnus, the Queen, their entourage, and the royal advisors. Among the soldiers was Ponnae. She kept in step; her face showing no emotion. The tight uniform and heavy armor made her feel safe.

Relieved of her position as Lord Chastan's chamber maid following her recovery, she begged to be allowed into the royal guard combat unit. She trained harder than most, securing an assignment in the royal palace as part of the escort team. It was a start. The stronger she became, the more respect she would gain.

Except, she hadn't gotten much stronger the past couple of years. Her skills had remained stagnant as if her body was rejecting the extra muscle and mobility. She wasn't getting weaker, no. She felt less useful as others surpassed her.

A group of soldiers marching the opposite direction down an adjacent corridor caught her eye. Three of the men in the formation came into view and her body stiffened. She sucked air through gritted teeth and tried to remain calm. The last thing she wanted was to draw attention to herself while on duty. They didn't turn their heads, focused on staying in line. Of course, their sight wouldn't wander to acknowledge her. So stupid! She kept her head straight.

Ahead of her was Biandra, walking directly behind Lord Romnus. The others in the entourage blocked most of their view. Ponnae nearly reared back as Biandra turned and glanced her way with a knowing stare before returning her focus on the journey. Her eyes burned, blinking constantly to fight back tears.

The two had been through the pits of hell and forever changed. Biandra by the cruel torture administered by Halfar. Herself, sexually desecrated by the three soldiers marching past on his order. The excruciating pain lingered in her mind even after so long. Her body wasn't the weak part; it was her psyche. I need to fix it!

Her unit arrived at the war room and the royal guards stationed there took over. She marched with her unit that spread out to either side of the first entryway to stand and wait until their charge came back out.

Then they would resume their duties as escorts.

Romnus lingered in the war room after the advisors and military leaders, including Rass, left. He rubbed his lower lip with a finger, staring out into the hall at the escorts awaiting his entourage to appear.

Farin glanced over at him questioning from across the table. He saw Biandra with her head held low, anticipating what he was thinking. Dropping his hand onto the table, he sat straighter in his chair.

"I don't like seeing her that way," he finally said.

Biandra nodded. Farin was momentarily confused, then caught on.

"Oh." Her expression saddened. "Neither do I."

"You can bring her into the fold." Biandra raised her head.

"I do need another guard," Farin added. "It's not the best solution, but at least she would be closer to us."

"I'll make the request at daybreak."

He had seen the look of terror on Ponnae's face as the other soldiers marched down the adjacent corridor. There was no denying the mental damage done, possibly worse than the physical. The thought of the incident made him heated. His cousin had a lot to answer for in his lifetime.

Farin rose from her seat, slowly. She was still recovering from birthing twins. Romnus stood to help her get steady. He had been staying in their chamber, taking care of her himself, only letting a medical attendant come to take vitals.

"You should lie down for a while. We'll see the twins later."

Farin pouted, making her seem childish. "They're so cute, and tiny." She wiggled her fingers in yearning. "I can't help it."

They were indeed adorable. Romnus grinned. Like Halfar, he had never thought of mating and having offspring. It changed everything. He became overly protective, territorial. His anxiety increased tenfold. The same was true of Farin's oldest child with Chastan. He had taken on the role as his father figure. Being a parent was stressful.

"Yes, I feel the same. Still." He hooked his arm around hers and guided her out of the room. "You're not at one hundred percent yet."

He saw Farin's face flush with anger. She hated being unable to defend herself. The fourth royal house was making a move to sabotage his reign and remove her from the royal line.

They were too cowardly to go through the proper channel that required a fight for supremacy.

Halfar defeated all the other royal houses' best fighters to claim rulership. The sour feeling was because he was the previous ruler's offspring. Their bloodline reigned supreme once again. And now Romnus sat on the throne, the son of the previous ruler's brother. Gaining it because Halfar yielded to him. Biandra reached into her sleeve. He shook his head. He didn't want one of the sedative fruits.

As they crossed the threshold of the room's hallway, the escorts turned towards them and got into formation. The group on the right went in front and the other half brought up the rear. The giant entourage moved as one down the corridor. Along the way, a couple from the fourth royal house strolled the path.

"Lord Romnus," the female said, not bothering to bow, showing her disrespect. "Congratulations on your spawns."

"Another addition to the bloodline." The man also did not bow.

The entourage halted and Batis was on them swiftly, blade to their necks. They flinched in terror, not daring to move for fear of him running it across.

"You will kneel," he ordered through gritted teeth. "And address your Supreme Ruler accordingly."

The two dropped to their knees, heads hung low.

"Our apologies, Supreme Ruler," they chimed. "May your will see forgiveness."

"I'll keep it in mind." Romnus stared down at them with fury. "Rise."

They stood with defiant looks etched on their faces. Batis sheathed his blade and stepped back behind Romnus. The two continued their stroll, glancing back once.

"They're not even trying to hide it anymore," Farin said.

"Which will be their downfall in the long run." Batis ran his fingers through his thick hair. "I'm getting tired of taking down our own people."

Resuming their procession, the escorts led the entourage to the royal quarters.

*****

Kur rose abruptly from the bed and gasped in pain, clutching his chest. He sucked air through his teeth while leaning forward. Rass stood staring angrily at him in the entryway.

"Lay back down," she ordered.

He looked up at her as she approached, realizing it wasn't just him she was mad about.

"I missed the meeting?"

He eased back against the cushions.

"You weren't going in the first place," Rass snapped.

He returned her maddening stare with his own. "Tell me."

Rass stripped naked, then donned a flimsy, nearly see through white flowy robe, before climbing onto the bed. She stretched out and laid her head on his chest.

"We will have to see what the Razznians come up with. This was a shock to Azrom pride."

"There's no reason to bow out." Kur turned his head to her. "We need a different way to counter. The enemy is not invincible. They can fall as well."

"Lt. Treshur is at the rendezvous point with the other science leaders to reverse engineer that weapon. He hopes to have a report soon on their preliminary findings."

Kur was about to answer when he felt Rass' body sag into him. In only a few seconds, she had fallen asleep, clearly exhausted. That fueled his rage. If he hadn't been so badly wounded, he could assist on the battlefront. Dividing the duties so neither of them would be spent.

I want vengeance.

Knowing he would accomplish nothing so late in the night, he settled in and fell asleep.

****

Whispers followed Farin wherever she went. Constant talk about her age. A child ruler. There were looks of admonishment from the older population and envy from women in the royal houses who wish they had bed Romnus sooner.

Over the years, she had endured it, shutting them up with her knowledge and fighting skills. That no longer worked. With the birth of royal twins, her reign and Romnus' was solidified.

Now came the death threats and talk of finding Romnus a more seasoned mate. That their union was just for his amusement. A trial run, as she heard many say.

Four royals from another house strolled the main palace corridor. They bowed as they approached.

"Good afternoon, my Queen," they said.

Farin tilted her head in a small bow.

"Good afternoon to you as well."

They continued their walk. When they got a few feet away, she heard their voices.

"I can't imagine that satisfying Lord Romnus," the first female royal said.

"He can't even get his proper fill. He'd kill her," the one next to her added.

"There's always his room in the brothel." The third, a male walking behind them said.

"At least there it doesn't matter." The fourth glanced back and, immediately turned his attention forward with a shocked face. "We should hurry."

Farin had stopped walking. Her entourage halted as she stared at the white and grey marbled floor, trying to unhear what they said. The brothel. She had peeked into it once when she was younger. Lord Chastan had come out and steered her away. It was also Rass' origin. Her head rose, and she gazed, squinting at the figures at the far end of the hall. Her vision focused.

Up ahead, three of the soldiers who desecrated Ponnae years ago were surrounding her. She held her own, appearing unafraid, her hand on the hilt of her longsword. They laughed, teasing her to draw her weapon and show them what she's made of. Which she could not do or face prison. Farin moved, her guards following close behind.

"You look even better in a uniform." The first said, his fibgers running across her breast plate. "It's like that dress up they do on Earth."

"Should we be nice and let her strip down for us here in the hallway?" The second asked.

"Or we could just rip it off." The third grabbed her by the arm. "No whore should wear the royal robes of the court." He bared his teeth.

"It's insulting," said the first.

"Let go of me!" Ponnae struggled for a bit, trying to get out of the third one's grip. "I will not tolerate your behavior." She got free and stepped back, pulling her sword out of its sheath.

The three of them stared at her in surprise, then they became angry. The first pushed her as the tip of the blade was almost out, forcing her off balance. As the first came at her, she managed to get it out and swiped up at an angle, slicing his left cheek. She backed a few feet away and went into a defensive stance, sword out in front of her.

The first soldier howled in surprise, slapping the wound. Blood trickled through his fingers. He removed his hand and stared at the blood. His eyes turned black, and his hands morphed into pincers.

"You piece of trash! We should have ripped your womb out while we were at."

Farin had seen and heard enough.

"Stand down!" Her voice boomed in the massive, nearly empty area. The soldiers turned towards her, eyes full of malice, still morphed and ready to attack. Then they fell to their knees in horror. "Explain yourselves."

"May Azrom prosper in your reign, Queen Farin!" They slammed their fists into their chests.

"Ponnae," she addressed the former hand maid. "That means you as well."

Stricken with fear, Ponnae dropped to her knees, her sword flat on the floor.

"May your reign see Azrom forever victorious." She pounded her chest hard.

Farin's disgust fell on the three soldiers. They didn't dare look up any further, capable of seeing it from their view below.

"We were only giving her some grief," the first said.

"A little ribbing between comrades," the second continued.

"Is that so?" Farin zeroed in on the third one. He turned his head away to avert her vicious stare. "Speak!"

"Of course, my Queen," he finally answered. "What else would we be doing?"

Ponnae stared at the floor in shock. Her teeth clenched, she fought back tears. Farin exhaled slowly and loomed over them.

"You will leave this instant. I will be reporting this to your superior later. My suggestion is to inform them before I do."

"Yes, My Queen!" They stood and, in trained fashion, marched down the hall to the next section. Not one of them looked back.

Farin knelt before Ponnae. The woman was shaking, her head still hung low.

"It's okay now." Farin used a soft tone to try and ease her. "Please, rise." She held out a hand to her. Ponnae was frozen where she kneeled. "Calm yourself and rise," Farin ordered more forcefully, standing.

Startled, Ponnae slowly got to her feet. She dragged her sword up, looking at it as if the blame fell on it. Like it was a useless piece of decoration. Farin had seen her do this many times after her training sessions with the other guards in the courtyard. With shaky hands, she sheathed her weapon.

"My apologies, my queen," Ponnae said softly. "I am ashamed to have displayed such lack of discipline drawing my sword."

"I would say it was justified." Farin nodded upwards. "Come. I am here to fetch you." Ponnae looked at her in confusion. "You are now part of my guard detail." She looked over her shoulder at the ones behind her. "Is that understood?"

"Yes, my queen!" They replied.

Ponnae stopped shaking and took her place beside Farin. The moment Farin took a step forward, the entourage moved as one and resumed walking down the corridor. Ponnae's demeanor changed, becoming hardened, and she fell in step with the others. The perfect soldier. Farin didn't like it at all.

Entering the promenade that ran along the outside of the royal quarters, all but two soldiers and Ponnae dropped back and marched from where they came. Their escort duty was complete. With her small group, Farin continued towards the other side of the palace. Ponnae seemed to tense. She knew where they were going. The other two soldiers weren't sure what to make of her routing decision.

To their surprise, Farin didn't go to the main entrance of the brothel. Instead, she veered off onto a narrow walkway that led down and around to the back of the structure. She raised a hand for them to halt when they reached the base.

"Wait here." She saw Ponnae hesitate to reach out. "Just do as I ask. I'll be back momentarily."

Farin extended her talons then scaled up the the wall to a window set high above. She climbed in, disappearing from their sight. Stealth like, she moved closer to the secret chamber deep inside the brothel.

Even from where she was, the screams and moans found her. She braced herself for what she might see as she crouched down against the outer wall and eased into place at its edge.

Inside the chamber was Romnus on a pile of cushions piled high into a makeshift bed. Naked, half morphed, his giant pincer closed around the neck of a female, holding her down as he brutally rammed his altered cock in her, causing blood splatter. The female's eyes glazed over, going blank, and she stopped screaming. That didn't stop Romnus. He wasn't done yet. The whore lay motionless, her body twitching with each thrust.

On the cushions next to her was another female moaning in agony, her body spent, covered in bruises and lacerations from the pincers. Horrified, Farin sat rooted in place while her vision blurred. Pain filled her chest and she stifled a cry. Romnus let out an animal like roar that ended in the high-pitched tweeter sound.

The guards at the chamber's main entrance buckled from the sound. She forced herself to watch Romnus releasing his seed, some of it seeping out from the rim of the female's womb as he threw his head back in satisfaction.

To her horror, he tore himself from the female and pushed her onto the floor like discarded meat as he reverted to his normal form. Blood and other bodily fluids streaked his chest down to his groin.

He stepped away from the cushions and went into the bath adjacent to the room. Farin covered her mouth, feeling the sting of vomit threatening her throat. No, no, no! She backed away stealthier than before and made her way to the window she entered. Swinging one leg over the ledge, she sat atop it for a moment, taking deep breaths to calm herself.

She anticipated seeing his brutal side of sexual prowess. This was nothing like what she imagined. It was much worse. She slid down the wall, careful not to scratch too deeply in the stone.

At the bottom, her small entourage was lounging on some rocks. Ponnae gave her a sad expression. Of course, she would know. Chastan may not be as bad, but he was a sadistic monster when he bedded other women besides Farin.

"I'm done. Let us go. I am tired."

And she was. Mentally exhausted. So many things swam in her mind. None of them a solution. Nothing to ease her anxiety. *I should have known better!* Yet her curiosity got the best of her yet again. She walked in a daze, startled when Ponnae addressed her.

"My queen, we have arrived at your chamber."

Farin regained her focus and found herself at the entrance. The darkness of the room invited her in. She didn't bother to activate the hover lamps.

"Is there anything else you need?" Ponnae asked.

"No." Farin traced the edge of the bed. "You are dismissed." She glanced up and saw Ponnae lag the other two guards. "Go."

When Ponnae finally left, following the others, Farin crawled onto the bed and laid on her side across it. By her calculations, Romnus would show up within the hour, Biandra having slipped him one of the fruits despite his sated appetite.

A dark figure silhouetted by the sun behind them stood in the entrance. They stepped closer. Batis crossed his arms

"I didn't take you for a voyeur to go watch Romnus fill his primal urges."

Of course, he knew where she had gone. He was never too far, even though he was part of Romnus' entourage. Farin didn't move. Her body felt heavy. She couldn't keep her eyes open. Batis sat on the ledge facing her and caressed her head.

"Yeah. That was a bit too much for you to take. Sleep. I'll divert the beast elsewhere."

"Thank you," she whispered before sleep took her.

Empathy

For days after awakening, Trinon screamed in agony. The attendants could barely contain him. Jakar and Modas had to step in more than a few times. Ganna ran around in desperation to ease the pain. He woke up from a deep cryosleep not fully healed, breaking through the chamber with frightening strength.

Some of his wounds reopened, turning the bed beneath bright red. By the fifth day, his rage had subsided, relenting to tears. He sobbed uncontrollably.

"You're a demon." Ganna wiped sweat from his forehead as Modas released him. "But you're still a child in my book." She lifted the injection gun from the nearby tray and administered the sedative. Trinon went limp. "That's better."

Modas stroked Trinon's wet mane, moving strands from his face. Sadness, worry, fear; rage. It all balled up inside, ready to burst. On the first night, Jaron couldn't take her child's screams and refused to return to the medical bay. He didn't blame her. It took every fiber of his being to stay and keep his son down with Jakar's help. Und had stood in at the entrance horrified. The grief on his face plain to see.

Trinon turned his head and stared up at him with glazed eyes. The tears started drying. Modas took the wet cloth from Ganna and began wiping away the streak marks.

"It's alright, my son. You're safe."

Trinon mouthed something. Modas leaned closer.

"What did you say?"

"Und." Trinon whispered as he raised a hand and clumsily grabbed hold of his father's robe. "Did I make it?"

Modas leaned up, eyes wide. Worry etched Trinon's face.

"Yes. You did. He's safe and very worried about you too."

"Doubt…" Trinon's barely audible voice trailed off.

"Your name was the first thing he said."

"Huh." More tears fell. "Glad." Trinon fell into a deep sleep courtesy of the powerful sedative.

"He should be down for a few days with that." Ganna wagged the injection gun in the air before setting it back on the tray. "Now I can finish healing his wounds." She stood from the rolling seat. "I swear, your brood are a menace when we try to treat them."

"It's instinctive." Modas cupped the side of Trinon's face, then walked away from the chamber. "How long will it take for him to fully recover?"

"Longer than you think and he would like." She went over to her workstation. "I would say about a year's time."

"That's better than I thought." He continued to the door. "Jaron will be happy to hear it."

Modas headed for the family commons where the rest of his horde was out and about enjoying the afternoon. The young manbeasts were out practicing on the monolith while the little ones were being tended to by their parents. He saw Jaron spot him and stand from the bench along the wall.

"Is it over?" The bags under her eyes had gotten bigger since yesterday. "How is he?"

The other siblings looked over at him.

"Calm now. Ganna gave him a heavy sedative."

"Different than all the others she gave him?" Her tone was dubious.

She had every right to be. Nothing had worked to bring Trinon down. Ganna mixed a concoction made from the orange fruit of Azrom that could drop a Grulog beast.

"Yes. An experiment." Jaron hissed at that. Modas raised a hand up in defense. "It is safe, I assure you. Trinon is sleeping."

He watched her body seem to sag in relief. Und appeared conflicted. He turned away and went into the sitting area. Why is he so disingenuous? Modas wondered if it stemmed from Jaron. That automatic withdrawal from others.

****

Ganna checked the stats on Trinon's new chamber console. Satisfied he would be out, as planned, she went out the back way from the medical bay to her lab. Once inside, she headed into the secret room in the back to check on her other patient.

The hover lamps followed her to the cryochamber, and she stared down at the manbeast that lay unconscious inside.

Hon.

One of Jaron's children who also supposedly perished in Lassa's destruction. Different than the others, he had a blondish mane that resembled normal hair instead of fur. His DNA was also an anomaly. On occasion, litters of four or more will have a mated pair. The occurrence rarely happened and when it did, uncertainty arose from the parents.

It wasn't a stigma so much as a nuisance.

Hon was beautiful. He resembled Lassa of old. Ganna frowned. His core memories would be intact and that posed a problem. There were things Hon knew that shouldn't come to light yet. *I need more time.* Ganna drummed her fingers against the bottom of her chin. They needed to have a serious conversation when he awakened.

She checked his vitals via the display screen and did a visual of his body's condition. The new flesh was adapting to his original tone and all the limbs were back together, regrown where there were missing pieces.

"You look better than ever." Her eyes narrowed. *I never liked you.* "You horrid, little beast."

Multicolored speckles danced in the darkness behind Hon's eyelids as he forced them open. His pupils to retracted from the bright hover lamps assaulting his irises. He could feel the hard surface beneath him and knew he was in a medical bay. His fingers tingled. As he wiggled them, his talons scraped against the bed. The sound grated on his sensitive ears.

A sheen of dew covered his naked body. Cryochamber. He had seen one before long time ago when a field worker got hurt. Scanning his surroundings, he noticed it was not the same medical bay. This one was newer, more advanced.

How long was I out?

Then the memories flooded back. His body seized as the planet's destruction replayed in his mind. He felt his body being torn apart all over again. The desperation to get to Mota only to see him also meet his demise. Hot tears streamed down his face. A strangled cry came from his gaping mouth.

"Stay calm. Easy, now."

The female voice sounded familiar.

He turned his head towards her and almost pitched himself off the bed. She grabbed hold of his shoulderes and forced him still.

"Stop being childish!"

Ganna thinned her lips in exasperation. Hon narrowed his eyes, struggling to control the pain. He took a few deep breaths, never taking his eyes off her. He flexed his hands, ready to wrap one around her neck.

"Before you get all vengeful." Ganna released him. "You need to know a few important things."

Hon tried to sit up and gasped at the tightness in his chest. He laid still, relenting to hearing her spiel.

"And that's what?" He followed her to the seat she had next to the bed.

"First, our home world was destroyed. We are on a new planet. New Lassa."

"Why?" Hon clenched his fists. "Why is our planet gone?"

"Well," Ganna let out a sigh. "Halfar did not take being rejected by Chardon lightly. He sent a planet bomb."

He turned his head to her with a shocked expression. He felt sick. Only a few knew about their leader's tryst with the Azrom ruler. It was disgusting then and would always be, in his opinion.

"So that chapter is over?"

"Not quite." Ganna's face scrunched.

"What does that mean?" Hon waited for her to answer. "You can't mean…"

"They have reconciled. Even spawned two children. One of which is now Queen of Azrom."

Hon forced himself into an upright position and leaned towards her, gripping the rim of the chamber.

"How long?" He demanded. His teeth ground as he breathed through more pain. "Tell me!"

"Hmm." Ganna tapped her lower lip. "Over a century."

Eyes wide, Hon slumped over the ledge in horror.

"How many died?"

"Too many," Ganna spat as she stood.

Her hostile response surprised him. He didn't think she cared that much. *I guess I was wrong.* She came back with a clean robe and laid it in the chamber next to him.

"You should put this on before you get cold."

He slowly donned it, careful with his stiff limbs.

"Mota."

This time, Ganna's expression softened. She smiled. "I was able to restore only a few of your siblings. Even recovered your mother's core. Among them is indeed Mota."

"And the others?" Hon dreaded the answer. There had been eight of them, yet Ganna said a few. "No need to lessen the outcome."

"Jakar and Mara as well."

Hon stared at her, waiting for her to say more names. Rage welled up in him.

"That's all? Three of us? Me, making it four." Ganna nodded. "And we are supposed to just forgive Halfar and Chardon for their deceit that ended in the destruction of our planet?"

"I wouldn't say forgive. No one has done that. Nor should we." Ganna clasped her hands in front of her. "But the damage has already been done. There is nothing we can do to reverse it."

Hon felt his dirty blond mane drying from the cool air. It fell around his shoulders, cascading down his back. His eyes, the same color as his father's, grew dark.

"I have some streams for you to watch to get you up to speed." Ganna went over to an empty station with a holoscreen deck. "You have a lot of new siblings."

Hon eased himself over the ledge of the chamber and walked over to the station. "So my parents decided to replace their dead." The look of disdain Ganna gave him made him step back.

"Don't ever say such things again. Your parents were heartbroken. It is only reasonable that they would have more children."

"You're right. I'm sorry." Hon stepped forward again. "I didn't mean it."

He sat down at the station and waited for her to load the feed. When she stepped away, Hon scooted closer to the holoscreen as it began.

Ganna left her secret lab and went into the main one, where she made sure no one was waiting for treatment outside. Hon would be occupied for at least a few days, and she needed all that time to prepare.

*****

Barbon's little ones in the sandbox near the entrance peeked over their stall, tiny hands gripping the edge. They watched Mota walk over to the one in the corner and kneel next to it. He reached in and wiggled the first two. No longer small enough to hold in his hands, they were already three years old and big for their age. Being Jakar's that was a given. Adding his equally tall mate to the mix, Mota was sure they would probably surpass them all in size.

He looked forlorn, playing with them gently as opposed to his usual sessions of terrorizing children. Not today. He felt distracted, as if something had been injected in the air that only he could sense. The little ones mewed and giggled, making him smile a little.

There had been a few occasions when some of his family members had caught him like this. They tried to pry out what was troubling him. He understood their concern. Everyone was finding their mates, having litters and babies. The fact that even Mara had settled down amazed him.

Scuffling from behind made him turn. He saw Barbon's children no longer peeking over the edge. Instead, they were all climbing out, the first one in the lead. A year older than Jakar's litter, they could not be contained for long. Mota caught the leader's eye, and he gave the boy a sinister stare, stopping them all in their tracks.

They had seen what he did to the other children, leaving them alone since they were not in the same cluster. Mota stood and moved towards them. He saw the leader contemplating if they should make a break for it or climb back into the stall. Either way, there would be no escape.

He was feeling like a menace today and administering punishment to naughty children seemed the right thing to do.

Mota could feel Barbon and his mother's presence as they stood at the sandbox entrance with grim expressions on their faces listening to the crying and yowling coming from Barbon's children. His mother stepped forward, only to be held back by Barbon. He shook his head. Not yet. Neither could see around the edge of the stall, but he was sure they had in inkling of what was going on. After a loud yelp from the youngest one, Barbon moved.

Not the least bit startled, Mota eased away from them. Still hunched down, he was at the right height for his mother to smack him in the back of the head.

"Ow!" His hands flew instinctively to where she hit him, rubbing the sting away. "That hurt!"

"What do you think you're doing?" She snapped. "I've warned you."

Mota glanced up at Barbon. There was no sympathy in those eyes.

"They were almost out the door." Mota finally stood. "I didn't give them much of a choice."

Barbon simply nodded, knowing how his children were on a good day. He looked down at them, witnessing the sniffling. The oldest had angry tears. Mota could tell he was plotting payback when he was old enough to spar with him.

Bring it, as they said on Earth.

"That's not your job to discipline them." His mother exhaled sharply through her nose. "One day you're going to regret it."

Barbon leaned over the stall.

"Serves you right." The farthest two wiped their eyes.

"Don't encourage him!" His mother walked away to Jakar's children

They had sat up to see the show, leaning over the edge of their own stall, eyes wide in disbelief. Mota snorted, his sheepish grin resembling that of Trinon who also terrorized the young ones.

And then his mother looked over her shoulder at him with that probing expression. She saw right through him. He backed away, not wanting to be in the sandbox anymore.

Relieved that she didn't beckon him over, Mota turned around to leave. Barbon blocked his exit. The elder manbeast stared him down. There was a flash of admonishment, then it changed to what Mota could only describe as pity. Angered, Mota pushed his way around him and left.

Outside, he breathed in the cool air that picked up, blowing fallen leaves across the surface. He felt the tears coming and fought them back as hard as he could. It wasn't going to work. Terrified he might be seen, he flash stepped to his personal chamber in the family building.

His speed brought a gust of wind into his room as he stopped to open the door. Light objects went flying around, falling off shelves and tables. Slamming it shut, he walked over to his bed and flopped face down on it. Safe from prying eyes, he cried to his heart's content, letting the sorrow take him until he fell asleep.

Trinon stood on a hillside not far from the family commons and watched his older brother fall into despair. He knew that pain too well. Having snuck out of the medical bay, which he did on occasion, he had spotted Mota going into the sandbox.

Off in the distance to his left, he could see his father and Jakar doing the same. They didn't acknowledge each other. There was no need. Mota was hurting, and they had no idea how to help him.

Down below was Mara hanging back after Mota blew past her. The look on her face was the same. Seeing Ganna on her way to the medical bay building, Trinon headed back. To his surprise, she yelled up into the sky.

"I know you're up there, Trinon. You better be back in that cryochamber by nightfall so I can record your vitals."

He halted halfway down the hill, shocked at her outburst. Mara placed a hand to her mouth and laughed. To no one's surprise, Jaron came running out of the sandbox, looking around for him. Sighing, he carefully finished his descent. His body still hurt, limbs a little stiff. Not enough to stop him from climbing and jumping.

At the bottom, he went to the sandbox and let himself be confronted by his angry mother.

"What are you doing?" She yelled. "Why won't you stay put and heal?" He saw the tears and immediately regretted being caught. "Why won't you do as you're told?"

She tapped a fist on his chest and leaned against him. For a moment he didn't hug her. Afraid she would know how weak he was. Then he wrapped his arms around her.

"It's fine. I couldn't lay there all day." He pushed her away so he could look down at her. "I was bored." Her face scrunched. Uh oh.

"I don't care if you're bored!" She stepped out of his hold. "For once, you need to understand the situation you're in!"

Trinon's eyes grew dark, making her flinch.

"I know better than anyone."

A finger flick against the back of his head made Trinon bend forward.

"Don't talk back to your mother." His father stood behind him with an authoritative stare. "She was quite worried about you. As was I."

Mara dropped the basket of vegetables she was carrying and hugged Trinon.

"Ehhh!" Trinon tried to dislodge her. "Careful." She released him. "You're such a brute."

"You can thank Jakar and Mota for that," she said.

Mention of Mota made them all go silent. Barbon came out of the sandbox.

"He has his own demons to fight, it seems."

"I've noticed he always gets this sadness around him when he's playing with the little ones." Mara picked up her basket. "I think he's lonely."

Their mother clenched her fists. "All of you have finally found mates. He never seemed interested in doing so."

"Was he supposed to go chasing candidates like this one?" Trinon pointed to Mara.

She gasped, offended at the accusation.

"How disgusting. I'm your sister." Trinon shrugged at her. Her demeanor softened. "I could see why he would feel left out. I mean, even Und has a potential one in the wings."

Trinon raised his brow at that. The sullen and abrasive Und? Mating? He shook his head to get a visual that popped up out of his head. His mother seemed to notice and came at him. He had no time to react and took the smack on his arm.

It stung.

A tingling sensation went through Und as he leaped and scurried along the edges of the village to evade his pursuer. He was not in the mood for their aggressive advances today. He had received word that Trinon had escaped the medical bay. His focus was on getting to him. On his way, the Lassian warrior who had taken a liking to him years ago crossed his path.

Liula. Tall, fair skinned, and pretty, she saw no other but him. The village teased them both at every chance. It wasn't that he didn't feel a mutual affection. They had indeed mated whenever they felt the need. He just wasn't willing to commit to a life partner. There were too many things in the air.

Everyone's main focus should be the looming enemy. Yet his other siblings sought comfort in the arms of unions, having offspring amidst their race's chaos. He found it irresponsible. Even Trinon had found a mate while on a mission decades ago. The only reason he was not a family beast now was her untimely demise along with their unborn children during a battle on her home world.

I'm sorry about that.

Und wasn't unsympathetic. He knew how much pain Trinon was in over it. He simply felt his brother should have known better than to indulge while fighting to secure a planet's stronghold.

Duty first.

"Found you." That lovely octave sang in his ear.

He flipped around mid-leap and landed on his feet to face her on the ground. She stood beautiful as ever in a full-length leather robe over leather leggings and a lace up tunic half undone. Only the top of her cleavage was visible. Her full lips pressed into a playful grin. The longsword at her hip swayed to slant behind her.

The gentle breeze tousled her blonde, wavy hair. His groin tightened. No. He talked himself down silently. This is not the time. You have to leave. Make her go away.

"I'm on my way to see Trinon."

"I know." She stepped towards him.

Und moved back. He saw her frown. "Then you know I can't be delayed."

"What if I wanted to go with you?" She smiled awkwardly, hesitant to say more.

"I don't want to give my family the impression that we are together."

A strange silence enveloped the area. Some of the villagers seemed to stop what they were doing. A few gasped followed. People covering their mouths with their hands. Her expression fell and her body seemed to deflate.

"Are we not?" She whispered.

I don't have time for this. He stood straight.

"Why would we be? I have more important things to attend to. We can meet later."

He turned around and walked away, leaving her standing in despair. The looks from the villagers in the area made his skin bristle. They were judging him. Making his way back around, he caught her still unmoving figure. The look on her face made him falter.

That's not what I wanted. The hurt permeated her entire being. I did that. He shook it off and continued to his destination. I can apologize when I see her again.

By the time he got to the medical bay, Trinon was sitting in a chair while an attendant did a physical. Und stopped a few feet from him. The two brothers made eye contact. Neither spoke. He flexed his fingers, clenching and unclenching them into fists.

"I…" Und struggled to find more words.

"I know." Trinon smiled softly. "I'm glad I made it in time. And that you survived."

"But barely did!" Und yelled, startling Trinon. "Why would you do that? The only thing you accomplished was me going after them to avenge you!" Und fought back tears. "I thought you were dead." His anger intensified. "I was willing to scorch that planet and die for your sake."

Trinon reared back in the chair. The attendant placed a hand on his back and pushed him upright again. He finally took in Und's appearance. Realization struck. Und looked away, embarrassed.

"I saved you so you could escape with the others." Trinon said in an almost whisper. "You're my litter brother. How could I not protect you?"

Und fell to the floor, his legs bent beneath him. All the energy drained out of him. His hands flopped to the sides and he sat in a daze. Of course. For all the awful things he had said and done to Trinon, his brother only had one thought. Our bond. Shame and guilt came down on Und like a boulder. It hit hard and heavy.

Darkness loomed over him, and he looked up to find Trinon leaning over him, blocking the hover lamps. He cupped Und's face in his hands and they stared at each other for a long while.

"No matter what, I will always cherish you." Trinon's voice was soothing.

"I know that," Und replied raspy. "That's why it hurts." He hung his head, forcing Trinon to let go. "That's why."

The attendant tilted her head, waiting for Trinon to return to the chair. Und pushed him away. Wiping his face with both hands, he waved to the attendant.

"You better let her finish. She's about to get out of sorts."

Trinon laughed, slapping him on the shoulder. His bad one. He winced, careful not to show it hurt, and got off the floor. Trinon sat down and let the attendant resume the physical.

Und left the room rubbing his shoulder. He knew Trinon saw him regardless, knowing he too was still in recovery from serious injuries. Walking back towards the village, deep in thought, he was oblivious to the looks of disappointment and rage that came his way until his mother stepped in his path.

Behind her, Jakar, Mota, and Mara stood with similar looks. He glanced around and it struck that the village had indeed judged him. He frowned in disdain.

"You realize you're in the wrong, don't you?" Mota asked.

"This has nothing to do with any of you." Und spat.

"How can you be so callous?" Mara's expression angered him more. She looked at him like he was trash. "All she ever did was want you."

His mother stared at him with contempt.

"I never thought you were capable of treating someone that way. Behaving like that with your siblings is one thing. This…" Her eyes became slits.

"You're all making a big deal out of nothing. I'll see her later after evening meal or early tomorrow and apologize."

Jakar gave him a look of pity. "Good luck with that."

****⁕****

For days, Und waited in anticipation, bracing for her to accost him on the road or in the fields. Nothing. The times he did get a glimpse of her, she turned an empty stare towards him and went the opposite way. Anxiety set in. Another week passed, and he became angry. This is stupid! He never said he didn't want to see her again. Not once. Why did she take it that way?

He sought her out, only to be deterred by people in the village. His anger turned to panic. He didn't want to lose her. Not like this. The weight of his actions, the words he said to her, replayed in his head, making it worse each time.

In desperation, he burst into his parents' chamber where he knew his mother was resting for the day.

"Have you gone mad?" She rose from the desk in the corner. "What is so urgent that you…" She stopped, seeing his face.

Und stumbled towards her and fell on his knees.

"I can't fix it!" He cried. "Tell me how to fix it!" He slammed his fists on the floor.

"We warned you." His mother walked over and placed a hand on his head. "You can't hurt someone like that and expect them to just forgive and move on." She used a finger to lift his chin higher. "Do you love her?"

"I don't know!" Und sniffed. "I just know I can't lose her. I don't want her out of my life. That's not what I wanted."

His mother brought his head to her stomach and held him there. He couldn't stop the flow of tears. What have I done? He clung to the sides of her robes, not wanting to face what needed to be done. His mother was going to scold him for a good hour.

****⁕****

Ganna mustered up all her courage while she stood at Jaron's chamber door. She had managed to keep Hon hidden for months as he absorbed every feed from the last century. Now he had pulled a Trinon and somehow escaped her secret lab. It was only a matter of time before Hon ran into one or more of his family members.

She tapped the door with her knuckles and waited for it to open. Then she realized Jaron wouldn't open it without an announcement.

"It's Ganna. I need to have a word. It's urgent."

She could hear movement in the room. The door opened and Jaron stood blocking the entrance. Modas was sitting in a chair by the window. Oh please let Lassa's light shine upon me. Ganna gave her a smile.

"May I enter?" She gestured towards the room. "Believe me, you don't want to have this conversation here."

"Fine. Come." Jaron moved out of the way, shutting the door after she passed her.

Ganna pulled one of the other chairs closer to the desk area where Jaron went and sat. Modas gave her an icy stare. It would only get worse.

"I lied to you." Ganna began.

"Is that supposed to be a surprise?" Jaron eyed her incredulous.

"I'm being sincere!" Ganna snapped. Jaron leaned back in awe, ready to fight. "When I said there were only three of your children's remains."

Modas bent forward, eyes darkening. Jaron rose from her seat, fury oozing from her.

"What did you say?" Jaron moved towards her. Modas stopped her by raising his arm in front of her. She halted and looked over at him in confusion. "Why are you stopping me?"

"Wait." Modas turned to Ganna. "Explain."

"There was one other. Their body was in worse condition than Jakar's."

Jaron faltered. She remembered when they came to see his body in the cryochamber. Ganna pursed her lips. Taking a deep breath, she continued. Knowing what the next question would be, she answered.

"The other is Hon."

Modas gripped the arm of his chair with his other hand while Jaron stumbled back into her seat. They stared at her with shock and pain.

"Is he regenerating?" Jaron asked rapidly. "How long will it take?"

"About that." Ganna's brow raised as she gave a nervous grin. "He has already recovered." Jaron and Modas' expression turned ugly. Not happy. "He insists on being up to speed with the last century. Needless to say, Halfar needs to watch his back."

"Halfar can take care of himself." Modas had no sympathy for the former ruler.

"Where is he?" Jaron leaned forward. "I never saw him in the medical bay or your lab."

"Well," Ganna straightened in her chair. "He sort of escaped. I assume he's roaming the surface." Jaron's eyes went wide in disbelief. "Your children don't know how to stay put."

Jaron ran out of the room. Modas stood.

"Get out." His command was powerful. Ganna lifted herself out of the chair and hurried to the open door. "You should have told us."

His long stride overtook her, and he was first out of the room. She slowed down, making sure the manbeast was a good ways ahead.

"Well, that stretched my nerves."

She walked out of the family building into the morning air. It was going to be a hectic day.

****✳****

The first person Hon encountered was Mara. He watched her playing with her children and mate, laughing with joy in the fields. The whole idea of her being mated had him dumbstruck. She had been an unabashed slut, spreading her legs for whoever she fancied. Now she was a mother? The older of the children caught sight of him and pointed.

"There's someone standing over there watching us."

Mara stood from sitting on the grass, her movement that of a fighter getting into a defensive stance. She turned towards him and stopped midway. Her eyes were like saucers.

He half expected them to bulge out of their sockets.

"Hon?" Her voice was soft, cautious. Then, "Hon!" She shrieked.

Hon felt the verbal onslaught and stepped back as she rushed towards him. *That degenerate is about to hug me!* Not wanting to make too much of a scene, he let her slam into him, wrapping her arms around his upper body, pinning his arms.

"Oh, Lassa's light!" She let him go for a bit to look at him then resumed squeezing him. "I can't believe it." Then her face went sour. "Ganna." She spat out the scientist's name like a disease.

He agreed with that reaction. At some point, he wanted to get his hands around that woman's neck. For now, he had to deal with his sister.

"Let go of me." He looked sideways at her. They made eye contact. He sneered at her, making his contempt for her known.

She gave a devilish smile, throwing him off kilter as she squeezed him tighter. He struggled in her grip, feeling how much weaker he was from his injuries. He had not trained in the past months, and she knew that.

"Oh, Hon." She seethed, whispering in his ear. "How I've missed you."

When she let go, he fell back on his ass onto the grass. Looking up he saw the disgust in her eyes as she stared down at him.

"Did you know we have a little sibling named Trinon? His fighting style reminds us of you. Only that. He's nothing like you."

"So I've heard." Hon got to his feet. "Can't wait to meet him." He glared at her.

Her son came up behind her and her face changed, lighting up with love.

"Who's this, mother?"

Mara pulled her son closer, hugging him at her side.

"Why, this is my brother, Hon. He just woke up like I did long ago."

"Oh."

The boy moved to greet Hon. Mara held fast to him.

"He's still a bit sore. I may have used too much pressure when I hugged him."

"Nice to meet you," the boy said, waving.

"Oh, we will get to know each other soon enough."

Hon walked backwards, not daring to take his eyes off her. Behind Mara, still on the ground, was her mate, Dellus. They locked eyes and his calm demeanor struck Hon. His expression told a different story. He didn't like Hon. Not even a little. Feeling he was far enough away, Hon turned around and headed into the village to find his family commons.

He spotted Jakar stepping out into the front yard. Beside him was a tall female with a darker skin tone and a litter of four. They took off towards the fields, racing past Hon. Him too? Jakar's mate was obviously not in her right mind to endure a permanent union with that monster.

As expected, Jakar turned his gaze on him, eyes narrowed. His mate leaned away from him in surprise. Hon smirked. This was probably the first time she had seen his true face. Like Mara, the two hid themselves well. He advanced and saw Jakar's body move in his signature defense stance that seemed normal but was deadly. Hon raised his hands in surrender.

"Brother, you should know I am in no condition to spar with anyone, especially you." Hon got within a few feet of him. Jakar stared down at him with distrust. "Think about it for a second."

"Who is this?" Jakar's mate asked. She also went on the defensive.

"I see Ganna clearly had more secrets up her sleeve." He turned to his mate. "This is my younger brother, Hon."

"Oh!" Her body relaxed. "The one Trinon reminds you of."

"In a way." Jakar turned his attention back to Hon. "Are you going to keep your ways or change for the better?"

"I only want to be reunited with my family," Hon replied sweetly. Jakar's mate flinched.

"I'm not playing with you anymore, Hon." Jakar's gaze burned into his chest.

Hon was about to say something nasty when he heard the familiar footsteps of his parents. He turned, ready to put on an air of nonchalant acceptance until he saw them.

The bright red streaks in his mother's hair signifying elder status shocked him. Even more so was his father who had not aged physically yet his being conveyed otherwise. He balled his fists in anger. Tears filled his eyes, blurring his vision. He couldn't move.

His mother came to him, wrapping her arms gently around. He leaned into her and sobbed. For all his big talk, one thing was certain. He missed them. His father came to his side and embraced them as one.

After nearly two hours of family time, Hon had enough. He bowed out, citing he wanted to explore more of the planet. In truth, he went straight for the outdoor sparring arena where the Lassian warriors practiced. There were about thirty of them in various modes, cleaning their weapons, honing their stances, and engaging in light maneuvers.

In the ring was Talas, spinning his sword before going into a crouched stance in front of another warrior who did the same.

Hon watched with disinterest at the mediocre skill of the other warrior. Then his attention turned to Talas and he became furious. He could see by the way Talas moved that he was only using a third of his skill.

Not one sincere strike delivered!

Incensed beyond fury, Hon stepped forward.

The moment the warrior got close to the edge of the ring, he yanked him out, tossing him behind into the field. The other warriors stopped what they were doing and stared at him in awe. One of them raised a brow at Talas as if this had happened before, then flinched.

Talas stood with his sword tilted down. His expression was priceless in Hon's opinion. Sheer miscomprehension. He didn't know how to react. Hon let out a laugh.

"Is this it?" He called out. "The great and mighty Talas now a pawn toying with his people. Where is your superior swordsmanship?" Hon jumped up into the ring. Without warning, he attacked.

On pure instinct, Talas countered.

"Come. Show me your true strength." Hon sped up his relentless attacks. Talas kept him at bay, frustrated he couldn't dodge. "Where is your heart?"

Hon didn't let up, pushing Talas to the brink. The other warriors stood in awe, spectators for an unprecedented event. No one had ever seen Talas move that fast.

"You're no more than a weak and pathetic elder teaching nothing!" Hon spouted.

Talas' demeanor suddenly shifted to an almost non-presence. As if on autopilot, he turned his sword blade up and matched Hon's speed, countering each blow. The two became a blur in the ring, gasps sounding from the crowd.

Then Talas seemed to come to his senses, faltering. Disappointed, Hon pushed further and found an opening.

He was about to deliver his blow when something came between them. It was so fast and menacing, it scared him. Hon jumped back to the other side of the ring. Standing in front of Talas was a manbeast he had not met yet. Talas was panting heavily, slumped over, his eyes red from strain. Sweat ran down from his hairline. He was angry, his attention solely on Hon.

"I need you to cease your attacks. We can't have our best warrior out of commission." The manbeast said.

Hon stared at the tall manbeast with a brown mane and tanned skin. Not fair in tone yet nowhere near the same complexion as Jakar or Modas. The facial features gave him away. He looked more like their mother.

"You must be Trinon." Hon's eyes narrowed. "I hear you remind others of me. How sad."

"Hmm?" Trinon cocked his head to one side. "How so?"

"I'll show you." Hon figured he could feign more strength than he had and bent down, talons out, ready to strike.

To his surprise, Trinon's face changed from playful to deadly. *He knows I'm bluffing. And he won't show mercy.* Talas grabbed hold of Trinon's robe and pulled himself upright.

"Please," a voice came from the fields behind Hon. "Stop." The hurt and fear in their tone made Hon freeze. "Please."

Hon straightened his stance and turned around. Mota stood, hands shaking at his sides, tears streaming down his face. All other thoughts abandoned; Hon moved towards him. They stood face to face, not speaking. Hon reached out and brushed his hand against Mota's cheek.

"I missed you." Hon cupped his hand to him. "So much."

Mota nodded, taking hold of his wrist and keeping his hand there.

"I know."

Trinon watched their interaction. A revelation dawned on him. He glanced over at Talas who had the same expression.

Off in the distance, they caught sight of Ganna looking horrified. She then turned away and headed back to her lab. Trinon glared at her.

"So rumors are indeed true in this case." Talas managed while out of breath. "What a deep secret to hold."

Trinon felt sadness emanating like a wave from Mota. He understood the reason for his brother's over reaction to seeing newborn litters. He had carried and lost them. And the only timeframe that aligned with it was the destruction of Lassa. More lives taken out of jealousy and rage. Halfar would never be able to atone for his sin.

Talas stood, not needing Trinon's assistance and gazed at the two.

"What a horrifying match."

Trinon turned to him. "How so?" Then he thought of the incident that just occurred and he let out a heavy breath. "Never mind. I get it."

"No, you don't." Talas stepped away from him and stretched his arms. "You didn't endure Hon from birth to adulthood. He's a menace."

"Well, my first impression isn't all that good."

"He's going to come after you." Talas said matter of fact. "Only problem is," he hit Trinon in the chest with the back of one hand. "You are far deadlier."

Trinon's body sagged with defeat. He didn't want more sibling rivalries. That Hon at half strength was able to push Talas irked him. He glanced again at Talas limbering up. Talas had a secret. He had an idea of what it was. From the other side of the sparring ring, he caught Kelin, Talas' mate's stare. His eyes narrowed, and his lips pulled back to expose teeth.

So, he knows as well.

***

Chardon received word of Hon's return at the same time as a request from Farin. In male form for the day, he sat at his desk in one of the council chambers pouring over documents on the main feed. The holoscreen flickering before him, displayed reports from every department.

He rested his elbows on the desktop and hung his head, clasping his hands together so his forehead set on them.

The amount of drama was getting ridiculous. Most of it stemming from Ganna. He was glad she would be leaving again soon to meet up with the other scientists. To think she had Hon in a cryochamber the whole time she was away, and no one was the wiser. Chardon let out a deep sigh and let his head fall back against the top of the chair.

A ping from the feed made him raise his head. Across the screen was a new message. It came from a communicator on the planet surface. He read the words with disdain.

Hon is causing chaos. Will update soon. Chardon peered at the sender's name. A Lassian warrior who was part of Talas' advanced group. Seeing the time of day, that meant Hon was at the training arena. What for? It made no sense. Then he remembered.

Hon was a nasty piece of work. He was always 'playing' with others, causing more harm and injury than necessary. He was a highly skilled fighter, close to surpassing Jakar and Modas. Until Trinon. Hon would have a hard time trying to win over his younger sibling.

Not wanting to deal with that, Chardon turned his attention to Farin's request. Her child needed a detail she could trust for a while. The fourth royal house was acting up again. Chardon frowned.

Did they not learn their lesson from before?

Then it hit him. This was perfect timing. He would send Trinon. A limited vacation of sorts to speed up his recovery. And he would gladly protect Farin as he had always done in her formative years. The other part would be to get him as far away from Hon as possible. No need to test those waters.

The door swung open from Jaron who entered looking exhausted and rightly so. Chardon could only imagine the range of emotions running through her. From rage to sadness, joy, and murder.

The last being towards Ganna.

"Have you decided on the rest of your day?" Chardon asked, laughing.

"You jest," Jaron pointed at him accusingly. "I'll have you know I still have intentions upon that woman."

"And I have said this more times than needed." Chardon sat up straight and met her stare. "We cannot kill her."

Jaron rolled her eyes in protest. Chardon continued.

"By the way, Hon has been terrorizing the people." He heard the sucking of air through teeth as Jaron looked to the ceiling in defeat. "I don't have to tell you how this will turn out if he doesn't rein that in."

"He hasn't changed."

"Why would he?" Chardon stared at her, confused.

"I don't know." Jaron exhaled. "I somehow thought he would come back with the knowledge he attained and do better."

Chardon gave her a dubious smile. "Who's jesting?"

Jaron's lips went thin.

"I'll handle it later. What do we have?"

She sat in the chair opposite Chardon and scrutinized the holoscreen. They had more important work to do.

FOUR: WAR on ALL SIDES

A Debt Owed

Glowing red eyes scattered across the Razznian night sky. Behind them were one hundred bulbous, insect like ships hovering in formation above various air docks. On the surface below, the sea churned, foaming as it reached the shoreline. The tide was low, allowing uninterrupted frolicking.

There would be none of that tonight. Sars and his unit stood along the beach wearing brown cloaks over their battle suits. His reptilian eyes peered across the water as if expecting the horizon to reveal some new secret. A soft wind fluttered his cloak. He was tired and angry.

Planet Razzna was still in recovery. The contaminated water had been treated, and so far the remedy worked. The sea no longer appeared to be a black sludge. Lord Kraznan was grateful to Azrom for getting supplies from the outer rim. The Dreridians on the other hand. Those greedy bureaucrats! Two years after production went back into full swing, they demanded shipment for back orders.

Sars gathered his cloak around him and folded his arms. He breathed deep, his nostrils flaring, then receding when he exhaled. *And now there is a race worse than Azrom and us combined.*

Razznians were of equal might compared to Azrom. Both their species had been at war numerous times. Was it really a war? When it came to the common goal, there was no debate. They joined forces into an alliance with New Lassa. That part the Dreridians didn't care for.

The swishing of sand made Sars look behind him. A sentry from the palace came slithering towards him. The thick tail created grooves behind him. His dark red robes with black embroidery added to it, cascaded down over the top of the tail, skimming the sand.

"Commander Sars. Lord Kraznan requests your presence immediately. Please bring your troop."

"When does he want us to arrive?" Sars asked.

"Now, Commander Sars. I am here to escort you."

So it has begun.

They had been tracking the enemy after the attack on the Tolitha system. Hearing the report from Kur's mission, Lord Kraznan had gone silent for months. He held no meetings or entertained guests. The idea of it shocked even Sars. To push back an Azrom battalion, no matter how small, was a feat not seen in centuries. Nearly a millennium.

Sars nodded to his band of handpicked soldiers, most from his nest. He followed the palace sentry with them in tow. The trek spanned two miles from the beach. His group leisurely strolled up the hillside and over. The disturbed sand broke the silence with a soft sifting noise.

Looming high above all else was the palace rebuilt to previous specifications. The crystal structure gleamed in the dark like a beacon. Sar's unit reached the forty foot double doors guarding by four other sentries. The two closest to them walked over and pushed the panels embedded in the stone on each side.

The doors opened with a loud rumble, slowly revealing the main corridor. Their race had been mocked many times regarding the scale of things within the palace. As a reptilian race, their need for so much space baffled others. Sars agreed. It is nice though.

It took another twenty minutes to reach the lift that would take them directly to the throne room. They rode up, his soldiers having polite chatter. Sars didn't engage. He glanced over at the escort who met his gaze. Razzna would fight soon.

The lift stopped at their destination, and they exited into the throne room. Royal servants were already moving about, intense scowls on their scaly faces. Lord Kraznan sat solemnly on his throne. He hadn't registered the flurry of activity below him.

"Lord Kraznan. I present to you Commander Sars and his unit as requested." The sentry made a small bow and left the room.

Their emperor came to attention, sitting a little straighter. He looked down at Sars.

"Ah, my favorite soldier." The emperor spread his arms as wide as he could.

Sars kept his composure after hearing that. He noticed a few of the military leaders in the room frown at him.

"I am humbled you feel that way, my lord." Sars bowed his head, then raised it.

"You know why I have called you, yes?"

"I have an inkling." Sars grinned. "Reconnaissance."

"Yes, yes." The emperor drummed his talons on the armrests. "And proceed as needed. We must not let this enemy get access to our system. Nor our allies, for that matter."

"We owe a great debt to Azrom. Lord Romnus especially." Sars clenched his fists. "How many ships can I authorize?"

The emperor turned to the nearest military leader.

"What say you?"

The military leader's forked tongue flicked out while he huffed. It went back in and he finally answered. "It depends on the goal. I won't have a bunch of ships out, leaving a gap in our own planet's security."

"To prevent their advance, it may be in our best interest to form a blockade," Sars replied. "That gives the alliance time to create a trap to snare the enemy."

Lord Kraznan was intrigued. The military leader narrowed his eyes at Sars.

"Wonderful plan." The emperor leaned back, relaxed. "Twenty ships should do."

The military leader balked. Sars frowned. It was a start. Not quite enough, but it would send a powerful statement.

"That is generous of you, my lord. Thank you."

"Now." The emperor's stare went cold. "Go find a way to get rid of them."

"As you command, my lord." Saras and his unit bowed. I will do just that! His soldiers raised their heads along with him and turned back to the open lift.

****⁕****

Hisses and rattles filled Sars' senses as he and his unit entered the nursery. The hot house was at peak humidity, which suited the newborns hatching. Rows of circular nests made of brown moss and twigs atop a layer of soil ran the length of the room on both sides. Halfway down on the right were five clustered together in a hexagon. Attendants slithered about checking on the nests, moving out of his way when he reached it.

These were his and his men's offspring. Already hatched, ready to leave their nests in another year. They all seemed to be getting along. A fight would break out every now and again, but nothing serious. Sars undid the collar of his uniform to let in sticky air. Compared to the heat inside his suit, it felt almost cooling.

"How big do you think they'll be by the time we get back?" His second in command, Beldur, asked.

His men spread out to surround the cluster and peered down at the young reptiles. Since he and his men were from the same nest, their offspring didn't vary in species. The newborns all had scaly snake skin, not the thick hide like bigger predators.

"Hmm. They should be in the rearing houses by then." Sars replied as he caressed the top of the nearest one's head, feeling the smooth scales. "I want to recommend their training regimen in the next few years."

His third in command, Clexis, nodded in agreement. He used one hand to turn one of his over onto its belly. It flopped lazily to its side first, squiggling into position.

"Maybe not combat for mine." Sars looked over at him in surprise. "I feel we don't have enough scholars. It used to be we had great representation across the system. Now we barely have the numbers to leave Razzna for negotiations."

The rest of Sars' men fell deep in thought. Sars had not thought of that. His third in command was more a strategist, helping him with decisions on each mission. He was part of why they had such tremendous success with the drug trade while stranded on Earth.

Razzna indeed used to send trained representatives to other planets to negotiate trade and swap resources. The countless battles with Azrom somehow took precedence, and that tradition was lost.

"If they all have your wit, then I think that would be ideal." Sars stepped away from the nests. "Let's depart. We have a lot to check off beforehand."

Karne, the fourth in his unit, looked down at the baby reptiles. "Get big and strong."

They all walked off to leave.

Dolin, his navigator, and fifth lingered a bit for one more glance. The weapons specialist, Gren gave him a curious stare.

Sars led them on the long trek out of the hothouse and across the sands to their armored dune buggy. Dolin got in the pilot seat and hit the ignition. They all strapped in, and he sped towards their ship waiting at the docks. With a sharp lurch, the vehicle stopped at the dock entrance.

"That was a rough ride," Clexis snapped, rubbing his neck.

"One day you will learn to drive properly," Beldur chided.

"Sorry." Dolin's tone didn't convey it.

Sars didn't comment on the driving. That was the only time Dolin seemed reckless. He reverted to a young one learning to operate the vehicle and feel its power beneath. As the pilot for their ship, he was one of the best with his meticulous checks while watching the gauges. He and Karne were a well-oiled machine. Their combat skills were a bonus.

The massive shipyard loomed up to sky. Its height reached close to one hundred feet to accommodate the front of each ship docked in the circular ports. The rest stuck out free floating for ease when backing out. Like everything on Razzna, it was excessive in size. On another planet, it would be a small city. It was the opposite of their reptilian nature to huddle in small spaces and stay warm.

This was one of twenty scattered across the planet. Each ship was the size of a small skyscraper turned on its side. That was why only a third sat on the surface and the rest hovered above. Maintenance techs scurried around the hangar, making sure each ship was ready for travel. Sars was taking all of them from this hub.

They reached their ship and walked up the steep ramp, bending forward to lessen the stress on their legs. Inside, the rest of the crew gave small nods to them as they passed. The bridge was already busy. Two second in commands assigned to both the pilot and Dolin were doing the checks. Sars eyed his men who looked dubious of the newcomers' routine.

"Go make sure it is up to your standards," Sars suggested.

The two nodded and headed towards their helpers. Beldur walked over to communications while Gren and Karne left all together. Sars knew Gren headed for the weapons bay. There were a few new additions to the usual crew he used for bigger missions. It only made sense, having lost many in the battle with Azrom and New Lassa.

A giant mess.

It took the last fight to make all three races realize they were only hurting themselves and proving the Dreridians right. So much loss of life over misunderstandings and pride. Lord Romnus saw the remedy and acted, much to the distaste of the Dreridians. That didn't stop the trade commissioner from slapping sanctions on them out of spite.

A young reptile in a bodysuit uniform stepped up to stand by his side.

"Commander Sars. I am Lieutenant Prac, here to assist you in the battle plans."

Sars sized him up. Fresh out of the academy, he must have had high scores to land a position on his ship. The red beady eyes were full of ambition. His thick tail swished behind him. He resembled a salamander which let Sars know he could be cunning with the right training.

"Glad to have you on board. Have you studied the enemy and our plans for engagement?"

"I have." Prac clasped his hands behind his back. "Ugly creatures. I think Azrom was correct in their execution. Their mistake was not having a second ship to back them during the attack."

"They were trying to be sneaky." Sars said.

"That's not a trait they possess." The young soldier snorted. "We, on the other hand, are."

"Yes, but this time we have no need for that. They will know we are there to stop their tirade."

"About that." Prac turned to face him. "I think we should be sneaky to start." Sars' men still on the bridge looked up and over at them. "Please hear me out."

"Continue." Sars insisted. He tapped his earpiece and connected with Clexis so he too could hear what the soldier had in mind.

"We've seen footage, read all the reports, but have yet to engage the enemy. I propose we study them for ourselves. Keep our distance until we have assessed a strategy that benefits us."

Sars could hear soft sputtering in his ear. He was certain his lieutenant had thought the same and was not too happy with the newcomer. As if knowing that, the newcomer added, "I am sure your strategist feels the same. I look forward to their guidance as well."

Definitely ambitious.

Sars gave his men a curious glance. They had devious looks on their faces, liking the young soldier already.

In the hours of predawn, twenty Razznian ships rose through the atmosphere and into the darkness of space. An open vortex sat waiting for them to travel. Its gaping mouth appeared swirled at slow speed to the naked eye yet in reality, dizzying.

In tight four-point formations shaped like a diamond in the center, each cluster went single file through the vortex. It winked shut as the last ship's rear passed its threshold.

Exiting the vortex, the ships landed in the next system from the repair planet. They split and moved to hide behind the moons. On Sars' ship, the bridge listened to communication being picked up from a planet on the outskirts ahead. The enemy was about to attack another unprepared race.

Not being able to risk exposure, Sars made the hard choice to not assist. Instead, sent a reconnaissance to observe. He and his unit would be among the same as their mission on Earth when Azrom tried to conquer that planet. They didn't get too close and never engaged either side, grabbing the spoils of the carnage on occasion for a quick meal.

He had his core team board one of the smaller ships and they jumped to the planet's location. On arrival, they all hissed at the scene. Hidden on the other side of the planet, they could see the enemy ships formed in an arc, bombarding it with weapons fire while a scourge of fighter ships descended on the surface. Balls of fire erupted from the blasts.

The assault would decimate the planet if it continued.

"Prepare the suits," Sars ordered the weapons bay.

He had made sure twelve were loaded from the main ship.

"All of them?" Gren asked through the commlink.

Sars thought for a moment. "No. Eight should suffice."

"As you command."

Prac came up to him.

"Am I to stay behind in your steed?"

"Absolutely not," Karne cried out as he entered the bridge. "You are going to get your scales wet with a real mission."

Sars stifled a laugh. That was the plan of course. He couldn't have said it better. This will be the true test of your ambition. Whether the young soldier could hold his own and follow directions to prevent exposure would determine his role going forward. He watched the soldier try to hide the excitement on his face.

"Are the two record keepers ready?" Sars asked Karne.

"Yes. They are heading to the drop hangar to suit up."

"Let's begin." Sars motioned with his hand for the others to follow. His unit left their stations, and the backups took the helm. "Time to meet the enemy up close."

In the inner chamber before the drop hangar, Sars' unit of eight sat on the benches checking their jump suits and weapons. They did a commlink check to make sure they could all hear each other. The suits were custom made for their race at the behest of Sestis who commissioned the Dreridians for them. The first time they had used them was to infiltrate Azrom.

Sars slapped the shoulders of his suit to test its integrity. It had been a while since he used it. The harsh environment of space could break down the material fast if they weren't careful. Prac was admiring all the bells and whistles of the suit as he fitted it to him.

"Sealing antechamber. Please stand clear." The ship AI said.

All eight stood and lined up in a row across the edge of the room. They shut their helmets and waited for the outer shield to drop. The room became a vacuum, and the wall before them opened to a platform. They stepped onto it and went to the first section of clamps on the floor. The wall sealed behind, enclosing them in semidarkness.

Sars kicked his feet into a set of clamps, and the rest did the same. He tapped his inner commlink.

"Ready for launch."

"Opening drop hangar. Prepare for sequence."

The floor tilted forward at a seventy-five degree angle and the hangar doors opened to reveal the nearest planet amongst the dark. He watched the countdown on the small display inside his helmet and braced for the launch. One by one they were shot out towards the planet at bone break-ing speed. The suits protected them even as they punched through the stratosphere and began the burn.

They split into four teams of two as they got closer to the surface. Blasts sent debris hundreds of feet into the air forcing them to dodge to stay on course.

Sars and Beldur went to the center of the chaos where he was sure most of the enemy forces had converged. Confirmation almost hit them literally in the face as a piece of metal the size of a house came careening past them.

Up ahead, they witnessed the red tendrils doing their damage on a group of fighters farther away. They seemed to be defending the structure behind them. Sars immediately knew it was a massive power grid that probably supplied most of the planet. It spanned nearly five miles in diameter with multiple spikes that reached to the heavens. Its sides were ridged like coils spiraling inward.

Destroying it would cripple not only the entire planet but possibly the system, alerting the Dreridians. He didn't want that right now.

Sars clenched his fists as he hissed. His forked tongue slipped out in anger. His second turned to him. It was inevitable now. Sars tapped his commlink.

"Change of plans. We are meddling." An awkward silence fell over them. "That does not mean we expose ourselves. Is that understood?"

"Affirmed." The answer came in succession.

"Two teams. Prac and one recorder to me."

Within minutes, the two soldiers came zooming onto the scene, slowing their suits until they landed on their feet close to Sars and his second.

Sars drew his weapon from the side holster. He didn't like the phasers, opting to dig his claws in his prey, but on a different planet he had not studied and the nature of the mission, he had no choice. He nodded to the others to draw theirs.

Using the propulsion system of the suits, they got behind the enemy and began taking them out, one by one. A shot at the back of the neck that exited through the throat. Because of their speed, they remained a blur. The enemy attempted to track them, homing the red tendril weapon for a solid hit.

That did the trick. Seeing the disruption, the planet's fighters didn't hesitate to take advantage of the situation. A second wave of their battalion emerged with battle ships in tow and laid waste to the area where the enemy was.

They formed a blockade around the power grid's perimeter. Any enemies left on the ground retreated, seeing no way to counter. They retrieved any undamaged red tendril weapons and fell back.

"Now that's interesting," Prac said.

Sars and his team had moved to hide near a cave set in the mountains. The other team was finishing up their task of sabotaging the enemy ships in the vicinity. The fewer rides back to their main ships, the better.

"Yes, the reports said they were very meticulous about not leaving their signature weapon behind." Beldur scanned the area. "And from the footage, we had assumed they were wearing full body armor. That is not the case."

"Their skin resembles that. The fact that we were able to take them down by hitting their exposed necks is a win." Prac added.

The second team arrived at their location. Karne crouched down by Sars.

"Neck, midriff, thighs, all open for attack. They are arrogant, to say the least." He brushed some debris from his legs. "And those ships."

"State-of-the art." The recorder slid over behind the group to his counterpart. "More advanced than I've seen in a while."

"It would make the Dreridians drool," the other one said.

"So," Sars squinted, making his eyes mere slits. "They really are not from the five systems."

"I hate to state the obvious," Prac interrupted. "But from what I have seen so far." He paused, making eye contact with Sars. "We may have met our match. As much as we hate to admit it, Azrom has more might. And they were bested."

Sars seethed inside, knowing it was true. Razzna was a great military power, but second to Azrom. Even the Dreridians didn't dare go after them. And they were a super power all their own. He rested his arms on his knees as he crouched down, staring at the battle dying out in the horizon. The enemy was getting…bored?

"I guess if it's not a quick and easy win, they lose their taste for it," Beldur said, observing the same. "Kind of cowardly, in my opinion."

"Very interesting." Prac casts his gaze on Clexis.

Even through their helmets, Sars saw the two were plotting something.

****

The brief battle over, the group jetted back to their entry point and waited for the enemy ships to move before Sars could signal the reconnaissance ship to bring them back aboard. Instead of using the suits to fly up, they would be transported. Another system acquired less than a century ago to cut the time for meetings between what would soon be a true alliance between Azrom, New Lassa, and Razzna.

The two recorders took more footage while they waited. One of them turned to Sars.

"I think we may have been spotted." She pointed to a group of fighters standing on a mound. One of them held a pair of vision goggles over the top half of their face. "We better hurry."

"Yes, they may decide to communicate with us," Beldur said.

"Or take us out," Clexis admonished. "For all they know, we are another race looking to reap the spoils."

"They do seem to not have put down their weapons," the first recorder said.

Just as the group of fighters started to move, the one with goggles pushing them atop their head, the group felt the familiar fizzle in the body and on their skin as a beam of light shot down upon them, dissolving them from sight.

They appeared on the transport platform waiting for the scan to find any repairs needed for their body or DNA to be complete, followed by treatment. The technician behind the console had his head down, watching the multiple screens flooding with data.

"All clear. You may step down."

The antechamber shield dissolved allowing them to make their way back to the drop hangar and remove the suits. Sars took a deep breath through his nostrils as he lifted the helmet off. He set it down and switched off all the connections, cutting the remaining power.

Prac had a grin on his face, still experiencing the high of his first spy mission despite how short-lived it was.

Placing the suits in a bin for inspection, they headed to the main hold where they strapped in for the return to the main ship. Sars tapped his wrist band.

"Get us out of here," he ordered Dolin. "And make sure we're not seen."

The giant screen above showed the mapping system. They would need to open a vortex further out now that the enemy ships were moving into formation and headed towards them. The navigator found a spot and the pilot took the ship around the planet's moon, circumventing the enemy ships, to the other side where the main ship had opened a pathway per their received coordinates.

The small ship arrived at an open dock, and they disembarked, heading back to their stations. The recorders parted ways in the main corridor to dump their data. Clexis and Gren headed to the weapons room while Karne and Beldur followed Sars to the bridge.

Prac, back in his uniform, stepped into the area, beaming with pride. He turned to him. Sars had an urge to cackle.

"Will you be needing me for the rest of the rotation?"

"No. I believe Clexis would like a session with you."

"Of course. If you please." The soldier bowed his head then pivoted on his heels to leave.

Sars stepped onto the dais in the center of the bridge. He would send a report to the home world later. Right now, he had to calm his nerves. He could tell by the looks on his unit's faces, they too were feeling frustrated and angry. The scan data uploaded to the suits when completed showed they had all suffered injuries they didn't know they had.

The science group working on the enemy weapon needed to know. There was something else going on. It may have to do with a discharge of sorts. That didn't bode well for the alliance.

Moving to the edge of the nearest solar system, the Razznian forces formed a blockade across the planets. Once the enemy arrived, they would open a channel and try to deter them from going any further. To turn back whence they came.

The translator program ran nonstop, sending the same message until it received a hit.

After nearly a month, they received an answer.

Enemy ships appeared out of the dark with weapons firing full blast, hitting the unexpected Razznian ships in the center of the blockade. They dispersed to span both sides of the formation while still firing.

"Shields!" Sars yelled into the all-commlink.

On the main screen, he saw the blasts get absorbed into the cocoons surrounding the outer ships. His own rocked after being hit by a stray assault that crippled the ship before him that was on the front line.

"Do not let them break the line!"

That was easier said than done. He watched in horror as one of the enemy ships moved forward. Front and center on its face sat a giant cannon that resembled the red tendril's weapon. Sars' reptilian eyes opened as far as they could, and he turned his head to Dolin. The soldier glanced over his shoulder at him and nodded.

The cannon fired a web of thin red lines and swiveled to blanket the entire blockade, hitting the first line of Razznian ships. The tendrils ate their way through the shields right as the blockade winked out of existence.

On the communication screen were two words.

We refuse.

The enemy blast continued, hitting a nearby moon that was directly behind the now gone Razznian forces. Its red threads disrupted the atmosphere, making its way to the surface where a mining operation was in progress. The warning alarm came too late. The areas not under protection of the shields met a gruesome demise.

Surprise Attack

Lord Pondur sat in his study, sipping on liquor from the delicate chalice he held between his thumb and index finger. He watched the sunset turn the sky shades of orange and pink, casting a shadow over the industrial district sprawled below. His windows spanned the entire length of the study, giving him a full view.

He straightened his heavily brocaded jacket and got more comfortable in the ornate high-back chair he had set in front of his desk for that very reason.

He loved to watch his empire at work. It never stopped. Trade had no schedule. Profit was to be made every nano-second. His craggy face scrunched in admiration as he took another sip, his eyes squinted over the rim of the chalice. Loud bustling outside his chamber door made him flinch. His solace ruined, he turned to the door sliding open.

His accountant and the head of commerce were arguing as they came into the room. Lord Pondur saw them not even acknowledge him.

"Gentlemen," Lord Pondur lowered his chalice. "And I am using the term loosely at the moment." He set his drink on the small table beside him. "There better be an acceptable explanation for disturbing me so late in the day."

The two creatures stopped mid-sentence and stared at him in terror. They bowed their heads low, their bodies at a ninety-degree angle.

"My apologies, Lord Pondur!" They yelled.

"What is the urgency?"

The head of commerce raised his head and cautiously looked up. When the accountant did the same, he straightened his posture.

"One of Yaos' mining moons has been attacked."

"Caught in an unfortunate incident," the accountant corrected, in a haughty tone.

"An attack is an attack, regardless of its outcome!"

Lord Pondur raised a hand to stop them. They briefly stared at each other, then returned their attention to him.

"Explain." Lord Pondur addressed the head of commerce. They were trying his patience.

"The Razznians had formed a blockade to prevent that enemy scourge from advancing further into our system. The goal was to negotiate and have them return to their system without any more bloodshed."

Lord Pondur tensed. He already knew the outcome before it was said.

"The enemy answered by opening fire on the Razznians before they could open talks."

"That is correct, my lord." The head of commerce replied with a grimace. "They fired a larger version of that damnable weapon on the Razznian fleet. They were able to jump, but not before suffering damage. The blast kept going, hitting the moon."

The accountant raised the tablet clutched in his hand.

"The estimated loss of life and property destroyed puts the operation at twenty percent capacity. Two thirds of the workers, dead, and forty percent of the equipment, useless. Some completely gone. The blast literally ate them."

Rage burned in Lord Pondur's eyes. The two advisors stepped back from him.

He had made a mistake. Thinking the enemy was merely a nuisance to be taken care by New Lassa. That they were nothing of importance to bother with since the mighty Azrom would step in and assist. He turned to the head of commerce.

"Is there word from Azrom?"

"I have not checked my lord." He turned to the accountant.

"There is nothing disrupting their trade." He typed on his screen with a short, stubby talon. "I do see a report from the newsfeed in the defense logs. He frowned before clearing his throat. "It seems, there was an attempt from Azrom as well and it went badly."

"Badly how?" Lord Pondur braced his hands on the armrests of his chair as he leaned forward.

"General Kur and his battalion sustained life-threatening injuries. They barely retreated alive."

"When was this?" Lord Pondur shouted in shock.

"From this report," the head of commerce moved back one more step. "Over a year's time ago." He winced.

"Azrom was sent fleeing for their lives, and the Razznians ran with their tails between their hides!" He suddenly remembered hearing about a group of scientists having a clandestine meeting without his own being invited. "We are being kept out of the loop."

"To be fair, my lord," the accountant stepped forward. "You did wash your hands of the matter and advised New Lassa to handle it."

Lord Pondur's shoulders slumped as he settled back in his chair, resting his arms on the sides.

"I did indeed." He let out a loud sigh and reached for his chalice. "That was a miscalculation on my part." He took a sip, letting the liquor course through him. "I want full reports from both of you by end of day."

"Yes, my lord!" They made hasty bows and left the room.

Lord Pondur set his glass down and stood, walking around his desk to the commlink. He tapped the call icon.

"Lord Greggor. A word if you please."

"Of course, my lord. I am on my way," Lord Greggor replied through the audio.

Lord Pondur sat back down in his chair and resume drinking while he waited for his head of science to arrive. Within a half hour, the robust creature brought his wide girth through the doors and bowed his head before approaching.

"I am sure you heard the news. There was too much noise about it in the halls."

"Yes. Quite dastardly of them."

"The science meeting you caught wind of."

"Yes?" Lord Greggor tilted his head in curiosity.

"I want you to find where it is and assess the reason for our non-invitation."

"Oh, I have already found that out."

"Is that so?" Lord Pondur made a flourish hand gesture for him to continue.

"It seems during an Azrom mission they retrieved one of the enemy weapons. The one with those nasty tendrils, for reverse engineering. From the reports, the mission ended deadlier than they anticipated."

"Yes, General Kur barely lived through it." Lord Pondur gave him a stare, waiting.

"I have a spy who is serving as an escort for them on the planet where it is being held."

"Hmm. But I want you to be there. We need to know everything about this new threat. I will not be deceived again."

"I will be on my way by end of the week."

"Good. I don't have to tell you." Lord Pondur sipped.

"A full report and my findings on a solution will be in your hands en route to my return."

Lord Greggor exited the room, leaving Lord Pondur to stew in his fury. He didn't like being wrong about anything. Especially threats that affected trade.

Lord Greggor went to his office and began preparing for his trip. With the reports from his spy, it was clear the other scientists had no clue how to break it all down. There was a reason Dreridians dominated the sectors regarding trade and technology. They had researched far past the five systems. That was how the universal translator came into being. And he had already deciphered the language of the enemy. They were a nasty race of creatures and the new weapons they had were not Dreridian. That made Lord Greggor nervous.

****

Heavy traffic on Planet Hallios sky highway greeted Lord Graggor. Vehicles spanned bumper to bumper on both sides of the spaceport leading out to the city. Lord Greggor sat patiently in the back passenger seat of the transport taxi. The autopilot kept the vehicle in a hover state, inching forward with the line.

He opened a small box from his satchel and scanned the variety of snacks he had packed. Picking one of the little meat rolls, he shoved it in his mouth, chewing slowly to savor the flavor of slow braised tissue from an exotic species marinated in a spice rub of his own creation.

Beyond the traffic on the horizon was the tall spire of the science building. A prominent pillar in the five systems, it was a meeting place for many scientists to conduct experiments and brainstorm projects. He had been to many seminars there.

The vehicle finally moved freely again, and he was on his way to crash the party thrown by New Lassa, Razzna, and Azrom.

His spy had informed him they were at a stalemate. Lord Greggor grinned, a small laugh escaping his cragged lips. Of course they are. He had no doubt they were trying to dismantle the weapon without getting what composed the red tendrils on their persons.

His transport docked on the pad that separated the top sections of the spire from the rest of the building. The hatch opened to allow him to step onto the platform. The ride was prepaid, so the vehicle didn't linger, taking off immediately.

One of the science bureau representatives came through the sliding doors to greet him. A tall, slender male with four tentacles for each arm. He wore a lab coat over a flowing cream-colored robe that moved like liquid as he floated. His bald oval shaped head gleamed under the hover lamps.

"Lord Greggor. It is good to see you." His tentacles wiggled individually. "I was surprised you were not in the meetings with the others."

"Yes, I had important business with Lord Pondur."

"Of course, of course." The being appeared to float while turning around. "Please, let me show you to the multilab."

"Have you been able to see their progress?" Lord Greggor tried to pry out what little information he could. "It would be helpful to know what I've missed.

"Oh. Let's see." One tentacle rose to scratch his temple. "From what I could decipher, and mind you I am not one to snoop, they are having a hard time extracting the 'damnable fluid'."

They strolled down a wide hallway of gleaming white. From floor to ceiling, everything was pristine, with little to no debris. A small cleaning robot scurried around behind anyone who walked. At the end of the hallway, they made a right turn and came to two large double doors.

"Considering the work and the space needed for collaboration, I put them in one of our more spacious labs."

The being used a tentacle to pull a key card from the breast pocket of its lab coat and scanned it on the side panel. As the doors slid open, Lord Greggor could hear the arguments flood out.

The Razznian scientist happened to glance at the open door and paused. Then his beady, reptilian eyes narrowed.

"It sounds like you are all having a disagreement."

Lord Greggor walked over to the large white oval table they were standing around. He turned to the bureau representative. "Thank you for guiding me here."

"My pleasure. I hope you find the solution to your problems." The guide tilted his head then left. The doors slid shut.

Lord Greggor faced the group.

Ganna had a nasty look on her face. Lt. Treshur seemed put off by his presence and the Razznian was staring at him like a meal. Until Lord Greggor gave him one back. They all knew the rumors regarding his unnatural girth for a Dreridian. The Razznian relented, moving away from him.

Lord Greggor eyed the weapon sitting on the project table a few feet away, each piece digitally labeled. The cartridge, four inches long and a little over one inch wide lay in the center. A small thing yet so deadly. The red liquid sloshed around inside it even as it sat motionless. Like it had a life of its own.

"So, that is the thing that has us all terrified." Lord Greggor walked over to get a closer look.

"It is not something to handle lightly. Nothing we have tried to use can withstand the corrosion." Ganna's sharp tone grated on his ears.

"Everything gets eaten." Lt. Treshur came to his side. "I am quite fascinated by it, to be honest."

"Your general has a different opinion about that," the Razznian said.

"That was a tragic event," Lord Greggor interjected. "Now. Shall we proceed?"

"Were you not listening?" Ganna asked in exasperation. "We can't extract it."

"Let alone study its properties," Lt. Treshur added.

"Tsk!" Lord Greggor took a piece of the weapon and went over to the equipment section. Turning it around in his hands, he placed it in the diffuser and switched the machine on. The other scientists followed him, curious about what he intended.

The piece was resistant at first, warbling like a snake, then melted into the dish below, a thick ooze that was now malleable. Lord Greggor brought over the replicator and chose an extraction tool, along with a new sample dish.

He connected the two machines, and the dark ooze transferred into the replicator.

Behind him, Ganna seethed. The Razznian looked dumbstruck. Lt. Treshur folded his arms, placing one hand on the side of his face.

"Well, aren't we silly for not thinking of that?"

Within minutes, the replicator created a syringe crafted from the weapons's material, with a matching sample dish.

"Now we can really get started." Lord Greggor turned to them. "You should have had me in the loop from the start. We would have been much farther along."

"Hmph!" Ganna was beyond irritated by his display.

Lord Greggor snickered at her mild tantrum. She had bested him many times. It was his turn this round.

"We still have no idea where the enemy comes from. That alone would give us a clue." The Razznian went over to the cartridge. "There's no way they are not in the Dreridian database."

"We haven't mapped the entire universe," Lord Greggor scoffed. He took the syringe and dish to the table. "That said, we do know something." He saw them waiting for him to continue. "Hah," he sighed. "Their language was in the translator. An obscure one we captured some time ago."

"That means we can communicate with them." Lt. Treshur smirked. "As if that did us any good."

"They will have to play our game soon enough." Lord Greggor leaned over the cartridge and watched the liquid move. "We will not tolerate disruption in trade.

∗∗∗∗∗

Alarms sounded in the checkpoint stations along the ley line of the Dreridian system's major planets. The one closest to the home world moved into position at an angle, scanning the area. The operator frantically tapped the icons on his console to find out why.

A blip finally appeared. And it was too late. A vortex opened right between the satellite check station next to him and his own. From his line of sight, he saw a horde of ships send a barrage of firepower towards the home planet.

He had already hit the warning signal to the military liaison, certain the others had done the same. With that many alarms, the weapons systems would go online.

A wide beam from the home planet shot out into the vortex, taking the first few ships coming out of it down. As those dropped off, another round of ships took their place, firing at will. Like an opened floodgate, the enemy ships spread across in an arc, hitting the satellite check stations.

The operators bailed out in time, transporting to the planet using the emergency system. The planet and the enemy exchanged constant blasts, explosions erupting on the surface.

A larger enemy ship came into view, its cannon zeroed in on the center of the planet. Red light formed from thread like tendrils that rained down below. There was a plume of angry rust colored mist followed by a bright explosion.

There was a split-second lull where neither side fired.

A huge arc of light curved like a wave up from the planet, moving towards the enemy ships. Sensing their demise, the enemy's front line seemed to halt. Smaller ships spewed out and made their way behind the ones already retreating into the still open vortex. The ones not yet out, reversed course.

The enemy ships left behind, along with the abandoned satellites, were obliterated right as the vortex snapped shut.

Lord Pondur sat in the highchair of his study, his chalice halfway to his lips, with eyes wide in disbelief as he watched the blasts from the sky hit the refineries outside his viewport. He saw the planetary defense system engage, the giant cannons rising from underground and swiveling to lock on their targets.

Fires were ablaze across the planet.

The red veins of light hit the shielded manufacturing dome. The tendrils ate through a few sections while seventy percent of the shield held. Lord Pondur knew there would be casualties where they had hit. The shields recovered and blocked the rest of the tendrils. They didn't dissipate until they fell along the edges with nothing organic to attach to.

The arc weapons' system initiated, and he witnessed it flare out into space.

Behind him, his communications screen went haywire, flooding with reports.

And then the light show ended.

Chaos and destruction lay in its wake. Snapping out of his stunned demeanor, he realized he had cut his breath short. Exhaling loudly, he set his chalice down on the side table and slid off his chair.

He went to his desk and tapped an icon on the side. On the wall across from him, a map of the planet displayed. Tiny dots began to populate, showing the damaged areas. A few hot spots, but nothing dire that couldn't be repaired in the next few months.

That was not the issue.

Lord Pondur's eyes turned dark. The crags around his sockets seemed to fuse, forming smooth scales. How dare they? It was obviously a test that, if successful, meant they would have continued their attack. An attempt to destroy the Dreridians.

The commlink on his desk blinked. He tapped it.

"The enemy has fled the system," his Defense General announced. "The first wave of their ships was destroyed. We are tracking the vortex signal."

"No need."

"My apologies, my lord?" The General sounded perplexed.

"They will no doubt try again. They now know what weapons we have."

"Yes, but my lord. That was only two of our nearly hundreds of defense systems."

Lord Pondur managed a thin-lipped smile despite the tightness of his face.

"Exactly."

There was a long pause. "Should I contact the other departments?"

"Yes. And make sure there is a detailed damage report."

He would have to see the costs for everything and adjust trade accordingly. His fury knew no bounds.

This was an act of war.

****

Lord Greggor heard his personal commlink sitting on the main table chirp. The other scientists stared at it. Then Lt Treshur's went off. Ganna stood straight, apprehension on her face. The Razznian stared at his and within moments, it too went off. They all glanced at each other. It was ominous indeed. He left the huddle looking over the specimen data displayed on the lab table to see the message.

He picked it up and read the message twice. His expression turning from anticipation to anger.

Lt. Treshur relented and went to his, having a similar reaction. The Razznian held back, dreading what the message from his home world would be.

"Well spit it out!" Ganna exclaimed. She walked over to them. "What has happened?"

Lord Greggor gave her an irritated stare, mixed with his rage. She leaned her head back, mouth down-turned.

How he hated her.

"It seems the enemy is quite bold. They have attacked the Dreridian home world."

Ganna's face fell in awe. The Razznian hissed loudly, his forked tongue slipping out and vibrating. Lt. Treshur set his commlink down.

"Surely a test. They have realized all four of our races are connected. They need to know how much fire power it would take to bring us to our knees."

"Well, that's idiotic on their part," Ganna snapped. "We all know there would be no winning against Dreridian weapons."

For once, Lord Greggor agreed with her sentiment. He watched the Razznian go to his commlink and the look of surprise on his scaly features let the others know his news was something different. He turned to them, setting it back down.

"Our attempt at a blockade failed. Obviously, since the enemy came for the Dreridians. There is also a new bit of information."

"What is it?" Lord Greggor felt his senses tingle.

"The tendrils have another feature. It appears even the residual mist causes damage to the body. When the units on the mission returned via transport, repairs had to be made before they could be released from the platform."

Ganna frowned. Lord Greggor felt the same. This was not ideal. They had yet to crack the smaller molecules of the red liquid. It had not dispersed in their presence. He assumed they were safe from its effects at the moment.

"We have dabbled too long." Lord Greggor walked back to the table. "Time to dig deeper." He removed his lab coat, then took off his suit vest. Donning the coat back on, he turned to his associates. "They'll be in for a surprise next time."

"Yesss." the Razznian replied. "Let's create weapons more deadly to counter."

The four of them returned to the specimen.

Lord Greggor would contact his trusted assistants later after their next findings. He was sure the others were going to do the same. They needed their entire teams there to speed up the process. The thought of Lord Pondur watching the home world being bombarded with enemy fire made him briefly hesitate at his task. *My Lord must be beyond livid.*

****

Something bugged Emar. He couldn't put his finger on it. Most of his data was solid. He was sure of it. The other percentage made him wary. *What am I not seeing?* He sat at his station, running through the data feed on his right screen. He swiveled back and forth; hands clasped together at his chest. The room was silent, with the other workers already gone for lunch. He had one last thing to do then he too would be off to eat.

The left screen let out a ping, and he turned to see a reply from the request he had sent to the Dreridians. Coordinates to a meeting with Azrom so his people could plead their case to Queen Farin. It would all fall into place after that. Or so he hoped. That nagging feeling wouldn't go away. *And now for the second part.*

He found the previous message with the information on New Lassa. Only coordinates for a gate entrance were given. The leader had crafted a dire spiel to orate for when he met the Lassians. Like the representatives from the Tolitha system, they would land on New Lassa and request assistance. Except they weren't going to need it. It was simply a ploy to get a layout of the planet.

A plan on two fronts. Bring Azrom to its knees and New Lassa gets payback. The Dreridians would have no choice but to renegotiate their terms. Emar felt a tickle of apprehension. *Or so we hope.*

****

Adan saw the communications feed light up and he stared at the report in horror. Emar sat at the station with his brow furrowed. This was not part of the plan. Poking the Dreridians was like a lone being picking a fight with a galactic monster. The equivalent of a straw tossed into a vortex, not making even a blip.

"What do we do now?" Ryben asked.

"Huh?" Adan turned to him. "We stick with the plan. If they want to die off early, that's their problem. As long as they keep their end of the bargain, we get what we want."

"True." Emar laced his fingers as he swiveled in his seat. "I think we can take advantage."

"Absolutely. While everyone is preoccupied with the shock, no one would predict someone going after Azrom and New Lassa." Adan smiled.

"Yes, but they also poked the Razznians," Ryben added.

"Hmmm. That is a problem." Adan sat back against the edge of the station with arms folded. "That could get messy."

"Last I checked, Razzna and Azrom were enemies. From my research, it seems Sestis was also trying to get the Razznians under her thumb too." Emar smirked. "She really is a cruel female."

"Okay, first we hit the child Queen and see how that goes." Adan pushed himself off the edge. "She is coming to the meeting with her entourage and no large unit of soldiers. We'll be fine."

Adan's group dispersed to get ready for their voyage to the neutral meeting zone. Emar could not shake his unease. Everything was going according to plan on their end. He didn't like the mess the enemy was making with the other races.

It muddied the waters.

Bad Planning

The opening gate at the top of the royal palace brought a gust of hot air across the ankles of the greeting party comprised of Romnus, his entourage, and Farin with her own. From the black vortex, Trinon stepped out along with Chardon, Halfar, and Chafar.

They had only gotten a few feet out of the vortex when Farin rushed forward embracing Trinon. He winced, not letting her see his reaction as he held her to him. He met Romnus' face and the Supreme Ruler nodded.

"Farin, don't!" Chardon cried out.

"It's fine." Trinon raised a hand. "I'm fine."

Farin suddenly pushed away from him, her face full of sadness. She gasped, realizing her mistake.

"I'm sorry." Her eyes downcast, she moved closer, hesitant to hug him again.

"Don't be. I'm practically healed to almost full strength. It would take more than a tight hug to bring me down."

Farin didn't believe him. She looked over at her parents and brother.

"Brother," she addressed Chafar.

"Sister," Chafar deadpanned as usual.

She attacked him, wrapping her arms around him.

He struggled to get out of her grip.

"Let go." He tried to shove her away. "Get off me."

When they disengaged, Chardon burst out laughing. Chafar was not amused. He didn't like being affectionate, especially towards his sister.

He found her too boisterous.

Romnus came to stand by Farin. "Thank you for letting us borrow Trinon for a while." He tilted his head towards her small entourage. "I felt she needed to have her own escorts for when I am not with her."

Trinon glanced over Romnus' head to the group. His eyes narrowed as he spotted Ponnae in full royal guard uniform, weapon at her side, standing at attention with the others. Farin saw the look on his face.

"I know," she whispered to him.

"We have a feast waiting for us in the banquet hall."

Romnus turned to join his entourage.

They all followed him down to the lower level, taking the outside stairs. A unit of royal guards took up the rear. Their capes fluttered in the Azrom breeze. The sun was high in the midday sky. It being close to Autumn; it generated little warmth.

The banquet hall was empty when they arrived. Halfar raised his brow curiously. Romnus went to the lone table set in the center and gestured for his guests to sit.

"I figured it would be best to limit the invitation. We can talk more freely that way."

The royal guards left the room to stand guard outside. Only Romnus and Farin's personal entourage were allowed to stay. They sat at the end of the table closest to the entrance as a security measure. Chardon and Halfar sat together with Chafar next to his mother. That put him directly across from Farin who grinned at him. Trinon sat to her left with Romnus on her right. Batis and Biandra sat across from each other, not making eye contact. Ponnae looked at both in confusion.

"So, tell us." Halfar settled in his seat and leaned back as he reached over, grabbing a carafe to fill his glass. "Is it the fourth house again?"

"They won't take the hint," Batis answered as he, too, poured himself a drink. "You'd think they would have given up by now."

Fourth cousins removed through multiple matings, the fourth house was ambitious in nature yet cowards in reality. Not once had any of them competed in the succession battles. They felt gaining control of the planet could be acquired differently.

"It's tiresome." Halfar said.

"Still, Farin's life is in danger yet again," Romnus replied.

"I am not helpless!" Farin gripped her cup, sloshing the liquid she had just poured. "I can defend myself if need be."

"You are still recovering from birthing our twin sons," Romnus retorted. "I don't need you overexerting yourself when others can protect you."

Farin appeared dissatisfied with his answer. Trinon eyed Romnus with skepticism. There was more to it than that. What are you really afraid of? He dropped his hands into his lap when he saw them shaking from a spasm that hit his lower back. Damnit!

Farin gently ran her hand down his back and pressed where it began. He looked over at her. She kept her eye on Romnus, still gripping her cup. She finally raised it to her lips and took a big gulp. Her face scrunched from the hard liquor.

"Gah!" She shook her head, eyes wide. "Oh!"

Halfar snorted. "It will take a few more decades for you to handle this." He turned to Romnus. "Did you do this on purpose?" He tossed back the remains of his drink.

"I had forgotten." Romnus grabbed a different carafe. "How about something sweet?"

Farin nodded, still reeling from the effects of the liquor. Romnus poured her a new cup with sweet wine. Trinon stared down at his cup and tilted it a few times. He took a sip and swished it around a bit before swallowing.

"Not bad." He took a bigger sip.

Chardon and Halfar seemed impressed. Trinon hid a laugh. They had no idea how much he needed the hard drink. It coursed through him, easing the pain in his back, helping to unfurl the knot Farin was trying to release with her fingers.

He barely heard the conversation, having two more cups of the stuff. Farin had long removed her hand, gesturing with both as she talked. He only needed to know two things: who was the enemy, and Farin's schedule.

After the meal, Trinon fell in with Ponnae and the other two guards that made up Farin's entourage. Despite his slightly blurred vision altered from the alcohol, he was fully alert.

Glancing at Ponnae, he grimaced at the icy demeanor. Almost as if she had shut herself off in order to keep the concentration etched on her face.

I don't like it all.

When they reached Farin and Romnus' chamber, Farin turned around and gave Trinon a gentler hug.

"I am so glad to see you."

"I'll always be by your side, Farin. Even when I'm not." Trinon squeezed her then the two let go. "Get some sleep. We will escort you to the late afternoon meeting."

Farin bowed to them and headed into the room. Trinon went to the empty chamber next door where he had stayed before. Ponnae took the one on the other side, while the other two went farther down the promenade to a different one.

Exhausted and feeling his body relax more from the alcohol, he flopped face down on the bed. He struggled with the sleeves of his coat to get his arms out. When he was finally free, he tossed it on the foot of the bed. He used his feet to push his boots off, hearing them drop onto the carpeted floor.

Sleep took him in an instant.

****

Trinon woke in a panic, pushing himself off the bed then stood beside it in terror. His vision cleared and he scanned his surroundings. He regulated his breathing and leaned forward, resting his forearms on the bed. He punched the cushions with his fists.

He had dreamt he was back on the battlefield. Shoving Und out of the path of the red tendrils that shot forth from their blind side. Feeling those tiny vines eat through his skin as it went past his clothes. His body had seized and he couldn't move, dropping to the ground in agony, unable to scream.

He sensed a presence and looked over at the entrance. Ponnae was standing in the entryway alone. Her expression told him she understood. And he knew she did. Wiping his face with one hand, he turned around and found his boots. She waited patiently for him to get himself together.

The sound of the other two guards coming down the stone corridor made him hasten. They were almost at Farin's chamber. Trinon walked to his entrance and looked down on Ponnae, towering over her by a good foot in height. She didn't return his stare, simply pivoted like a royal guard and went to meet the others. Trinon followed.

Farin was already up, moving about in her chamber. She caught sight of her entourage and smiled.

"First up," she announced proudly. "The nursery!"

Of course. Trinon grinned. He would get to meet Farin's little ones. Watching the way she moved, he could tell she was in no way up to par with her former self. He knew better than anyone what she was capable of. Romnus was correct in his assessment.

"I'm sure your parents and Chafar are already there." He allowed Farin out of the chamber. "You may not get to pry them away to get a turn."

The two male guards positioned themselves in front, with Ponnae and Farin in the center. Trinon was directly behind them. He would usually stay a suitable distance, observing from afar. Not this time. He needed to make sure he could cover the area in the shortest time.

"Well, they are going to have to share." Farin clapped her hands. "They're my babies and we have to get to the meeting on time."

"Mm Hmm." Trinon laughed. He addressed Ponnae. "You really need to loosen up. This is not the kind of entourage where we try to be serious."

Ponnae seemed to falter, her steps off beat. Farin nudged her in the side with an elbow, making her step sideways.

"Right. If I wanted that, I would have joined the royal councils group. They are stiff rods of non-joy."

"Pfft!" The soldier on the left in front of Farin sputtered. The other glanced over at him. He was trying not to smile.

"I…" Ponnae regained her stride. "I just…"

"We know," Trinon said.

They walked through the main hallway of the nursery and found a group of spectators crowded in front of the viewing window. Inside, Chardon and Halfar each held a twin, cooing at them. Among the group was a trio in royal attire, looking on with grim, disgusted expressions.

Trion recognized them from before, when he had to deal with the internal strife of the palace decades ago. Fourth royal house members. The one closest to Trinon glanced over to see who was near and did a double take, looking up after finding himself staring at nothing but a black coat. His eyes widened. The other two seemed to feel his distress and turned to see what the issue was. They stared at Trinon in shock.

Oh, yes. I have returned. Trinon gave them his signature smile. They flinched from him.

Farin went into the room to negotiate with her parents to let her hold one of her own children. A few spectators laughed at the interaction. Chafar was with them, not cracking a grin. Instead, he too was alert, keeping watch on the fourth royal house members.

A chime went off.

Trinon turned his head to the sound. One guard at the end of the hall held a small device in his hands. The spectators made an about face and walked towards the exit of the hallway. They chatted and laughed, discussing the royal twins. The fourth royal house members glanced back, eyeing the viewing window.

Trinon leaned over towards Ponnae. "Do they really think they could get near those infants with us at Farin's side?"

"They can only hope?" Ponnae replied. "Something, or someone, must be emboldening them."

Trinon thought about that. Before, it had been the previous royal council who spearheaded the cause. They had all been executed. The new council seemed to have learned a valuable lesson from that. Yet there was this feeling of foreboding. He hated when he noticed it. Because he turned out to be always right.

****

A unit of twenty royal soldiers in full gear stood ready to board the convoy ship. It had minimal weapons in case of an encounter. Romnus waited at the bottom of the ramp for Farin and her entourage to arrive. He had misgivings about letting her go to the meeting alone.

She had no business negotiating with a planet Sestis had slighted. Even Chardon had volunteered to go in her steed, but she would not have it. As Queen of an empire, Farin felt duty bound.

The small entourage that protected his mate arrived with her in the center. She looked, and he was almost glad, not quite regal. It was to make the outworlder's feel at ease and not intimidated. Trinon had a strange look on his face. Was it worry or amusement? He couldn't tell.

Farin came right up to Romnus and kissed him hard.

"Make sure you miss me while I'm gone."

Something about the way she said it didn't sit well with him. "Of course I will."

She tilted her head, giving him a sly smile. "Hmm."

"I don't want you to linger. They were wronged, that is a fact. But do not promise them anything. All you need to do is hear them out and report to your mother. Chardon is their Regent."

Farin looked away, eyes rolled up an angle toward the ceiling. Trinon flicked the side of her head.

"Ow!"

"Listen to him." Trinon counted the soldiers opposite him. "I guess that's enough."

"It's a meeting, not a battle mission," Farin retorted.

"That's what the first meeting with the representatives was." Trinon walked halfway up the ramp. There was dead silence. Farin's demeanor changed. Damn it. "Hurry. We have to go now if we want to arrive on time."

The soldiers marched up the ramp with Farin accompanied by her entourage. Romnus met Trinon at the halfway point and grabbed his arm. Trinon stared down at him.

"If it turns out like that." Romnus didn't finish. He stared deep in Trinon's eyes.

"I will get us the hell out of there with no second to spare."

The look in Trinon's eyes told Romnus all he needed to know. It was something he had never seen come from the manbeast. Hatred. Deep-rooted and deadly. Farin would be brought back safely. Romnus let him go, then walked back down to his own entourage.

Batis leaned forward and whispered in his ear.

"That manbeast is not the same anymore. You may want to tread carefully."

"And why is that?" Romnus glanced back at him.

"Because he's always been fiercely protective of Farin."

Romnus remembered when he married Farin that Halfar warned if he ever harmed her or made her sad he would come for him. That would be true regarding Trinon as well. Before, he was sure he could take the manbeast in a fight. Now. He wasn't that confident. Batis was right. Trinon was not the same.

*****

A small greeting group from the host planet, Folza, awaited the convoy ship as it docked in the space hub above the capital city. Not an industrial powerhouse by any stretch, the planet was profitable. The sprawling structures appeared only decades old, despite having been constructed centuries ago.

The city was not bustling with traffic: vehicles or foot variety. Everything seemed to move at a leisurely pace. Farin and her people walked down the ramp of their ship. The greeting party made a slow procession towards them. No one was in a hurry.

The lead representative was intimidating. Her slender frame was straight, her exposed arms lean muscle. She was easily taller than Trinon. The sleeveless flowing robe was an iridescent pearl, pleated with a golden chain around the waist that dangled to one side. Her associates, two shorter females in similar blue attire, remained silent behind her.

"Greetings to you, Queen Farin of Azrom." The leader's voice had a musical tone.

The two entourages met at the halfway point. Farin stared up at the female in awe, like a child seeing magic for the first time. Trinon poked her in the back, making sure their host did not see. Farin closed her mouth and became serious.

"Thank you for hosting this meeting. There aren't many neutral planets that would let others come to settle their disputes."

"We like to have a smooth trade system. Discontent leads to loss of revenue."

She sounds like a Dreridian. Farin gave a nervous smile. Not so neutral, huh?

"Has the Barrima party not arrived?" Farin scanned the foreign ships in the hangar. "I would like to get our negotiations underway."

"Of course. They have indeed arrived." The leader's expression became hooded. "We have escorted them to the meeting room. Please," she turned sideways and gestured towards the exit with a long, beautiful sweep of her arm. "This way."

Farin glanced back at Trinon while they followed the two shorter hosts. He too had the same look on his face as the leader confirmed the Barrima party's arrival.

What was wrong with them? Did the race they were about to negotiate with not pass the smell test? Was something rotten already?

The host planet's leisurely pace was deceptive. Whenever a dispute could not be resolved, they decided for them. Which ended in tears or a mutual contract agreement. Or it ended in bloodshed, the host not tolerating any attacks during negotiations and taking down all parties.

The last part the host planet never announced ahead of time. Farin was only aware of it because of an incident where two other races previously under Azrom rule met their fate that way. Afterwards, the two made peace and resumed their partnership.

Which meant the Barrimans had no idea what would happen if they were not there in good faith.

Walking through the shimmering walls of the space hub mesmerized Farin. She felt trapped in a wonderland. Species from other planets roamed around, flowing between the docks and the center where entertainment was located. Multiple bars, eateries, and shows were available for visitors, including a virtual tour of the planet. The stay accommodations were considered a tier above exquisite.

The group surpassed the center, going around it to another set of corridors. They took the one on the right and headed to nearly the end before stopping at a pair of closed sliding doors.

Made of the clearest glass material, the doors allowed anyone walking past to see everything going on in the room. The host believed in truth and transparency.

"We are here." The shorter host on the left waved a hand against a sensor on the side of the door frame. It slid open. "Your party awaits."

Farin led her entourage into the room and came in view of the Barrima representatives. She counted ten, all male, wearing dreary brownish grey jumpsuit uniforms. Dirty boots and goggles gave the air of a race in dire straits. Farin noticed instantly it was more than just for show. They were obviously a race with minimal resources flaunting it for, what, sympathy? That left a sour taste in her mouth. *Now I see.*

The host leader stood at the end of the large table while the other party rose as Farin approached. They didn't bow, only nodded in acknowledgement.

"Good to finally meet you, Queen Farin," the man in the middle of their line spoke. "I am Veris, second commander of Barrima's military. Our leader, Master Adan, could not be here due to more immediate dangers that recently arose."

"Oh! And what would that be?" Farin cocked her head to one side.

"We encountered a procession of hostile beings in our system. We can obviously defend ourselves. But an air of caution was necessary."

"Huh." Farin's lips curled inward, her cheeks puffing out.

"Sit." The host leader raised her arms, extending them to each side.

Both parties sat across from each other. Farin was in the center, facing the second commander. Trinon and Ponnae flanked her with the other two in her group as bookends. Her battle unit had split in two. The first positioned near the corridor entrance while the other guarded the ship. She was certain the Barrima group had a larger force elsewhere.

A small ding sounded, and the doors frosted for privacy, though not by much. Farin rested her hands on the table. The whole thing didn't sit well with her. Their leader was too busy to meet the Queen of Azrom with the fate of their planet at stake? She glanced over at the host leader, who kept a constant eye on the Barrimans.

Veris stared at the Queen of Azrom and immediately felt a sense of foreboding. He had seen Sestis before and had records of her mate, who had identical features. He also knew more about the mighty Azrom under Halfar's reign. This female was nothing like Sestis.

In fact, she resembled Halfar more than anyone.

Those murky green eyes set in a fair, almost pale, face with dark hair. He flexed his hands to prevent making fists.

What is happening? He decided to clarify his fears.

"Queen Farin, how fares your mother? We have not seen Regent Sestis since she came to assess our planet."

Her entire entourage's expression changed. The female soldier let out a gasp. The tall being with the animal mane leaned back in surprise. Queen Farin's eyes darkened, a fury rolling in the gleam of them.

"That woman," she seethed.

Her hands balled into fists. Then her demeanor changed. She sat straighter in her seat.

"Lady Sestis met her end when a planet bomb destroyed our home world over a century ago. I am the child of Lord Chardon of New Lassa and Lord Halfar of Azrom."

Veris felt his entire insides tighten. He remembered the communications kid saying something about his data being a mix of old and new, the feed sporadic. This was a big deal. They had created a plan based on a false deduction. He tried to glance slyly at his men, not wanting to draw attention to the act.

"Your Regent is Lord Chardon." Queen Farin continued when there was no response. "I am only here to find out what your planet requires, so I can relay it to my mother."

"Of course." He nodded, not sure what to say anymore. His head was full of scenarios on how to back out of the situation.

"What is your planet's trade? What is your race known for?" Queen Farin asked.

"Uh, well." He regained his posture. "We do repairs on mostly armada ships. The bigger they are, the more we get to show our expertise. But we seem to be too good at it. Our revenue drops with ships not needing repair for generations. We thought we would branch out into the other systems when our debt was handed over to Lady Sestis."

"Securing more clients and projects." Queen Farin propped her elbows on the table and laced her fingers. "That would have been the best route. She didn't set up any trade meetings?"

"She came to declare herself our ruler, told us we were worthless to her while making that promise, then left us to rot." He could hear the malice in his own voice.

"I am sorry to say that your planet was not the only one she deceived for her own greed."

"We had heard as much. Since Azrom seemed to assist the Lassians, we figured you would be the one to talk to."

Trinon, visibly twitched. Queen Farin's eyes narrowed. Their reaction perplexed Veris. What had he said that made them go on guard suddenly?

The host leader placed her hands flat on the table. Her shimmery eyes went pure silver as her gaze fell on him.

What did I say? He yelled in his head, recapping it in his mind and not finding the issue.

"This procession of hostiles," Queen Farin raised her wrist and tapped it. A hologram of the enemy displayed in midair. "Did they happen to look like this?"

Commander Veris's eyes bulged. What triggered her ire hit him. His race wouldn't be on standby if the enemy was nearby. They had attacked every other planet on a whim. The only reason they had not done the same to theirs was because they had sought them out and made a deal.

I messed up!

He was about to respond when the room rocked. Hairline fractures ran across the floor and the walls shifted off kilter. They all turned to the floor to ceiling windows and saw a vortex opened in the sky above, causing havoc in the space hub while a slew of laser blasts pummeled the surface, destroying parts of the dock.

The host leader stood slowly, pivoting to the doors. She did not turn around as she addressed the Barrimans.

"Once we have dealt with this disruption, we shall deal with you."

Trinon took hold of Farin and brought her to her feet. The rest of her entourage stood, surrounding her.

"What was the plan, then?" Trinon asked, keeping his tone even. Inside, he seethed.

"You must understand." Commander Veris stood with his arms up in defense. "We did not have all the information."

"Which is more reason why you should not have implemented whatever this is." He tilted his head towards the chaos outside. The room shook again. "What are you..."

He didn't have time to finish. The windows blew out. A ship hovered in their wake, firing rounds into the room. Before Trinon could get a tighter grip on Farin, a tether shot out and wrapped around her, yanking her into the arms of a soldier dressed in the same uniform as the others. The ship sped down towards the docks.

Containing his rage, Trinon looked over at Commander Veris. The horror on his face let him know he had lost control of the reins. Jumping out of the room into the smoky air, he made a beeline following the ship.

He landed on different platforms along the way to launch himself faster. He spotted the group at the main hub entrance, taking advantage of the attack. They were forcing their way in, Farin struggling to get out of her captive's grip. He could see her yelling at the man full throttle. He appeared taken aback by her strength and words, not expecting so much resistance.

Trinon almost laughed at his plight. The soldier was about to hit her in the head with the butt of his weapon right as Farin extended her talons when the landing they stood on broke apart from an enemy blast. Trinon was there in a flash as he saw Farin's eyes and mouth open wide in fear, thinking she was meeting her demise. He snatched her, then leapt to the other side of the hub.

From his position, he saw Commander Veris arrive on the scene with the rest of his group to rescue his men. They used the confiscated ship still intact below and got to the same area as Trinon. Ponnae and the other two blocked them from getting any closer.

"What the hell happened?" The captor yelled. "I thought this was supposed to be easy!"

Commander Veris grabbed the man by the front of his uniform. "You were to wait for my signal," he replied, gritting his teeth.

"They attacked. I thought that was the cue."

"We need to call it off!" Veris released him, pushing him away. "We were wrong."

"What?" The captor and his men looked around. The situation became clear. "This wasn't the plan?"

"She is not Lady Sestis' child."

The other soldiers in the group stared at their second command in disbelief.

"Then whose child is she?" The captor asked heatedly.

"Lord Halfar. Of Azrom." Commander Veris locked eyes with him. "You see?"

The captor and the others went slack jawed. His gaze shifted to Farin. He finally got a good look at her. Trinon saw the way he backed up in horror.

"If you're done chastising each other," Trinon said angrily. "We need to get to safety."

All of them made their way on foot to the docks, not chancing getting shot down in a transport vehicle.

They reached a wall with a large hole blown out, its edges crumbling from the disproportionate weight. On the other side was the dock that held the two ships. And their additional forces engaged with the enemy.

The Azrom unit was being pushed back despite the help from the Barrimans. Trinon froze for a second. His mind not willing to let his body move into the fray so quickly. He had to find a way to defeat the enemy and get Farin safely back home.

Move! He screamed at himself. I am not afraid! I'm not. So. Please!

Out of the corner of his eye, he saw Farin move with lightning speed. No! That did it. He was a split second behind her. They took out the first four enemy fighters in the front line, which allowed the battle unit to get some distance. An enemy from behind came at Trinon.

He didn't think, just struck out with his talons. A diagonal line appeared from the right side of the enemy fighter's face down to his left ribcage. The skin splayed open, revealing a cluster of bulbous cells. The fighter fell backwards, dead before he hit the surface.

Trinon felt his hands shake. He stared at them as if they were not his own. His vision blurred, and he shook his head to clear the haze. A loud ding, like a chime, rang out. It echoed through the air from a planetary PA system.

"Commencing cleanse of disruptors." The female AI voice announced sweetly.

There was a pause in the fight as even the enemy looked around, confused. Trinon felt the hairs on his body tingle. His head snapped up. He pivoted towards Farin, tackling her, then yelled, "Get down!" to the others in the room.

The enemy wasn't fast enough, which he counted on. A bright, shimmering light shot through the hole in the dock wall and hit the enemy forces. Some managed to retreat, scrambling to their ship. The vortex in the sky warbled as the same light from a different angle hit it, bringing the enemy ship bombarding the planet to the ground, its power source dead as the vortex shut.

Trinon felt the slight brush of air tearing at the back of his coat. He didn't dare look to see what was going on behind him. After what seemed like minutes, the same chime erupted.

"Cleansing complete. Please stand by for repair and rescue."

He eased up onto his knees and turned his head to the docks. Bile threatened to rise from his esophagus, and he clamped a hand over his mouth. A few of the others weren't so lucky.

Farin sat up, eyes wide with shock and went, "Ewww!"

Lying on the dock floor was a mess of disintegrated flesh and tissue still squirming with life for a few moments before going still. Some pieces identified as the enemy. The host leader came towards them, her entire body shimmering, almost blending into her robes. The shorter hosts remained unchanged.

"And now," she stared down at Commander Veris and his crew. "We deal with you."

Trinon could not decipher the level of terror in their eyes. He just knew they were not coming out of the situation unscathed.

FIVE: ALLIANCE

Terms of Engagement

Commander Veris pleaded with Farin, stating his race only wanted to be prosperous again. That their botched kidnapping was a misstep. The host representative cut his pleas short by ordering her guards to seize his party. Not wanting to stay a moment longer to witness what punishment the host planet would deliver to the Barrima people, Farin's entourage gave their apologies and waited on their ship to be cleared for departure.

They sat in silence in the main cabin. Trinon kept himself together, not letting on how devastated he felt inside. He turned his head so no one could see it etched on his face and caught a glimpse of Ponnae. She, too, was not doing okay. They locked eyes. A mutual feeling passed between them.

"We are cleared for departure," the pilot announced over the commlink. "Docking clamps removed. Please strap into your seats."

There was no need to repeat it. They all hurriedly did as instructed. It was time to leave.

The ship rose from the platform and eased its way out of the hub. The dusk sky now cleared of enemy ships. The ones not crippled had fled, towing their damaged ships with them. Another thing to report on.

Trinon wondered what the enemy's real reason for not leaving behind any of their technology or bodies. He found it excessive.

Farin slumped in her seat, already falling asleep. He didn't blame her. She was in no condition to fight, and this exhausted her. That feeling of uselessness niggled at him again and he fought back the urge to respond, keeping his hands loose, jaw unclenched.

The wounded soldiers seated behind them would rest in shifts on the journey back to Azrom. They had triaged themselves, not wanting to burden the hosts any further. Azrom pride strikes again.

Trinon closed his mouth and exhaled slowly through his nose. He couldn't really say anything about it since Manbeasts were just as bad.

The viewports darkened, the overhead lights dimmed, throwing the cabin into semidarkness as the ship entered an opened vortex. It shot through the gaping hole in space and Trinon was out like a light, his body giving up the battle to stay awake.

✳✳•✳✳

Romnus and his entourage awaited on the palace rooftop for the ship's arrival. Trinon could see the worried look on the ruler's face as it passed, heading for the shipyard. They turned and walked down the side stairs where a transport vehicle sat at the bottom. He knew they would get to the hangar within minutes of them disembarking.

Farin was nervous the moment she woke up in Azrom space. She wrung her hands together, furrowing her brow in deep thought. Trinon half snorted. No matter what she said to Romnus, he would not be pleased. A vibe of disappointment emoted from the entire group.

Should we have seen this coming? Was there something I missed? Trinon knew Farin was thinking the same. To be ambushed like that stung.

With the ship secured, the ramp opened. They all released their harnesses and walked down to be greeted by Romnus who was already heading towards them. He took one look at them and his face contorted in anger.

Farin flinched. Trinon held her steady with a hand on her back. Seeing her reaction, Romnus changed his demeanor to a more accepting one.

"Farin, my beloved." Romnus reached for her, pulling her into his embrace. "It is good to see you back safely."

Trinon saw him eye the wounded, then his glare landed on Trinon. There was no blame in his expression, merely frustration at the outcome.

"I feel the same." Farin clung to him, burying her face in his massive chest.

"Not to be harsh," Rass said from the rear of the group. "But you rested enough on the way. We need a report before you retire to your chambers." He motioned at the soldiers. "With me," he ordered.

The small battle unit assembled in their marching formation and followed Rass out of the hangar. Romnus dropped his arms. Farin hung on. He gently pried her away from him.

"General Rass is correct. What happened?"

"It was a trap." Trinon said matter of fact. Romnus reared back his head. "And I disagree. We need proper rest. Because right now, I can't really think straight, let alone give a report."

"That's fair." Romnus circled an arm around Farin's waist. I will take her with me for now."

He turned, surrounded by his entourage as they left Trinon, Ponnae and the two guards standing in the hangar. Relieved to have Romnus and his people gone, Trinon relaxed a bit and headed to the other lift that would take them topside. Ponnae and the two guards didn't speak even when they reached their quarters in the palace.

Trinon settled on the edge of his bed with his legs straddling the corner. Safe, no longer in danger, his entire being faltered. He felt himself crumble inside. His hands resumed shaking.

A strangled cry escaped his mouth, his lips curled back, exposing teeth. The tears formed, falling to the carpeted floor. He bent over; one hand clasped over his eyes.

Fear. As much as he didn't want to admit it, that's what it was. He had never felt it with this level of magnitude before. His breathing became labored while hearing the soft hiccups coming from him as he cried.

A hand. Small, delicate. It brushed his back. He looked up, startled. Ponnae stood above him on his left. She didn't speak. Her other hand came around his head to pull it to her. Her kindness was too much for him. He relented, sobbing against her. He grabbed the sides of her cloak and held on. Beneath him, he could feel her tremble. She truly understood.

****

Romnus glanced over at Batis, then Kur and Rass. They sat around the giant oval table in the war room across from Trinon, Farin and her entourage. In the center of the table, the information disc placed on the platform displayed a hologram of multiple screens combined into one image in midair.

One of the footage the host planet had sent.

"So what you're telling me is that this rogue planet has made a deal with the enemy?" Kur sat back in his seat; arms crossed. He had one leg resting on the other. "We have a problem."

"That means the enemy does indeed know how to communicate." Rass drummed his fingers on the table, then stopped. "They had no intention of doing so with New Lassa."

"I think they saw New Lassa as a nuisance interrupting their attempt at conquest." Trinon finally spoke. He had been quiet, for the most part, and could see Romnus and the generals were getting worried. "We went to stop the carnage they had no intention of ceasing."

"I agree on the reasoning for the silent treatment." Batis said. "If it were Azrom, we would have done the same."

"But now they know New Lassa is not some weak race and has the backing of Azrom through me." Farin lightly clenched her fists and set them on the table before her. "They are moving at full speed."

"Their audacity knows no bounds." Kur rocked forward. "They will come for Azrom. If they were stupid enough to attack the Dreridians, that is their next step."

"Hit the most powerful first. If you can take down the mightiest, the rest of the system is easy." Rass frowned. "I don't like that."

"They were lucky, the first time. It won't happen again." Romnus' eyes burned bright.

✳✳•✳✳

With the Lady Farin asleep along with Lord Romnus, Ponnae joined her entourage in strolling the palace halls during their free time. Trinon towered over them, walking behind. The amount of people walking the main corridor was scarce, giving them a wide area to spread out. They kept close regardless. Ponnae was glad about that.

It allowed her to relax a little and take in the scenery. Being on the fourth level gave those on the outer halls the perfect view of the Azrom landscape. Rolling hills covered in flowers and a vast mountain range against the deep azure sky. The sun was slowly descending behind the hills as daytime ended.

Laughter. Loud. Vulgar. Ponnae felt her body stiffen, her stride shortening with her slowed pace. Across the way, coming towards them, were the three guards from before. They moved freely, harassing passersby and intimidating servants trying to avoid them.

The one on the right caught sight of her and tapped the soldier next to him, interrupting his taunting of a female servant hunched over in fear. He looked over, and the third did the same.

Their attention now distracted elsewhere; the servant was free to scurry off hurriedly. The three approached the entourage, disgusting grins on their faces.

"Look at this. The wench got herself on a royal detail." The first one called out.

The second one snorted. "Guess it's better to only have to bend over for two." He eyed the two male guards. "Not all that great, is she?"

Both guards instinctively went for the hilt of their swords, then hesitated, remembering their code of conduct. Their hands did not move from where they hovered.

"Oh!" The third laughed. "Haven't had a taste yet?" He glared at Ponnae. "It's all used up and tainted, but beggars can't be choosy, right?"

Ponnae was about to speak when a presence full of malice and fury radiated from behind her. She dared not turn around. The three guards' expressions turned to terror. They backed away from the entourage, their mouths gaped open in fear.

She glanced down towards her right and saw black talons extended. Her gaze moved up to her counterpart next to her and saw his head tilted up, staring at Trinon, his eyes wide with fear as well.

She turned away and took a deep breath before looking herself. Her already stiff body froze in place. Her back went erect, and she felt like her insides were being scrambled. What she saw on Trinon's face, his entire demeanor changed, was nothing she had ever seen before.

One Earth phrase she had heard came to mind that properly defined what she witnessed. Demon.

Trinon was used to others being unaware of his presence, despite his stature. He did it on purpose, so not to intimidate anyone. The three guards were in his view before Ponnae, or he knew who they were.

When Ponnae's body seemed to deflate and her steps slow to a crawl before stopping, he felt her fear.

The moment they started spewing their disgusting words, his neck hairs bristled. The two guards were stuck in a hard place on deciding to attack should the three move towards them. He had no such dilemma. That last remark snapped Trinon out of his friendly mode. His vision turned red, his brow scrunched forward as his talons extended.

This I won't tolerate!

The three guards backed away, drawing their swords. They stood together, ready to fight. Trinon swung his left hand, the rest of the entourage ducking down to give him full range. His talons sliced through the swords, cutting them in half. The metal clinked onto the marble floor, causing people witnessing the scene to winced at the sound.

Not deterred, the three stepped back further and regained their stance. Trinon moved forward. They will get a lesson in pain today. He was ready to deliver.

"No!" A voice rang out. "Not happening, manbeast." Batis came into their line of sight. He stared unflinchingly at Trinon. "Stand down." When he didn't move, halted in a lunge, Batis stepped in front of the three guards facing him. "Right now, Trinon."

Trinon straightened his posture and moved back to stand behind Ponnae and the two guards. His talons retracted, and he forced his vision to return to normal. He felt drool formed along his mouth and wiped it with the back of his forearm.

They all watched his demeanor shift instantly to that of a jolly giant. He forced a big grin, scratching his mane as he laughed, squinting.

"Sorry, guess I got a little mad." His eyes still showed fury when they opened. "I don't like that sort of thing."

"I get that." Batis nodded to the two guards flanking Ponnae. "You can move your hands from those hilts too." They reluctantly complied. "Continue on."

Trinon dropped his arms to his sides and waited for the others to start walking. When they were far enough not to hinder his long stride, he followed, eyeing the three guards once more.

****

Batis exhaled slowly. No one noticed his true feelings of terror at that moment. That was not the gentle manbeast they all knew. Transformed into some other beast, he was no longer beautiful. Batis scratched his chest, wondering what exactly made a manbeast. Shaking off his fear, he turned to the three guards formerly of his unit.

They looked relieved. Lowering their broken weapons, the guards grinned. The first one let out a "hmph!" The other snorted, following it with a sheepish grin. The third frowned.

"Commander!" The first one smiled. "Thank the gods of old. That manbeast has lost his sense of place."

"That thing was going to cut us down," the second one said. "Damned monster."

In one swift motion, Batis unsheathed his longsword and swung it across the three guards' chest. There was a heavy silence as bystanders and the guards stood in shock. Their breast plates cracked, and the lower sections fell to the floor. Red lines appeared to drip where they had once connected.

The three guards looked down right as their wounds opened from movement. They cried out in pain, clutching their chests, hoping to stop the bleeding. The third one looked up at Batis as he went down in a pool of his own blood. Batis saw the question in his eyes. Why?

"The fact that you never once saw anything wrong with what Lord Halfar had decreed and continued to terrorize that handmaid shows your lack of honor."

Batis sheathed his sword. His hands tingled from the strike. He hadn't used his longsword in decades, usually opting for his short blade or crossbow. The guards struggled on the floor, gasping for air, then went still. Not dead, they were unconscious from blood loss. He glanced at the bystanders.

"I'm certain I said to continue on." His tone was dark. The people left the area, leaving him with his fallen former subordinates. "I should have done something about all of you long ago," he addressed them.

A group of guards arrived with the medical insignia on their collars. They positioned a floating stretcher next to the guards and heaped them atop each other onto it.

One of the medical guards wore a backpack with hoses attached. He pulled one out and sprayed the blood on the floor. It stopped flowing and turned to a gel like substance. He retracted the sprayer and pulled on a different one. It had a wide nozzle and when he positioned it over the gelled blood, it sucked up the mess.

The floor was pristine. Nothing had happened. Batis was thankful for the quick clean up. The medical unit surrounded the hover stretcher as they left. There would be rumors. He couldn't stop them from spreading. But there was no evidence of the near carnage. For he was sure of one thing.

Trinon would have torn those three guards apart.

****

Trinon stepped into his private chamber and punched the wall near the entrance. He had not felt so much rage in a long time. And that he couldn't contain himself made it worse. He could only imagine what he looked like to the others.

I'm losing it!

Looking under his raised arm planted on the wall, he saw a figure in the entryway and noticed Ponnae standing awkwardly. She finally let out a sigh and went over to his bed. She climbed on, scooting all the way to the headboard, then sat against it upright. To his amazement, she raised her arms for him to come.

Hesitant at first, he remained by the wall. She moved her arms forward, insisting. He went to her, laying his head in her lap. She caressed his mane, gently running her fingers through its thickness. His body sagged into her, and he closed his eyes. This too he hadn't felt in so long.

The last time someone showed him such affection was when he was with his now deceased mate. She was more vibrant and full of humor than him. They had been a perfect match. He sometimes thought of her, bringing his mood down. Ponnae was different in every way.

Quiet, Loyal, determined.

She refused to let what happened break her.

He wrapped his arms around her waist. What she didn't realize was that the damage had already been done. She could never erase it any more than he could in his case. They were now two beings trying to find out what they were alive for.

****

"He has to go." Batis sat leaned against the back of his seat in Romnus' private study. "If you saw what I did, you would say the same."

"Yes, we have heard the rumors." Rass tapped his fingers on the table. He sat sideways; his other arm thrown over the back of his chair. "But the whole purpose of him being here is to protect Farin."

"The fourth house has backed down tremendously. I think they understand what measures we will take if necessary." Batis reached forward to grab a piece of cured meat from the tray in the center of the table, then flopped back. "It's not like you don't have a second unit watching your beloved at all times."

Romnus eyed him with contempt. Batis scoffed. Not much of a secret.

"It hasn't even been a full year." Kur twirled a tiny bone he had stripped of its meat. "I'm actually surprised he lasted this long without harming anyone."

"Trinon needs counseling. Something is very wrong with him." Rass unhooked his arm from the back of his chair and placed both hands on the table. "Farin will understand."

"She's probably the first to observe his behavior. She just won't say anything unless she needs to," Batis added.

"I'll talk with her." Romnus frowned. "This new enemy changed many of us." He looked over at Kur who was oblivious to the scrutiny. Rass seemed to bristle. "A new way of thinking will be forthcoming."

"Yes." Batis chewed on his snack. "Azrom might has its limits."

****

Farin stood back and watched Trinon sitting on a bench facing the outdoor maneuvers arena where Ponnae practiced with her full unit when she wasn't on guard duty. She saw the distress on his face as he witnessed her focused movements.

It saddened her. The moment Trinon stepped on Azrom soil, she knew he was no longer the joking prankster she loved.

I have to do it. She gathered her courage and went to stand by his side.

Trinon didn't acknowledge her at first, opting to keep his sight on Ponnae. He moved his head towards her.

"I would chastise you for walking around alone, but I know your secret guardian, who isn't all that secret, is close by."

Farin rolled her eyes. Yes. Romnus left no stone unturned.

"Good. Then you know why I'm here."

"I've frightened the masses."

"No, Trinon." She folded her arms around his shoulders. "You frightened yourself."

She felt him go rigid in her embrace. The truth hit hard. Farin squeezed tighter. He turned his head forward.

"I'm sorry. I came here to protect you."

"I know." Farin buried her face in the back of his mane.

"I have a request."

"Oh?" Farin raised her head and leaned over his right shoulder. "And that would be?"

"Release Ponnae of her title. Let her live on New Lassa."

Farin sighed, slumping into him. She should have known that was coming. Seeing Ponnae do military maneuvers made her heart hurt as well. There was no reason for the former handmaid to continue living on Azrom with so many memories keeping her soul caged.

"Granted." She felt him relax a bit. "But on one condition." Trinon finally turned to look at her. "You have to take care of her. Make sure she's safe, always."

Trinon's eyes narrowed. "Of course I will." He angled his body towards her, shifting his weight on the bench. "I just don't like the guardian Romnus picked to be in your shadow."

"That's no longer your concern." Farin released him and stood.

"Until I leave, it is." His tone was harsh.

You really don't like him. Farin giggled, causing Trinon to stare at her in exasperation. She gave him a mischievous grin. Have you forgotten? I can take care of myself. He seemed to catch her thoughts and snorted, turning away from her.

****

For half a day, Ponnae fumed. Her commander had come to her chambers early in the day to announce the royal decree that she be removed from duty. She had protested, picking up her gear to leave, regardless. Ordered to not join Queen Farin and the other two guards, she languished, still wearing her uniform in her quarters.

The thought of taking it off would seal the deal. A new outfit sat in a neat pile on the edge of her bed. A simple blue tunic, light brown leggings, and a matching robe with a sash. The only thing she would keep from her guard gear were the boots.

Her head hung planted in her hands to cover her face. She had stopped crying an hour ago and felt too exhausted to even move from that position. All the training she had endured physically and mentally was all for nothing. And she knew its truth deep down. A battle was nearing. Her death would be instant on the front lines.

Ponnae finally sat upright and glanced at the clothes. Defeated, she stripped off her uniform, placing each piece in its own neat pile. The new clothes fit perfectly, and she wondered if Queen Farin had picked them out.

Who else would know her measurements besides Lord Chastan? The fabric was soft, hugging her body. She had never worn that kind of attire before. Having gone from handmaid to soldier, it was an extreme transition in wardrobe.

Footsteps approached. She turned around to see Trinon halt in the entryway, then lean against its arch. He eyed her for a moment, taking in her new look. She felt her body shrink from the scrutiny as she blushed.

"Come with me," Trinon's voice pleaded.

His demeanor matched her own.

Ponnae figured out Trinon had made the request. And Queen Farin would have granted it no question. Her argument to stay would fall on deaf ears. She stared down at the Azrom issued longsword. The only thing that kept her empowered over the years.

She could feel Trinon's displeasure. At the last moment, she snatched it up, clutching it to her chest, and went to him.

"I'm sorry," she whispered. "I can't leave it."

"I know." Trinon pivoted around to follow her down the outer corridor.

They walked in silence towards the other side of the palace where the stone staircase led to the rooftop. The gate operator was visible halfway up, his hands maneuvering over the console. With ships being allocated for missions, this was the best and quickest way back to New Lassa. Waiting for them was Queen Farin, flanked by the two male guards, Lord Romnus and his entourage.

Ponnae held the sword tighter as Queen Farin's eyes narrowed at it. Batis let out a small laugh.

She cringed at the sound.

"Let her keep it," Batis said. "She's earned at least that."

"I'll allow it." Lord Romnus had a similar look on his face. He didn't like it either.

"Thank you." Ponnae loosened her grip on the sword.

My sword.

The gate opened, bringing the whipping hot air that was in contrast with the icy cold of space. The black tunnel of stars swirled behind the operator's right shoulder. Queen Farin came forward and embraced her, squeezing hard.

"I wish you happiness. To find some small bit of peace."

Ponnae struggled to stop herself from falling apart. She felt the tears run from her eyes uncontrollably. Her arms moved on their own and returned the hug. When Queen Farin let go, she stepped away, shamefully wiping her face. To her surprise, Queen Farin moved towards Trinon with fervor, her expression angry.

"Down," Queen Farin ordered.

Trinon knelt before her, his head just below hers. She cupped his face in both hands and the two stared into each other's eyes for what seemed like too long, in Ponnae's opinion. No one said a word, not sure what to do.

"You," Queen Farin finally spoke. "I need you to find out who you truly are."

Trinon's head jerked back, but her grip was firm, not letting him move any further. Ponnae could tell he wanted to run. To not see how he looked in her eyes.

"Because I need you. Always." Queen Farin pulled his head to her bosom and held it there. Trinon's arms hung limp at his sides. She let go so he could raise his face to her. "Understood?"

"Understood." Trinon got to his feet, towering over her. "I'm sorry, Farin." He brushed a hand across her cheek. "I thought I could…"

"I know." She stepped back to stand with the others. "Now go. We have a lot of work to do. Here and on New Lassa."

Trinon's expression turned sour, as if he had tasted something bad. Ponnae pursed her lips, not wanting to know what the manbeast was thinking. She walked to the opened gate and waited for Trinon to stand beside her.

"Ready?" He asked, not looking over at her. She nodded. "Let's go home."

Home. Ponnae liked the sound of it. She was born on Azrom yet never felt it was a place where she would prosper and be safe. A new beginning was on the other side of the vortex. Together, they walked through the gate.

To Start a War

Adan tapped the keycard in his right hand on the ship's navigation dashboard. He was filling in until its operator came back from a break. He glanced over at the communications board. Nothing had come through yet from Commander Veris. He was certain everything had gone as planned.

No news was good news, keeping chatter down so it wouldn't alert New Lassa before the main event.

He crossed his legs, stretched out on the edge of the dash the other way, and leaned back further in the seat. He admired the workmanship of the cockpit. The outside was pretty good, too. This was the best way to impress their new overlords. Show them their skills. The ship used to be a hunk of junk. Abandoned by a more advanced race that weighed repair costs over waiting for reinforcements.

No big deal. He grinned. Got a nice ride in the process for next to nothing. The rest of the bridge crew conducted their tasks in silence. There really wasn't much to say until they arrived at their destination. Everyone was nervous.

Except him. The ire he felt for the Lassian woman, and her kind fueled his actions.

The bridge doors swished open. His navigator walked to his station and motioned for him to vacate.

"I am your superior, in case you forgot," Adan said.

"No. But I am the navigator, and you're preventing me from doing my duties."

Adan swung his legs down and stood, gesturing for the man to take his place.

"How much longer?" He asked.

The navigator stared up at him in shock as he sat down.

"You should know. What were you doing all this time?" He shook his head and focused on the multiple screens in front of him. "Looks like one more day and we will be in New Lassa space." He turned to Adan. "When do you want to start the hail signal?"

"Let's see if they notice us first. If not, then we wait until we're closer to the planet." Adan smirked. "Don't want to scare them too soon."

"Good call. The kid would be pleased."

Referencing the young communications tech on their home world made Adan smile. The information was flawed, sure. But he still maintained that the bulk of it was solid. He couldn't wait to meet the Lassians.

****

Ganna stared dubiously at the satellite feed. Her lips curved into a crooked smirk. The reconnaissance system linked with the gate console for easier decision making she had put in place after the debacle with Halfar.

She had returned from the neutral science zone a month before; the others citing a needed break. They had hit a snag. The enemy's new toy even perplexed the great Lord Greggor.

She stood next to the gate operator under the early morning sky. Both looked up at the two giant holoscreens in midair. Anyone within a five-mile radius could see them. Which was part of the plan. The manbeasts wouldn't have to look too hard from the hilltops with their superior sight. She glanced over at the gate operator, finding his mood matched hers.

Another unknown guest had arrived. She marveled at the ship while the system identified its origin. At the bottom of the left screen, a message blinked.

Yaos system D Class destroyer. Decommissioned due to critical damage. Sold on repair planet Barrima in the Rendal system for parts salvage.

Is that right? Ganna tilted her head in amusement. They're making a statement. She addressed the gate operator.

"Scan for weapons."

"Already doing that."

"Compare it to the original ship schematic." He gave her a quizzical stare. "Just do it."

He entered a string of commands, and the ship's blueprint appeared on a smaller screen below.

Ahh ha! Ganna grinned.

"What is it now?" Chardon's voice rang out.

Chardon came up to the console, followed by Jaron, Modas, and Talas. "That thing looks ominous." He pointed to the ship that came out of nowhere hours ago.

"Looks can be deceiving." Ganna gestured towards the lower screen with a hand. "It has been extremely modified. Seventy percent of its weapons have been stripped, leaving the primary weapon system and a few strategic bays intact."

"Where does it come from?" Jardon watched the other screen change to reverse tracking.

The system pinged and the Rendal II system, farther out than they thought, came on screen.

"It's from one of the planets under our Regency." Ganna tapped an icon on the console and the image zoomed in. "The same planet this ship was dumped on."

Her eyes went wide as she thought of the possibilities. Their own repair shop. She frowned after the next thought invaded her mind. They would have to share with the alliance.

"Well?" Chardon aked. "Have we hailed them yet?"

"Doing that now," the gate operator replied.

Talas let out a sigh. "How many left on that list to meet and greet?" He scratched the side of his head. "That woman did us no favors."

Sestis.

They all said her name in silence. Ganna crossed her arms to hide her fists. She had gone along with that ambitious sow longer than she should. Everyone at present, including the gate operator, had no love lost for her.

"Let's see what they came for, hmm?" Talas glanced over at the new space hub's landing pad off in the distance.

"We can give them a guided tour." Jaron quipped.

****✳****

The ship eased out of the jump into New Lassa space. Adan caught his breath as he saw the planet loom before him. It wasn't so much the relatively small size, but the number of satellites surrounding it. Standing on the raised dais in the center of the bridge, he counted ten in all. A lot for such a little planet. He called it so because it was a third the size of his own.

Did that make it normal sized, then? He pondered.

There was a guiding strip made of giant strobes leading from one satellite to the surface. What looked like a transport gate sat on the dark side of the planet. The sun was not as bright as most. A closer look found it being bombarded with projectiles. They're injecting it with more energy.

A sense of foreboding hit him. This was no super power. What greed Sestis portrayed now appeared to be a desperate attempt to attain that status. A tiny planet with a weak sun and an over the top defense system? They had been invaded before, and would not be caught sleeping again. A monster awakening.

"Now, that's impressive," Ryben said, whistling.

"We're being hailed." The communications tech said. "Are we sending the auto message?"

Adan contemplated sending it even though it would probably look disingenuous. He rubbed his chin and glanced back at the others.

"What do you think?"

"Go audio only." The first man suggested. "Make it sound dire that we land or something."

"Scratch that," the tech called out. "We were scanned. They know about this ship."

"Huh," Adan exhaled. "Okay." He cleared his throat. "Open a channel. Set it on delay."

The feed on the holoscreen above the communications station went blue and a small dot blinked in the corner.

"Greetings, New Lassa. I am Master Adan from planet Barrima. I am here to request dire assistance in light of a crisis on our planet. We were given your gate coordinates by the Dreridian council that oversees regencies."

He paused for effect then continued,

"As ownership of our planet has been given unto your hands, we were advised your race is obligated to hear our plight. We request permission to land and meet our Regent to discuss options."

Adan nodded to the communications tech who hit the send icon.

Now we wait.

*****

Four hours went by with no response, making Adan nervous. He tried to speculate what would cause the delay. He paced the small dais of the bridge, arms crossed, a finger tapping his lower lip. His brow furrowed. The crew watched him, waiting for him to say something. The commlink pinged, startling him, and he halted his movements.

"Permission granted." The communications tech swiveled around as he announced it.

Adan's shoulders sagged in relief. "Good." Regaining his composure, he motioned for his entourage. "Let's get moving."

They left the bridge and headed for the hangar. As they entered, the two smaller ships sat clamped down on each side. Adan went to the one on the right, pulling its control panel from his vest. They ran up the ramp before it was fully down, eager to be underway.

Everyone went to their stations on the tiny bridge while Adan took to the captain's seat in the center. The ship powered up, and the pilot did a check of the systems before maneuvering it out the open hangar doors into space.

Adan gripped the curved rails of the seat and leaned forward, staring intently at the main viewscreen. He wanted to see their approach to the surface in full. The heat shields came down, darkening the screen. Not enough to obscure his view.

New Lassa was plain. Nothing stood out. No beautiful swirls, discernible features, or anomalies. A brown, yellow, and green orb with a few pale clouds. It almost appeared as if dipped in wet soil, muddied. After the burn died out, entering the atmosphere, the shields rose to reveal the landscape below in true color.

"Prepare for landing," the navigator said.

The advanced technology littering the planet was an eyesore in contrast to the dullness of the surface. Yellow grass, patches of greenery. It matched the outer aesthetic. Adan stared at it, confused. None of it made sense. The ship settled on a platform in the middle of a field. Tall grass swayed around it and got shorter along the pathway leading to a clearing.

Making sure their weapons were concealed, Adan and his entourage exited the ship via the ramp and walked down the path. Ahead of them at the clearing, a group of people came to stand in its center. He squinted to get a better focus, scanning the individuals and could not find the Regent Sestis among them.

Did she not feel obligated to attend? Was it beneath her? Did she even remember their planet? He seethed, then reined it in. He was not to show hostility.

His people halted ten feet away from the New Lassians. Adan stared at them. He noticed they were a hodge podge species. Three unique ones, in fact, and an obvious Azromian. He glanced over at the overly tall one with talons and a large mane. Another humanoid one with eyes that seemed to have an inner glow. The third was rough around the edges, a hunter type.

The Azromian stood out from all of them.

Sinister, murderous, murky green eyes and a slender build with a hidden power. Behind him was a solver haired woman whose gaze fell on the ship instead of them. The ravenous look in her eyes made him uncomfortable.

Realizing he was scrutinizing them a bit too much, he gave a polite smile and bowed. His entourage following suit.

"Greetings, New Lassa. I am Master Adan, the leader of Planet Barrima. It is an honor to meet you." He brought his head up and looked around at them. "Is the Regent Sestis not coming?"

The taller of the glowing eyed ones frowned. He took a closer look, and saw the similarity in features he had with Sestis. The other Lassians' expressions turned sour.

What is that? He watched the first step forward, hands clenched at his side.

"Lady Sestis has been deceased for quite some time." His hands unclenched and hung loosely. "I am Chardon, her former mate. The title of Regent has fallen to me."

Adan struggled to hide his shock and failed. His eyes widened, and his mouth opened slightly.

"Regent Sestis," he whispered, then stuttered, "Is dead?"

"Correct."

Chardon waited for him to gather his thoughts.

"How long ago?" Adan's face scrunched.

"Well over a century," Chardon replied.

"And not long enough," the other like Chardon with red strands in their hair added.

"Good riddance," the slender blond ruffian said.

Wait! This isn't right. Adan went through more questions in his head and finally asked, "Did you know of our plight? Did she tell you her plans for us?"

Chardon lowered his gaze and shook his head.

"We were visited by another group of representatives from a different system about the transfer of power. The Dreridians only recently informed us of the other planets Sestis had acquired."

Oh no!

The mostly solid information now showed its cracks. And a major one it was. Adan didn't know what to do next. All the sinister plans he had implemented would backfire. With horror, he thought about the current one.

We've made a mistake!

Off in the distance, a vortex appeared.

Adan and his entourage looked over to see the transport gate open.

Trinon strolled down the walkway out of the vortex with Ponnae close behind. He nodded to the gate operator as it shut down. The wind created from their entry ceased.

"Welcome home." The gate operator eyed Ponnae.

"It also pertains to her. She will live here from now on."

The gate operator gave her a small head tilt. "You are just in time." He gestured to the ship in the field. "WE have yet more guests courtesy of Sestis."

Trinon's face blanched as he focused on the outworlders. Then his eyes narrowed. He looked down at Ponnae, also enraged.

"Is there a problem?" The gate operator became defensive. "Are they an enemy?"

"Hmm." Trinon held up a palm. "Wait here, just in case."

Trinon and Ponnae walked over to the clearing. His mother gave him a puzzled stare. His father seemed concerned.

"Trinon. What brings you back home?" Modas asked.

"Yes." Halfar glared at him. "Were you not supposed to be my daughter's guardian on Azrom?"

Master Adan seemed to rear back, as new information hit him. Trinon stared him down, his anger on full display.

Chardon noticed, eyeing their guests in a different light.

"Do you know this race, Trinon?" Chardon asked. He kept his gaze on the leader and his people.

"There was an ambush on the neutral planet, Folza. A plan to kidnap and harm the Queen of Azrom. The enemy was lured there as cover. The host planet is not pleased."

Halfar stepped closer to Adan. Chardon spread his arms to block him.

"Is she alright?" Halfar asked through gritted teeth.

Ponnae came next to Trinon.

"The Lady Farin is well. She is also quite angry. I have her report for you, Lord Chardon."

Mater Adan stood straight, clearing his throat as he gulped.

"The Queen of Azrom is your daughter?" He asked cautiously.

"And mine," Chardon replied.

"I…don't understand. I thought she was Sestis' child. That you gave her to Supreme Ruler Romnus as a gift."

The looks of horror and fury from every Lassian made him fear for his life. Trinon could smell it on him. He almost pitied the newcomers. Yet again, they were operating under flawed details.

"That is completely false." Chardon tilted his head. "Where did you hear something like that?"

"They didn't," Trinon said. "They merely speculated based on incomplete data."

"Which means you didn't come here for a friendly chat, did you?" Talas placed a hand on the hilt of his longsword. "Let me guess, you are sending the enemy the gate coordinates for New Lassa?"

Trinon tensed.

His mother was on Adan in a flash, pinning him to the ground by his neck. The first four soldiers in his entourage drew weapons while the other ten hesitated, not sure what action to take.

"Master Adan!" The man closest to him trained his weapon on Jaron. The leader raised a hand towards him.

"Commander Ryben, stop!"

"Please," Ryben said. "We made a mistake. You can't fault us for wanting vengeance."

The man was on the verge of panic.

"But we can." Trinon stepped towards the guests, towering over them. "You didn't check your information."

"Due diligence is key. You have to cross reference all that." Ganna said, wagging a finger.

"Everyone remain calm." Chardon raised his voice so they could hear.

He went and leaned over Adan, making sure Jaron was letting him still breathe. Then he turned to Ryben standing not a foot away with his weapon still on Jaron. The others adjusted their mark to Chardon.

"We can fix this." Adan stuttered.

"Did you send our location to the enemy?" Chardon's stare bore into him.

He glanced over at Ryben who Trinon grabbed by the neck, lifting him nearly a foot from the ground.

"Answer."

Flailing, still clutching his gun, Ryben stared into his eyes. Trinon knew how animal like he appeared at that moment and didn't care.

"Not yet," Ryben finally replied. "Our main ship is waiting for the signal."

"I do want to talk," Adan managed to cry out. Jaron stared at him in awe. "Our planet does need help. That has not changed."

"You want to ask for help after you come here under deceptive means?" Chardon gave him the same look. "Why? Why should we help you now?"

"Please." Ryben's eyes darkened, brimming with tears. "We made a mistake."

"You're covering your hides," Ganna scoffed.

Trinon let Ryben go, dropping him on the surface. The man rubbed his neck before getting back on his feet. He saw his mother let the leader up as well.

Tapping his wristband, Ryben raised it to his chest.

"Do not send the coordinates."

"What?" The voice on the other end shouted. "Why? The plan was to…"

"I said," Ryben cut them off. "Don't send it. There's been a..." he paused for a moment, "miscalculation."

"Do you need emergency extraction?"

"No. We are staying to negotiate. Stand by."

"Negotiate?" The voice exclaimed.

"Just…"

"Obey the order!" Adan yelled into his own wristband. "No one is dying today."

"Oh, that's a bit optimistic on your end." Talas grinned. "What made you think we were some easy target you could pick off on a whim?"

"The only ones not getting off this planet alive would be you," Jaron added.

Adan finally got a good look at his surroundings. Around the perimeter of the ship and the pathway were energy users, orbs glowing in their hands, warriors with longswords drawn, and manbeasts scattered throughout.

"I see that now." He stood. His entourage scanned the area with terrified expressions. "Forgive me."

"Now that that's out of way." Ganna turned towards the commons. "Let's talk about the ship you came in and how you modified it."

The way she smiled made everyone flinch. Trinon caught Ponnae's perplexed face. He didn't want her to find out the reason for their reaction. As for the guests, they were getting what they deserved. Ganna's undivided attention.

On board the main ship, the communications tech huffed at the end of the leader's order and sat back in his station. He looked around at everyone on the bridge.

"What do you think?"

"Miscalculation, my eye." The soldier standing guard at the doors snorted.

"Yeah, we come this far, and they back out?" Another crewman said.

"We didn't come here to be afraid all of a sudden." The communications tech loaded the coordinates and sent them to the enemy. "When the enemy signals their jump, we call our cowardly leader back."

"Roger that. Don't want to see those ugly aliens and what they're going to do to that planet." The maintenance tech swiveled away from his console. "Feel kind of bad for the population."

"No different than their leader abandoning us to fend for ourselves. They didn't care about our population," the crewman said.

The commlink made a ping and a 'message received' blinked blue. "Done." Feeling a sense of pride, they resumed their tasks.

The entire council in attendance, along with Adan and his people, crowded the conference room. An awkward silence lingered while they all sized up one another. Talas and Jaron made their own assessments early and ignored their guests to converse privately in a corner.

Ganna eyed them with suspicion, her wristband blinking. She reached over and tapped it after glancing at the message to shut it off.

Chardon sat across from Adan. The man had shaken off his nervousness and now sat smugly, leaning back in his seat with one arm flung over the top. He was dead set on negotiating after his little stunt.

Halfar sat glaring at him, ready to strike if he so much as sneezed. Chardon kept one hand below the table and stroked his thigh for comfort.

"I know you think we are being bold, but you must understand." Adan brought his arm around and rested his muscular forearms on the table. "We were desperate. Our planet is on the brink of crumbling. What else would you have us do?"

"Huh." The head of politics gave him a stern look. "I don't know. Maybe come find us like the other races under our regency did and plead your case."

Adan pursed his lips, having no counter. Chardon set his elbow on the table and laid his head in his hand. All of this could have been avoided if they had only done that in the first place.

Their actions reminded him of Earth and how the humans there made assumptions and asked questions later.

Ganna gave Adan a dubious side glance. "I want to know more about the modifications on that ship." Adan turned to her. "It's expertly done."

"Of course it is." He frowned. "We take great pride in our work."

"Which makes me wonder if Sestis didn't really look into your planet's expertise." The head of science interjected. "That seems like a missed opportunity on her part."

"Yes," Ganna said. "We could have been utilizing it this whole time."

She huffed at the thought of lost experiments.

"So," Chardon let his hand drop. "What's the problem you need remedied?"

"Our planet system is shot," Commander Ryben replied. "We barely have enough resources to keep it going, let alone do a job."

"That ship is the last thing we were able to fix with available parts," Adan added.

Ganna and the head of science leaned back in shock.

"Impressive!" They said in unison.

Commander Ryben's wrist band beeped, and he stared at it for a moment, his brow furrowing. Adan looked at him.

"What's wrong?"

"We're being hailed by the ship to return at once."

"Why?"

"Oh, I can tell you that," Ganna answered.

"As can we," Talas said, referring to himself and Jaron.

"What's going on?" Adan was up, his body tense as he stared down at Ryben.

The man went pale as he read the message running across the tiny screen. He slowly raised his head to him.

"They sent the signal." He let his arm go limp in his lap. "The enemy is en route."

"What?" Adan yelled.

Chardon was about to stand, his eyes wide in disbelief. Halfar was again enraged. Jaron held up a hand, gesturing for them both to ease down.

"We figured as much," Talas said. "They won't get anywhere near New Lassa."

"Well, they will be in the same space." Ganna nodded her head sideways. "They just won't get to the surface or close proximity."

"I don't want them here at all!" Chardon protested.

Ryben's wristband chirped excessively with from urgent messages. He didn't acknowledge them, his demeanor that of defeat.

"You need to move your ship, or it will be destroyed." Halfar sat further back in his seat.

"We can't have that beautiful piece of technology going to waste." Ganna stood. "It has weapons that can go online."

"That's correct." Adan plopped down in his seat. "Not enough to defend ourselves from those things' relentless onslaught."

Ganna synced her commlink with the data platform on the table, and an image of space floated on a holoscreen in the center. They all watched a patch of darkness swirl, growing larger to accommodate the large, ugly ships easing their way out of a vortex. The Barrima's ship was already turning towards the far side of New Lassa for cover.

Ten enemy battle ships came into view, weapons already burning bright, ready to fire. Chardon stared at the intrusion of their home world with fury. He turned to Ganna.

"Now what?" He pointed to the image. "We're clearly outnumbered in terms of firepower."

"Oh, Chardon." Ganna sighed heavily, then smiled. "Have faith. I made sure New Lassa was prepared for any enemy."

Giant mounds scattered across planet surface formed, then splayed open to reveal massive energy pods. Electricity danced around their domes as the accumulated blasts shot out into space. On the holoscreen, everyone in the room saw the enemy fire a wide beam of orange needles that curved along the planet.

And hit a wall of blue light that negated the attack.

They stared in awe at the image. Ganna grinned and turned to Talas.

"Did you like that?"

"I did." Talas and Jaron stood. "Let the real fight begin." He nodded to Jaron. "Time to show them our true strength."

Chardon's expression changed to something sinister. Even Halfar leaned away from him. The enemy's battle sense had caught them off guard the first time. Not anymore. And that they had the audacity to bring the fight to New Lassa?

No, this time, the enemy was getting their way.

"Bring them to their knees and get them out of our system," Chardon ordered.

The entire room felt his conviction.

Without saying a word, the council dispersed. He stared at Adan and his people. They would pay dearly for this. For now, he would use them any way he chose and make them fight along with everyone else.

~ACTS OF TRANSGRESSION~

CORE: BOOK FIVE

PREVIEW

ONE: CONGREGRATION

Meeting of the Minds

Every planet in the Dreridian system was on high alert after being attacked by an unknown enemy force less than a year ago. Battle cruisers patrolled the space, looking out for any vortices that may pop open. There was a movement of solemn behavior while trade continued to flow. New satellite hubs were being constructed to replace the previously destroyed ones.

The count so far was half.

On the home planet, Lord Pondur stood staring at the industrial district in full swing outside the panoramic windows in his office. Vapors drifted from the giant smokestacks, changing the color of the air above it for a brief second before dissipating. construction rings surrounded the main refinery. The upper half, caved in, exposed to the elements was still being rebuilt. His scrunched, craggy face deepened the crevices.

With his hands clasped behind his back, the quarter length dress jacket pulled tight around his shoulders. He wore a deep rust red tailored suit with charcoal vest and cream colored ascot. The collar was up, curbing around his nearly round head, The buttons on the vest and jacket were shiny gold with the Dreridian crest etched on them.

Casual, yet dignified. He had no meeting scheduled for the day. That said, he was always prepared.

A small spark of fury lingered in his mind at the enemy's audacity to strike his home. And not only his. Their relentless pursuit targeted the two most powerful races in the five solar systems, Razzna and Azrom, along with the newly formed Lassian force.

The enemy was a scourge on the system, disrupting trade.

A proposed alliance between the three made him uneasy. Granted, combining their resources would make them a might of staggering proportions. That also meant they could challenge him in the future.

Maybe we throw our hat in the fray as well? He figured having a spot in the alliance would help deter such an outcome. As powerful as they were, each race was still quite new; only acquiring their status half a millennium ago.

The Dreridians had scoured the galaxy setting up trade systems for over two thousand years making them the prime industry leaders. Others tried to build similar ones yet never achieved the same level of success. Lord Pondur snorted. The Dreridian reach was vast.

His door slid open for the head of science, Lord Graggor. The portly creature moved gracefully despite his size to stand next to him. Wearing a dark grey tailored three piece suit a shade darker than his cragged skin, he was the picture of an aristocrat like Lord Pondur. His two stone horns were short and stubby in contrast to Pondur's thinner, pointy ones.

"I read the reports. Everything is almost back to peak production." Lord Graggor laced his fingers in front of him and rested them on his belly. "The damage was minimal after crunching the numbers."

"What do you think about joining the alliance with those three imbeciles?"

Lord Graggor turned towards him in shock at the sudden outburst. He took a deep breath and reverted his gaze back to the scene below.

"We would be able to monitor them better. And keep them at bay in case they decide to go against us." His face tightened. "I think we may be giving them more credit than they warrant."

"I agree, They are still too young."

"We could," Lord Graggor seemed to be treading carefully as he spoke. "Mentor them. Get their leadership on track so trade is not affected so drastically like before."

Lord Pondur's brow lifted in surprise. He had not thought of that. Instead of the constant chastising, a lesson in true power would benefit them. He thought about their military might. Crass and barbaric, they would be of use when Dreridians didn't want their hands dirty.

"Why, Lord Graggor, that is a fascinating proposal."

Lord Graggor tilted his head to one side and shrugged. "I do what I can, my Lord."

"You came for a different reason." Lord Pondur frowned. "What is it now?"

"It appears the enemy was given the location of New Lassa's gate coordinates and attempted to raze the planet." Lord Graggor pursed his thin lips.

"Is that so? How did that happen?" Lord Pondur was not happy. He had a theory.

"Planet Barrima, under their regency was slighted by Sestis and they wanted revenge. Of course they realized their error but it was too late."

Lord Pondur lowered his head in defeat. It was as he feared. It further solidified his feelings of not helping the regency planets in the first place as a mistake.

"The damage?" He braced for the reply.

"Astonishingly," Lord Graggor began, "the Lassians were able to push them back. That woman," his disdain for the Lassian scientist Ganna clear, "had devised a defense system in such a short time."

"Really?" Lord Pondur was intrigued. "So they learn quite fast. Good." He nodded.

"What are your next moves, my lord? The enemy hasn't attacked any other planets in the past cycle. They are surely regrouping as they have done before."

"No doubt." Lord Pondur unclasped his hands and tapped his chin with one finger. "Send out a message to all our posts. I want to know where their main fleet is. Any information leading to its location will be rewarded."

"Monetary or credit?"

Lord Pondur turned a sour expression towards him. "This small distraction does not constitute payment. Trade credit will suffice. Add in free shipping for hauls outside their system."

"Very good, my Lord. A perfect incentive."

"Now, go find out what kind of defense system that Lassian scientist has created."

"On my way for inspection in two days."

Lord Graggor exited the office, leaving Lord Pondur to his quiet observations. The Lassians. He still had little information on that race. They appeared out of nowhere.

Or had they? The speed in which they learned and the complicated nature of their cores made him think they may have been something else entirely. Something jumpstarted their evolution.

When they came for a seat at the trade table, he was leery of them. They had not divulged their planet's location and being new the other conglomerates didn't push the issue since they had no intention of visiting. The gate coordinates had changed due to the new planet. What Lord Pondur wanted to know now was the location of their original home world. Something told him it was the key to all this. And I will find it.

~END~

ABOUT THE AUTHOR

Hi there. I'm Maquel A. Jacob. I have had a passion for the written word since the age of seven, reading everything I could get my grubby little hands on which included encyclopedias and the thesaurus. At twelve, I had my first encounter with a Stephen King novel and was hooked. I then became inspired to write my own brand of fiction. Combining multiple genres to keep things interesting.

I am a HUGE Anime fan, love a great bottle of wine and rock out to heavy metal music. Green and lush Oregon is where I currently reside spinning imaginary worlds in my head and daydreaming.

For cool limited-edition Swag, updates, FREE short stories, Newsletters
...and more, become a Patron
https://www.patreon.com/maquelajacob

Visit:www.majacobauthor.com

Like Maquel A. Jacob on Facebook plus
Follow on Tumblr and Twitter
all @MaquelAJ1
MAJart Works on Instagram
Also find me on Goodreads

www.ingramcontent.com/pod-product-compliance
Lightning Source LLC
Chambersburg PA
CBHW030623190726
48286CB00008B/2370